QUIVER

QUIVER

— HOLLY LUHNING —

PEGASUS CRIME
NEW YORK

QUIVER

Pegasus Books LLC
80 Broad Street, 5th Floor
New York, NY 10004

First Pegasus Books cloth edition 2011

Library of Congress Cataloging-in-Publication Data is available.

ISBN: 978-1-60598-192-5

10 9 8 7 6 5 4 3 2 1

Printed in the United States of America
Distributed by W. W. Norton & Company, Inc.
www.pegasusbooks.us

For my grandmothers,
Helen Seifert Luhning (1921–2009)
Hilda Lowe Jacobson (1922–2009)

"Beauty is terror.
Whatever we call beautiful, we quiver before it."

DONNA TARTT, *The Secret History*

QUIVER

Chapter One

She was easy to spot.

Her skin was almost blue-white. As usual, at the corner she said goodbye to the other girls; he saw her part from the heads of pink hair, tight black curls, a blonde pixie cut. Watched her follow a narrow asphalt footpath that led around the corner to a pedestrian tunnel under the busy motorway.

He'd been in the tunnel, walked its sixty feet back and forth. He had done this most mornings this week, on his way to the office. No one noticed him. He was just a man wearing a suit, carrying a briefcase, going to work. When a lorry passed on the road above, the caged fluorescent lights that hung from the ceiling buzzed louder. Sometimes cyclists whizzed towards him through the tunnel, but they always stayed on their side of the yellow line painted down the centre of the path. Each day before he left the tunnel, he stopped and looked at the yellow paint, imagined it blotted by a puddle of blood, a small broken body stretched across the line.

Today, while he waited for her to pass by, he sat at a table next to the café window and flipped through the pictures they'd sent him. Four snapshots of the girl with long, dark hair. The girl, with a rucksack, on her way to class. On a sports field, wearing muddy football cleats. Sitting on a lawn, sipping a juice box. Walking home from school with a group of friends, passing in front of the café.

He had an allongé and ate a cannoli, slowly. He glanced at his reflection in the glass: a translucent, freckled hand, copper hair he had cut every three weeks at the salon. Ironed dress shirt, slate sports jacket.

As the girl left her friends, she flipped her dark hair from her collar. Locks splayed over her heavy rucksack.

He walked into his flat. It faced west and had beautiful evening light. Unfortunately, he had been distracted and let the kitchen get messy. White dishes streaked with jelly and tomato sauce filled the sink. Bloated bread and pizza crusts clogged the drain. He was almost out of clean cutlery; a collection of dirty utensils was sunk beneath two inches of water. Small islands of white and green mould floated on the surface.

He cringed at the sight and smell of the mess as he walked through to the living room. He hated letting things go like that, but this project had kept him too busy for housework.

He put on John Cage's "Cheap Imitation." The speakers wired in each corner of the room pulsed with eerie piano. He sat on his black leather sofa, pulled the photos from his briefcase and set them on the heavy marble coffee table. A trio of flies migrated out of the kitchen. He stood and shooed them, then poured himself a glass of Scotch. As he swallowed the smoky liquor he looked at the pictures again.

The one of her sitting on the lawn with her hair up was the best, he decided. He liked the pictures, but he almost didn't need them anymore. He would destroy them tomorrow, according to plan.

The books and DVDs they had sent him were in a long box under the coffee table. The kit they had sent was there too. He sat down again, popped the lid off the box and pulled out the blue satin pouch. He untied the string, felt the metal blade and the ceramic talisman inside. Then he closed the pouch and started to think about which film to watch that evening.

Before he'd met them, he didn't have these books or movies about the Blood Countess. It was a bit lonely. He went to work at the software company, input data and printed reports. He'd earned a promotion last year, but still his boss wanted him to go faster, produce more reports and numbers. Sometimes on Fridays he went to the pub with some co-workers. He went to the gym twice a week. But these were all things that everyone else he knew did too.

Then he met them, and learned about how the Countess killed hundreds of girls. How people helped her with the girls and the blood. It kept her beautiful. More beautiful and exciting than filling a computer with numbers or running like a rat on a treadmill.

He'd never hurt anyone before. But he'd always thought about it. About what it would feel like to attack someone, to hold his hand on their chest while their heart stopped beating. Once, he had poisoned a stray dog, stood over the mutt while it convulsed and died, but that didn't stop his thoughts. It only fed him, teased him. When he met them it was like they could sense it immediately, but instead of looking away or making an excuse not to talk to him in the coffee line, like some people did at his office, they liked him more because of his fantasies. And now he had instruction, inspiration. He had a goal.

Between melancholy piano notes, he heard a squeaking in the corner by the fridge. This building was old, so if he didn't remember to keep the holes plugged the mice got in. He would do the dishes, get groceries and plug the holes after he finished with the project. But for now, he'd only had time to pick up some sticky traps at the corner store last week.

He chose a DVD from the box and put it on the table. Downed the rest of his Scotch, then stood up from the smooth leather sofa. He saw the mouse in the sticky trap. Its body shook, strained against the glue that shackled its feet. He picked up the trap, held it upside down, then sideways. He was amused every time the rodent squealed louder.

He put the trap on the counter. Thumb on the mouse's right back leg. Snap. The next one. Snap. Both front legs. Crack, crack. He batted the trap between his hands, laughed at the loose shimmy of the animal's body above its broken limbs.

He found a clean paring knife in a kitchen drawer. The mouse's squeals were quieter; its eyes fluttered. "In a moment, mouse," he said as he stroked the top of its head. He ripped the dull knife through the fur and sinew of the mouse's neck.

They bled best when cut at the throat.

Chapter Two

I moved across the Atlantic to speak to the man in the next room.

I am five minutes early, but the orderlies have him ready. Beige hospital pants and top, standard-issue sneakers: Martin Foster looks much like any other patient I might interview in a day. He's seated in one of Stowmoor's observation rooms and I watch him through the one-way window. He scrunches up his nose and cheeks to push up his tortoiseshell-framed glasses, then sticks out his lower lip slightly and blows his shaggy ginger hair off his forehead.

I know his file off by heart. He is thirty-one. He is five foot nine. No history of substance abuse. No prior criminal charges.

Two years ago, he abducted a fifteen-year-old girl who was walking home from school in Leeds. He beat her, restrained her and branded her palms with a small ceramic block that he heated with a blowtorch. The engraved block seared an imprint of the letter *B*, bordered by a circle of vines, into the girl's skin. He slashed her neck with a Renaissance-era dagger, bled her to death and bit pieces of flesh from her thighs. He said he believed her blood had the ability to wash away the freckles that still pepper his face and arms. Upon arrest, he told police he was paying homage to sixteenth-century serial killer Elizabeth Báthory.

I am one of his psychologists. Martin Foster is waiting for me to enter the examination room.

My family and friends wonder why I choose to do this. Spend the majority of my time in psychiatric facilities, around murderers, sociopaths, pedophiles. Insane and violent criminals. Even my boyfriend, Henry, sometimes says, "Watch it around those lunatics." I wonder if he worries I could catch it, be lured from my role of psychologist and succumb to some latent psychosis. Watch it, your sanity. Watch the line. What I don't say is that the line is hardly there. It's as blurry and fluid as the slope of the shore, from beach to the shallows to water over your head to the open sea. And I'm not really supposed to believe in that spectrum. I'm in the business of treating, of reforming those who stray from the norm. But we're all there on the slope. I think the difference is whether you've manoeuvred yourself into a position where your head's above the sea.

I do this because I want to know about extremes. About the sublime edges people retreat into and lash out from. I want to know about people who deviate from what society has authorized as acceptable behaviour. About their fixations and obsessions, those quick dark moments when the safety doesn't catch and they tell the lie, forge the cheque, steal the car, use the knife. What pushes them over the threshold of idea into action. Foster claimed he was pushed by Báthory. His obsession with her defines his violence and was the catalyst for the perfect and sudden bloom of his disorder.

The truth is, I don't spend the majority of my time with murderers, thieves or psychopaths. I spend most of it theorizing about them and analyzing their assessments. I assemble reports and photocopy files. I write articles and grant applications. And when I have the opportunity to be in a room with a patient, it's usually a brief and sanitary encounter, an intake assessment or an annual report. I read the file and the patient appears. I ask the pre-set questions and record the responses. It's clinical, it's detached and it's designed to be that way. The past actions of the patient, their sublime edges, become text, a piece of paper in a file.

I've been trained well. I push the paper and win the grants. I do the bulk of my assessments almost by rote. But with Foster, it's different. His case grips me, a boa constrictor. It breathes; he's more than text on a page.

I straighten Foster's chart, stack my folder on top and make sure I have two working pens. I open the door and walk into the room. "Hello, Mr. Foster. I'm Dr. Winston. We've met before briefly, with Dr. Sloane and Dr. Abbas." I sit down across from him.

"I remember." He leans forward, puts his elbows on the table. "You're the new girl."

I set my folder in front of me and line the pens up beside it. "I'm a new psychologist on your team, yes. I'm heading up your annual assessment this year."

He pulls his elbows off the table, slowly. "Wonderful." He crosses his legs, puts his hands behind his head. "Let's get on with it, then."

"In general, how are you feeling today, Mr. Foster?" I say, flipping open my folder.

"I'm quite fine, thanks." He smiles. He keeps looking at me. "Your hair looks lovely. A ponytail suits you, Dr. Winston," he says. "Very shiny, so much nicer than mine," he says, stroking his short red hair. "I haven't been able to get to the salon lately. Still, us gingers need to stick together, am I right?"

Involuntarily, I run my hand along my ponytail but stop myself halfway. "We're going to move right into the standard measures of this interview. I'm sure you've been administered questionnaires like this before. I'm going to ask you a series of questions—"

"You're not too freckled for a ginger." He's still staring. "Not freckled at all, really." Another smile. "Tell me some of your beauty secrets?"

"Mr. Foster." I pick up my pen and look directly at him. His grey-blue eyes don't blink. "Let's focus on the task at hand."

"But you know some of mine." He motions towards my stack of materials. "It's only fair you should share some of yours."

I ache to take this bait, to see what I could win from his cat-and-mouse. But I've been trained well. "Please answer the following questions with a yes or no response . . ."

I lead him through the standard battery and check anger, violent thoughts, sleep patterns, mood. I'm on question seven before he deviates.

"Do you often feel anxious or concerned about day-to-day matters?" I ask.

"Well, that depends," says Foster.

"It's yes or no. Do you often feel anxious or concerned about day-to-day matters?"

"These questions, if you'll forgive me, Dr. Winston, are rather dull."

"I appreciate your patience in answering them, Mr. Foster. We're almost through. So, do you often—"

"Feel anxious, yes, you've repeated the question once already. Well, I suppose it depends on what my day-to-day matters entail. And how you define *feel*. I believe most people say that they *feel* things right away. Like if something happens to make them upset, they're upset right then. But I don't see it like that."

It's a yes or no answer. I shouldn't, but I indulge. "Oh?"

"It's like I see the feelings first, and then I feel them later. Do you know what rage looks like? It's exquisite. And love. They're all beauties, radiant. I see them, like pictures."

"And this is important to you?"

"Very. Imagine if you could see emotions without feelings, appreciate them with your eyes, with your mind. Feelings limit the senses."

"But you feel at some point?"

"Yes, but later. Later."

I circle "no" for question seven.

"And you?" he asks. "Do you feel anxious day to day? A lovely girl like you in here with us loons?" He smiles.

I try not to smile back. "As a professional, I object to the use of the term *loons*."

"But seriously, Dr. Winston. It doesn't rattle you? You don't look over your shoulder when you leave at night?" He says this in a soft, cajoling voice.

This time, I bite. "Why would I do that? If the loons, as you put it, are in here."

"Well, before we were in here, we were out there. You never know who may be about, Dr. Winston." He grins, adjusts his glasses and presses his torso against the edge of the table.

"A risk we all take, Mr. Foster. Now, to finish . . ."

I insist that he stick to yes or no for the remaining three questions. When I finish, I stack my folder on top of his chart and stand to leave.

"What was your first name again?" Foster asks.

"I didn't say. It's not of any relevance."

"Do you know someone wrote about me? In a psychology journal. Someone named Dr. Danica Winston. The library here gets all the journals. I ripped out the article. I keep it in my room."

I grasp the back of the chair. "Oh? It has your name in it?"

"No. But I know it's referring to me."

I never thought he'd read the article.

"Well, there have been many things written about you," I say. "Your case attracted a lot of attention in the papers."

"The papers!" says Foster. "Oh, they love me! But they'll print anything remotely sensational. This was an article in a psychology journal." He lowers his voice and says in a mock-professorial tone, "It's quite serious."

Bill, the guard, raps on the door. "Everything okay?" he mouths through the small wire-reinforced window.

I nod to him, push in the chair and look at Foster. "You should be careful about ripping pages out of library material. Good afternoon."

I knock on the door and Bill lets me out.

I walk down the hall to my office, careful to take even, measured footsteps even though I want to skip with excitement. My first solo interview with the infamous Martin Foster.

Back in my office I open Foster's chart, place copies of the assessment questions inside and file it neatly under *F* in my increasingly full drawer. I've only been here a week and a half but already the patients' assessments seem relentless, a steady onslaught of interviews and filing. I thought I would get a break from administrative drudgery after I finished the long string of paperwork to apply for this fellowship at Stowmoor. It seems as if the last six months of my life have been devoted completely to filling out forms and asking for letters of reference and writing

a perfect statement of intent. And as Carl, my graduate supervisor, reminded me again and again, as prestigious as my fellowship is, it's not a permanent position. Moving to England means
I'll have to log extensive, supervised clinical hours before I can
become officially chartered here. And those hours won't count
towards certification if I move back home.

But still, I took the leap. And now I'm here, on Foster's case.
I slide his file into the cabinet. My fingertips quiver and not
even the fluorescent office lights can mask my glow.

"So it went well, did it?"

Dr. Abbas steps into my office. He does this at the end of
most afternoons. I haven't figured out if he's checking up on
me or just trying to be friendly. "That look on your face—it's
a look of satisfaction. Brilliant," he says.

"Oh, yes. The session went well," I tell him.

"Very good. Heading out for the day now?"

"I'm on my way." I log off my computer and tuck my notepad into my desk drawer. "Are you leaving too?" I ask.

"Not quite. I've got a late one." He runs his hand over his
short black hair, which hasn't yet started to show any grey,
even though his beard is salt and pepper. "Last-minute appeal
tomorrow or something." Dr. Abbas specializes in addictions,
and he's often called in to testify as an expert witness.

"Right, then," he says, turning towards the hall, "if you
hurry you'll still catch the 5:45 train."

I say goodnight to Kelly at the reception desk. James opens
the iron gate, then shuts it behind me. The metal clang vibrates
in my chest. I walk down the windowless grey stone hallway.
The air is cool, mildewy; I button up my jacket. The hum of
the florescent lights and the dull click of my footsteps echo as
I walk towards another gate at the end of the corridor. Finally,
I pass under a high, ornately sculpted archway. It is the main

exit through the eighteen-foot brick, razor-wired walls that surround Stowmoor Psychiatric Hospital. I remember Foster's words, but I don't look over my shoulder.

I turn the deadbolt of our basement flat.

The room is humid and smells like melted crayons. There are puddles of red wax on newspaper and a Portishead album streaming from the stereo.

"Hey there," says Henry. He stands up from behind the sculpture he's working on, a throne made entirely out of wax and steel wire. It's a deep wine colour and almost as tall as me. "You walked all the way from the tube without an umbrella?"

"Forgot again." I hang up my soggy coat by the door and make my way over to him. I step lightly on the newsprint, dodge red puddles.

"Over two weeks here, think you'd remember by now." He puts down the stainless steel carving pick he's holding and smoothes back the damp frizzies that have sprung from my ponytail. "This," he says, making a sweeping movement with his arm, "couldn't be avoided." Newsprint covers the floor from wall to wall, even in the kitchen. He's pushed our bed into the corner and covered it with a black tarp. The throne is in the centre of the room.

"The rest of my tools came from Halifax today, and I just had to get started. It's for the Fantasy and Disaster festival next month." He gestures towards the sculpture with a wax-covered palm, as if it's something I could possibly miss. "I called today, but they told me I won't get my studio at the college until Tuesday. I couldn't wait. You like?"

I shuffle through the newsprint and displaced furniture and look at the throne from the front. It's over five feet tall, with two thick, black metal wires protruding from the wax at the top of the chair back. The wires spiral downward and support a lacy web of red droplets. Wires curl out of the ends of the arms as well, covered in the same lace of wax. The rest of the chair is solid red, smooth and polished to a dull shine. The seat is slightly concave, and the front curves out and down into a red claw on each front foot. Henry has begun to sculpt a pair of eyes on the back of the throne; they're emerging from the wax, heavy lids, smooth like rocks you find at the bottom of a riverbed. The whole thing is fluid and sanguine, some large, distorted piece of flesh.

I look up at him. "You did all of this today?"

"Well, I only have a few weeks. And the wax had already come. So?"

"Interesting," I say.

"Interesting?" mimics Henry. "You don't mind if I keep it here indefinitely?"

"Well, how indefinitely?" When Henry cleaned out his studio in Halifax, he left a sculpture (inspired by sheep bowels, he said) in my living room for three weeks.

"Maybe it can be a new chair for the kitchen. I can make another one for you—matching thrones, king and queen of our basement studio suite?" He lifts my ponytail and kisses the back of my neck.

"No, no, no, kidding," he laughs. "It will be out of here next week, when I get my studio space. I'll get one of the keener undergrads to come by and give me a hand with it."

"Thanks," I say, putting my arm around his waist.

"So, how was your day with the crazies?"

I hop over his tools and clumps of newspaper and make my way to the kitchen table.

"Just kidding, cherry blossom." He smiles at me and starts

to clean the wax off his hands. "I know how you love them."

"It was good," I say. "Very good."

"Ah—finally met your favourite subject?"

"I can't discuss specifics." I try to sit on one of the kitchen chairs, but there's a foot of iron wire and some rags on the seat. I stand and fidget. I'm dying to share that I had time alone with Foster today. "You know, confiden—"

"Yeah, yeah. Confidentiality." He pulls off his wax-streaked T-shirt, tosses it into the hamper and leans his tall frame against the bathroom door. "What do you want to do for supper?"

"Did you want me to go pick something up?"

"I can run out. I've been in here all day; I wouldn't mind. Sit down, get dry."

Everything except the kitchen table is covered with plastic and newspaper, or heaped with piles of magazines and boxes. "Is it okay to take the tarp off the bed now?"

He grabs his keys off the hook. Tosses them in the air and catches them, a metallic jingle as his palm snaps shut. "Most definitely take the tarp off the bed." He takes an umbrella from the rack at the door. "Curry okay?"

"For sure."

"Oh—you got some mail. It's on the table. Back in a minute."

Beneath an empty coffee cup on the kitchen table are two envelopes. I set aside the cup, pick up the letters, pull the tarp off a corner of the bed and sit down. One is from Stowmoor, confirming direct deposit of my paycheque in the bank. The second has a return address in the city, probably an office. Not junk mail. The envelope is maroon, and my name and address are handwritten in a yellow-gold ink. Inside, I find a card.

Danica,
You are hard to keep track of. I asked your supervisor,
Carl, in Halifax, for your address—you do not mind? You
know I am in London now? So you must meet me. Friday,
September 27, at Tiger Tiger, 20:00. I have something new.
My hair is blonde now, but you will still recognize me.
                                                          Maria

I reread it five times. The Portishead album ends, then starts
again from the beginning, synthesizers and string instruments
calling from the speakers. By the time Henry comes back with
the food, I've tucked the card into the bottom of my purse.

Chapter Three

On Friday night the tube is full of tourists with street maps; they're headed for *Mamma Mia!*, *Dirty Dancing*, *Oleanna*. A group of schoolboys cluster in the middle of the car, their light blue dress shirts untucked and wrinkly. The train jerks to a stop, then roars on again, dirty underground air pushed into a wind. A tall teenage boy presses the length of his body against the pole I'm holding. There's no place to sit down or shift to, so I shimmy my hand up the bar away from the crush of his blue-shirted stomach to the gap between his shoulder and his cheek. On the up side, standing means I won't wrinkle my outfit. Taupe linen skirt and a navy halter, backless. Beige iridescent heels.

The train pulls into Leicester Square and I step into the human river that flows from the underground. A woman with a dark bob and a full-length leopard-print trench coat pokes my arm on the escalator. "What time is it?"

"Quarter to eight," I tell her. She pushes past me.

"Show's starting soon!" she calls out, stilettos clacking against the tile at the top.

Tiger Tiger is a short walk from Leicester Square. I'll be early. The Soho streets are congested with theatregoers, grey and black jackets over dress shirts, designer shoes hitting the cobblestones.

I pass a pub and decide to pop in to use the bathroom, but instead I gravitate towards the warm oak of the bar. I risk wrinkling my skirt, sit on a stool and tell the bartender I'll have a gin and tonic. I flip the beer mat over and over, take a big breath and consider staying here for the rest of the evening.

"It's happy hour, love. Four quid. You here alone?" The bartender sets my drink down. He has shaggy brown hair and looks like Noel Gallagher.

"Meeting someone later." I hand him a five-pound note. He smiles and says he'll be back. I drink half the highball in two swallows, gin fizz buzzing my nose.

I walk into Tiger Tiger at ten past eight. Dance music plays, and even though the floor won't be full until midnight I still have to pay a twelve-pound cover. It's early, but the speakers are pumping out an M.I.A. song about BMWs and Ibiza, backed by heavy synthetic bass. I turn left into the lounge, past a waterfall fountain that cascades down the wall. A few couples are nestled in the little booths scattered at the edges of the room. Candles flicker on the tables. A group of five young women are seated at a table in the middle of the space. They are drinking Bellinis, their long acrylic nails clicking against the large, round glasses. Two men, thirtyish—I imagine they're businessmen who just wrapped a huge merger in the city—are having Stellas and staring at the girls.

Maria isn't in sight; has she stood me up? She's done it before. But then I see three tables at the far end, raised on a dais. The area is dark except for one small lamp hung from the ceiling. Two of the tables are empty, but a figure with

blonde hair occupies the one farthest to the right. She's facing away from me, but then she drapes her arm over the back
of her chair and turns around. Automatically, I stand a little
straighter. Maria smiles, and even in the low light her chandelier earrings shine.

I walk over to her. "Danica! *Jó estét.*" Maria greets me with
two cheek kisses and a long hug. I take a slow breath and smell
her gardenia perfume before she releases me. I linger, then pull
away slowly. She's wearing a low-cut black silk dress, and her
hair falls in light waves past her shoulders. "You look wonderful," she says.

"And you," I reply. Maria is ten years older than me but is
easily one of the most beautiful people in the room.

"Sit." She points to the black upholstered bench across the
table from her chair. There is a martini waiting for me, three
olives.

"I didn't think I'd hear from you again." I wait a beat. "You
know, after you left in Budapest."

"Ah, Budapest. Nonsense." She flicks her wrist, dismisses
everything with a swish of her hand. "I ordered for you," she
says, gesturing towards the drink. "Send it back if a martini is
not still your favourite." She crosses her legs and takes a sip of
her red wine.

"So," says Maria, "you are working at Stowmoor? Your old
supervisor, Carl, he tells me this."

"Yes. Started a few weeks ago."

"Have you met Foster?"

Is she just fishing or does she know I have? I stifle a smile,
think how badly she would like to know about my tête-à-tête
with Foster last week. "Can't discuss that. Confidential."

"But it's only me, Dani." She blinks her doll eyes a couple

of times, blue irises bright next to dark liner and thick black lashes.

In the past this display might have swayed me. I'm still taken with the effect, but I say, "I can't discuss it, Maria."

"Fine. But I assume, then, there is something you *could* say."

"Your note said you had something?" I sip my drink.

"Yes, that. Carl told me you have moved in with an artist. Living in Shepherd's Bush. Not as trendy as you would hope?"

"Well, it's kind of exciting. There was a murder in the park by the tube station last week. And the grocery is close by."

She tries to make me feel like a ghetto-dwelling undergrad eating ramen noodles from a Styrofoam cup. How did she get all this information from Carl? I consider leaving. Maria leans back, re-crosses her legs, then leans forward again. She lowers her chin slightly, tilts her head and smiles.

"I have them, Danica. Báthory's diaries."

"You don't!" How could she possibly have them? We'd found nothing in Budapest. The diaries were only rumoured to exist; there was a reference or two in old history books, a note that sixty years ago someone read a report that someone claimed to have seen them. It was harder still to find any information on where the diaries might currently be. But we'd decided to search.

"I could not take them from the library. But for three days, they let me read them." Maria smiles, reaches for her silver clamshell purse and pulls out some lip gloss.

"What library? In the archives? How did you find them?"

When I was in Budapest, Maria had said the logical place to start was with the National Archives. We climbed up Castle Hill in mid-July heat; the archives office was in one of the grey stone buildings amid the spires and staircases. Maria led me through a wooden double door, down a hallway to a little office where three ladies worked at old cherry desks. Rows and rows of card catalogues lined the walls of the room. Maria spoke with the ladies for a few minutes. Finally, she turned to me with a translation: we'd need an exact catalogue number for any box we wanted to retrieve.

"How can we know what box we want?" I asked. "Where are the records of what's in each box? Can't they do a database search on the computer or something?"

"Dani, here it is different. The records, they are not all on computers."

I looked around the office again. There was an old microfiche reader in the corner and a mid-nineties-looking PC on one of the ladies' desks. "Are you serious? Where are the records, then?"

Maria waved at one of the card catalogue stacks.

"The entire archival records for the whole country are in card catalogues?"

"They have started, with the digitization. But for now, only paper records are complete. The ladies, they have said we can order up all the boxes of the Báthory family, and then we can look. But the diaries, there is no guarantee they will be in the boxes. They say people, before us, have tried to look and found nothing."

I began to understand why no one had officially discovered the diaries. Still, if we put in the work and went through absolutely everything, maybe we could find them. "Well, how many boxes are there? When can we go through them?"

"They said there are perhaps fifty. But Dani, things here, they take time. The boxes, it will take four months for them to arrive."

"Four months? Where are they?" I asked.

"They are in the storage cellars, below the castle. The archives, they are very large. Here, things are more complicated than I think you are used to, Dani," she told me.

In the dim light of Tiger Tiger, I wait as Maria finishes dabbing clear shiny gloss onto her lips, rearranges her purse and snaps the clamshell shut before she answers me. "They were not there, where I looked at first. It was a bit challenging. It was necessary to speak to several people."

"Who? Where were the diaries?"

"The diaries were not in the archives of the Báthory records. I consulted with some historians at the universities, in Budapest, then Szeged. The story, it is too long for tonight."

Of course it is. "But you saw the diaries? You read them?"

"I transcribed them, and translated them."

"Into English?"

At this, Maria laughed. "Always impatient! Now they are for the most part in modern Hungarian. But I have started on English copies and I have brought my transcripts here."

"How long will you be in town?"

Another laugh. "I am here for many months. On contract with the Museum of London. Did you not notice my address on the card?"

"Yes, but—"

"I am consulting on the Jacob exhibition. But they do not work me too hard yet. I am thinking of using my spare time to write the diaries in English. After that, I will go with the original plan. Publish a modern edition."

She finishes her wine, sets the glass on the table and looks at me without a shade of guilt. The original plan was for us to search for the diaries together.

"So you've started translating them already? How far along are you?" I had fantasized about pulling the diaries out of a long-neglected pile of manuscripts. I'd pictured Maria and I passing Báthory's words between us, the paper she had touched.

I had been fixated on the idea of finding the diaries. It had become a cherished distraction from the requirements of my program, the jumping through hoops, the ferocity of Carl's insistence that I compete for every possible award. One day I made the mistake of mentioning to Carl that I had an interest in finding the manuscript and maybe contributing to an edition of the diaries. "That's a vanity project, Danica," he had said. "Chasing after a myth. Where is the scholarly merit? How much time would this take away from your training?"

Maybe it was vanity that had motivated me. The belief that I was entitled to a more interesting reality than an academic life could provide. Even now I'm angry with Maria for continuing the project without me. But still, I'm compelled; if she has them, I want to see them.

"The translations? I really have not gotten anywhere yet." Her mobile beeps from her purse. She pulls it out. "Ah, text from Edward."

I've drained my martini. Maria slowly packs her purse, picks her coat off the hook on the wall. She wraps the grey fur over her dress and pulls a black belt taut around her small waist.

"You're leaving?"

"This place," she tilts her head and sniffs, "it is not where I wish to spend a Friday night." I take a second look, notice the frayed rayon seat covers and several blobby stains on the floor. The businessmen have accumulated a half-dozen empty beer bottles with labels half peeled.

I stand too. "But will you show them to me?"

"You would not think I would keep them from you?" she says as she pulls her hair out of her collar and lets it fall around her face. A man around my age walks onto the dais. "Ah, Edward," she says and kisses him. "Danica, here is Edward. He is an arts columnist at the *Guardian*."

"And sometimes I write for the less illustrious *Time Out London*, too," he says. Edward is handsome, what you would expect for Maria. He's immaculately groomed, and his chocolate-brown dress shirt complements deep brown eyes and a tan. "A pleasure," he says, holding out one hand to me while keeping the other around Maria's waist. I shake his hand half-heartedly and hear Maria introduce me as "a friend and colleague."

"Dani, I will be in touch," she says as she and Edward float down from the dais and across Tiger Tiger's lounge.

She lured me and won. I'm angry and disappointed. And embarrassed that I'm disappointed, that I even came at all. Of course she would drag me out and then abandon me, leave me sitting in a dark corner in a tacky club, alone on a Friday night. It's my own fault; I shouldn't have given her the chance. I have a Ph.D. in clinical psychology and still I fall for her. She's not a balanced, empathetic person. She's manipulative, selfish, opportunistic. I will recite all of this to myself repeatedly and not respond to her again.

But if she's telling the truth, she has Báthory's diaries.

I storm around the West End for a while. Theatre signs, lit up and pulsing, spur me to walk faster. I pass through the red glow from *Thriller*, the yellow glare from *Avenue Q*. Soon the streets are teeming with people filing out of shows, making their way to overpriced bars. I want to diffuse my anger among the chatter of the crowd and dull my craving to see Maria again. Groups of friends bunch together on the sidewalk, divide the flow of people striding around them. I'm jostled into the roadway twice and decide to push onto the underground and go home to Henry.

It's only quarter to eleven, but he's already in bed, flipping through a Marcel Duchamp book he's fished from one of our yet-to-unpack boxes. He takes off his reading glasses when I come through the door. I crawl on top of him, coat and heels still on, and land a gentle kiss in the hollow of his neck. "Hey, Venus," he says, pushing off my coat, undoing my halter. He turns me onto my back and pushes my hands above my head, and I welcome the weight of his body on mine. I close my eyes and try to erase Maria and her gardenia smell. Imagine the diaries dissolving, bookworms devouring every slip of parchment, every copy Maria might have made.

Chapter Four

Two days later, a message from Maria turns up in my inbox:

So lovely to see you the other night. The first of many meetings, I am
sure. For now, a snippet for you.
x, M.

She has attached a file called "BáthoryVienna." Immediately,
I click on it.

Vienna, November 14, 1599

I am much pleased with Dorca and Fizcko this
evening. This morning I was sure they would fail to
deliver what they have been promising me all week,
and that the only punishment to be witnessed tonight
would be their own beatings. But Dorca found such
a pretty girl, with truly sable hair, rare for a peasant.
And Fizcko constructed the perfect cage, barbs strong
and sharp as steel tusks. I told Helena Jo not to clean
after our play—I want to wake tomorrow and see the
rusted blood thick on the cellar floor.

Fizcko followed my instructions exactly. After

supper (the duck was not warm enough) he waited until I was comfortably seated in the cellar. The girl was bound, ankles together, wrists behind her back, a coarse-woven sack over her head. She moved little, having had no food since Tuesday; any longer and they are too limp for my purposes, any less and they are not desperate enough. She was crumpled on her side near the brick furnace, where she could feel the heat and hear Fizcko setting the long irons. Her hair spilled past her shoulders, out of the brown sack, long knotty waves of the purest black. She was without a dress, wore only a dirty ragged petticoat, a patched and rough corset, the kind poor women stitch together. Whenever Fizcko turned the irons, the clangs echoed in the cellar and the girl would let out a noise, goaded, I presume, by fear: a sort of half moan, tailed with a tiny, high-pitched shriek. Sometimes the shrieks would come in waves, three, four at a time, as if all her body could do was take in small snatches of air and force them out in minute spurts. I hoped her gag was tied tightly, cutting into the corners of her mouth, rubbing that pink flesh raw as slaughtered beef.

The cage sat directly before me. It was black iron, the bars set just wide enough apart for a girl to extend an arm, maybe a leg if she wasn't too stout. Just wide enough so Dorca could jab her with the irons, enough so I could see every futile movement she made, could watch exactly how she moved to impale herself on those tusks. There was a constellation of spikes, all at least eight inches long, protruding inwards. To the top of the cage was fastened a chain, which was threaded through a pulley; once the girl was inside, Fizcko would hoist her up. In this cellar space it wouldn't be very high, but high enough for the cage to swing at least a foot above my head. This old house used to be a monastery; thank God those Augustinians made such a sturdy, high basement. The bottom of the contraption was a steel grill, strong enough to hold a frantic dying girl, open enough to let her blood rain down below.

At last the pokers were heated. Fizcko gathered up the crumpled girl and stood her in the cage. He moved to take the sack off her head before I reminded him to stop and loose only her hands, so that she could do the rest. Fizcko locked the door to the cage and told the girl to untie her own feet, take off her blind and gag. She started to scream as soon as she saw where she was, locked fast in the maw of my spiked cage, with Fizcko hunched and dirty outside the bars, stoking the furnace. She cursed in German at him, and he brandished a glowing iron towards her. The girl whimpered and stumbled back, screamed again when her forearm scraped against a spike: a half-moon mark, fresh red, sprang up on her skin. She was an easy bleeder.

She kept looking towards me, taken, I imagine, with what she saw. Helena Jo bleached my hair just last week, so now it looks like white-gold silk. I had the girls do my hair up today, a twist at the crown. They put in the ruby combs that Ferenc brought back from the Turks. Just before supper I changed my collar to a stiff white lace. I must have looked like an angel, all golden and light and glittering. I could calm these half-starved, frightened girls before they died, kill them quick, draw a knife blade across their pale throats, their skin soft and easy to split as an apricot. I could explain to them that their virgin blood had a purpose, would contribute to the preservation of my beauty, that they are dying to serve one greater than themselves. But I would miss their screams, their tears.

I sit for a minute, then close the file. But the images remain with me. The scared girl, the cage. Báthory describing herself as an angel.

But there's no description of the actual murder, and Maria's only given me a half story about how she supposedly found the diaries. She hasn't sent or mentioned any photos, any documentation proving she's seen the real, original volumes. This fragment could be from anywhere; she could have written it herself.

On the other hand, she could be telling the truth and have actually found them. She has a background in curatorial studies, knows libraries and archives. She's always mentioning museums she hopes to work for or has been on contracts with, conferences she's attended. Always around successful, seemingly well-connected people. She could have met the right professor at a museum reception, learned about a yet-to-be-catalogued stash of papers in a university rare books library. Maybe she's poring over her transcriptions right now and translating more and more into English, building her manuscript for publication. I feel a flutter of jealously.

I became fascinated with Báthory years ago. During undergrad I'd often look through a plastic milk crate of one-dollar giveaways at the used bookstore in the strip mall behind my apartment. The bookstore was one of the only good things about living in the suburbs on a bus line that ran only until midnight, in an institutional, faux-wood-linoleumed, excessively scrubbed and whitewashed apartment block. One day I found her, in a book called *Weird and Wicked: Women You Never Want to Meet*.

I read and reread the chapter; she caught in me like burrs. The stories of her tortures, the images of what she committed, pricked me when I was walking between classes, shopping for a new dress, sitting under the dryer at the salon while my highlights developed.

I have been mostly lucky, or maybe unlucky, in that I've never experienced anything horrifying in my life. When I was about fourteen, one of my friends at school told us about her tabby cat, Frisco. She found him lying under the potentilla with three of his legs cut off, bone splinters and ground flesh at the stumps. He was half conscious, his pink tongue clamped between his front teeth. He had been roaming in the field; her dad was swathing the wheat and Frisco got caught in the blades. That he made it back to the house was pure adrenalin, homing instinct. He stayed under the potentilla until her mom wrapped him in an old bath towel. Her dad had to get off the tractor, find the rifle and shoot the cat.

It became a story boys at school would retell, one or two hunching over and flailing, miming the de-limbed cat, another pretending to hold a gun, aim, shoot. And shoot again and again until they were all laughing, playing charades with their imaginary guns and the memory of a cruelly injured cat. The rest of that year I'd sometimes see my friend stare blankly at nothing during class or at a party. I thought it had to be Frisco and the boys' constant re-enactment of the incident that made her chew her cheek, made her eyes fix on empty space. I imagined that the world was never exactly the same for her after she saw her pet maimed and dying. I've never had an experience like that, something that gnawed at me in every pause and that changed the taste of things. I know I should be grateful, but I'm curious, envious to see what it's like to pass through a version of reality and to see your world differently than you are able to understand it right now. Reading about Báthory didn't completely change me, but it spurred me, dug in just enough to encourage my curiosity of what it might be like to experience the horrific.

After that book I searched further in the library and online. I took a course called "History of Eastern Europe, 1450–1600," where we mostly learned about the Ottoman Empire, but I managed to put her in a footnote for my term paper. I kept *Weird and Wicked* on my desk at home. She was my spectre, my something sparkly amid the faux hardwood, the white walls, the never-past-midnight bus rides.

Technically, I was fixated. Though now I don't necessarily think about Báthory every day. I don't idolize her like Foster does. There've been long stretches when she hasn't even crossed my mind. But what my interest in her churned up is something that goaded me. What makes somebody lie, steal, kill? And how do you know who is capable of what?

It's hard to know for sure. Are people innately normal, genius or insane, if you can even define these terms? Or can these things be nurtured? The *Diagnostic and Statistical Manual of Mental Disorders*—the DSM, we call it—was first published only in the fifties. The *International Classification of Diseases*—the ICD, which they more often use here—has a longer history, but its goals are similar. With every new edition of these texts, new disorders are "identified." A disease is shaped and given a name. Someone decides that if you have certain traits, you have Disorder X. But open the most recent editions, the DSM-IV or the ICD-10, and you discover we all have traits classified as maladaptive. How many people do you pass on the street in a day? One in a hundred has psycho-pathic tendencies. When do tendencies and traits add up to an absolute, a diagnosis; when do traits prompt actions; when do those actions cause others harm? Where is the line between healthy and unhealthy, and who gets to draw it?

I'm supposedly trained to address these questions in a mea-sured and professional manner. Even when I interview foren-sic patients, the situation is extremely controlled. I read about a patient's history in a file, I go sit in a room across from him or her for a few minutes, ask questions from a script, calculate a score and stick one more piece of paper in the case history. It's my job to observe and to record. To be detached. I'm getting good at it. I can interview a criminal who shot someone during a robbery, then ran over two people with his truck during his failed getaway, write up the report and not think about him or his victims ever again.

But it's different with Foster. And Báthory. Twenty minutes after reading Maria's attachment I'm entering test scores in a spreadsheet, but my mind lingers on the image of the count-ess: platinum blonde, dressed in white, the cage with the spikes. No clinical assessment, no sanitized environment. Hot irons and a dirty basement and Báthory welcoming the blood. No limits on money, power or resources. For a time she was above any law or church. She was evolved into a perfect mani-festation of her disorder. Unfettered and terrifying beauty. Compare her to this spreadsheet in front of me, the patients corralled into small grey siderooms, the clockwork *click-click* of the nurses' med cart, all in some way necessary, perhaps even good, things. But not beautiful.

I pull up Maria's email message and hit reply.

Chapter Five

I suggest a lunch date on Saturday with her. Henry's started to teach a Saturday class, so I'm on my own for most of the day, anyway. "Only for a while," Henry says. "Just to make a bit of extra cash."

Maria picks the place, a vegetarian restaurant near Covent Garden. The area will be overrun with tourists and shoppers, on a Saturday especially, but Maria assures me we'll have no problem spotting each other if we meet directly across the street from the tube station. I still feel like a tourist myself, really, even though we've been here over a month now. I leave the house about an hour early to allow time for getting lost, tube delays, other unforeseen emergencies.

But I arrive at Covent Garden without incident and with over an hour before I'm supposed to meet Maria. I head to the market and kill twenty minutes in a makeup store that sells gloss and eyeshadow in tiny jewelled pots. I'm looking in the mirror, holding a bright teal shadow beside my eyes, when I see a quick flash, a blonde darting behind me. I turn and accidentally step on a salesgirl's toe.

"Oh, no, excuse me," I say. I look down and see that her shoes are open-toed.

"Not at all," says the girl, biting her lip. She looks at me. "You have interesting colouring. Very peaches and cream, but with your eyes, I'd suggest something gold," she says. Her lips are carnation pink. "Here, we have a few things that might work for you." I feel bad about crushing her foot, so I sit on a stool and let her pick out a colour. She dips a makeup brush in a glittering pot and swabs my eyelids. "This is called Be Bronze. Golden tones bring out the light in amber eyes. Look."

I glance in the mirror. Not bad, actually.

"Now, tell me if you like this." She dabs at my lips. "It's called Carney."

It looks like she's taken an orange highlighter to me. "It's a little bright," I say.

"Not to worry. But it's good to give something new a go. You never know." She hands me a tissue and I wipe off the lipstick, then check to make sure I haven't smeared it all over my face. In the mirror, another flash. Platinum hair. I turn quick, see the back of a coat, high-heeled feet rushing out of the shop. Maria? I throw the tissue in the garbage and step off the stool.

"Have you tried any of our fragrances? This is one of our classics, Make It Fluffy." The girl sprays a strip of paper and some of the perfume hits my sweater. It smells like musk and artfully rotting flowers.

"Um, thanks," I say. I give up the idea of following the woman and move towards the cash. "I'll just take the eyeshadow."

The salesgirl wraps the pot for me in red tissue paper and sets it inside a petite gold bag. I twirl the bag between my fingers and head back to the street.

It's overcast but not raining, so I walk back towards the

tube station and cross into Seven Dials. The musky perfume
sticks to my coat and hair; I walk quickly to try to shake it off
as I weave through the thick, quick crush of Saturday shoppers. A woman nudges past me, four-inch heels effortlessly
clicking on cobblestones. I hear another set of footsteps pushing behind me. Foster's words rattle in my mind. *You don't look
over your shoulder? Before we were in here, we were out there.* It's
only bothering me because I'm anxious to see Maria, to get her
full story of the diaries while fending off her inevitable questions about Stowmoor.

I window-shop mostly. But I can't concentrate on the dis-
plays. No matter what speed I walk there's a sound of steps
at my heels; someone keeping pace with me for blocks. Then
someone elbowing past. A man's late-morning coffee breath
warm on my skin as he shouts on his mobile phone. Each
time I duck to the edge of the fray to look in a storefront,
I see the window's reflection: a horde of translucent bodies
and heads jostling behind me. A head with blonde waves
like Maria's bobs close, then pulls away. I turn, watch solid
walking bodies, dozens of blonde, grey, white, brown heads,
a few pink and green ones. No Maria, no one paying me any
attention except to step around me as they hurry to their
next destination.

Exhausted by my own neuroses, I go into a boutique. I peel
off my rotten-flower smelling clothes and try on things the
saleswoman suggests: a black dress, short, with a tulle skirt
and corset-like ribbon ties in the back. A grey angora sweater.
A billowy sequined purple minidress. I survey myself in the
mirror. As my mother would say, it does nothing for my waist.
I look like a sparkly eggplant.

Someone in the change room beside mine pulls the brocade curtain back six inches, but doesn't come out. She must

be waiting for the mirror. I scurry into my change room, put my clothes on and leave the outfits behind. When I come out, the curtain of the next change room is wide open. A long, white, iridescent dress hangs at the back. The clerk takes the dress off the hook, holds it in front of her. "Your friend had to rush off?"

"My friend?"

"Yes. The woman who was in here."

"No, I . . . I didn't know her."

"Oh, I thought you two came in together. My mistake." She whisks the dress away. The slinky material glitters as she walks.

I look back at the empty change room and involuntarily shiver. I'm being ridiculous. What was so odd? Someone using a change room beside me? Get it together, I tell myself. I walk out the door.

Still a half-hour until I'm supposed to meet Maria. I merge into the flow of pedestrians, accidentally bump a woman who's carrying a takeaway coffee. The lid of the drink stays on, there's no spill, but she looks at me like I tried to push her in front of a bus. I apologize repeatedly, slip back into the crowd. I jostle along for a few minutes and spy a pink storefront with a clear Plexiglas double door. The window display is rose and cream and serene. I step inside.

Another cosmetics store. I pick up a sample jar of cream, dab a bit on the back of my hand. Dragonfruit Surprise Body Lotion. I sniff my hand. Mouldy fruit smell, mixed with the bad flower perfume. I smell like a compost heap.

A raven-haired salesgirl pops out from behind a caddy of bronzing products. "Are you familiar with our services?"

"Um, no. This is my first time here."

I'm struck by her perfect ponytail, the crispness of her pink blouse. Lip gloss so shiny I swear I can see a shadow of my reflection. "Our list is there," she points behind me, "on the wall, or you can pick up a pamphlet to take home with you. We take appointments or, if we have time, walk-ins. This week we have a special on lash extensions—partials are half-price."

"Partials?" I say.

"Yes, we attach the lashes to only the outer half of the eyelid."

"Attach, permanently?"

"Semi-permanently. The service comes complete with a care sheet, extra glue and a special solution to dissolve the adhesive if you wish to take them off."

"Oh, sounds interesting."

"If you want, I'm open right now. It only takes about ten minutes."

I think of Maria's doll lashes. I look at my watch—still a good twenty minutes until I have to meet her. "Sure," I say, and follow the girl to the back of the store. I sit in the makeup chair; she swivels me to face a mirror lined with bright, round light bulbs.

"I'll just grab the supplies," says the girl. "Here's some information about our services. I'll be back in a sec." She leaves a lavender pamphlet on the counter and skips away, dark hair bouncing.

I peruse the list of services that will make me more attractive, or happy, or both. The various treatments promise *rejuvenation, glow, definition* of my skin, my eyes, my very soul. You don't need a degree in psychology to know they're trying to create a feeling of lack in the consumer, one they will happily correct, for a fee. Still, I notice that they have eyebrow shaping on the list too. I look in the mirror. I should pluck mine more regularly.

"Right, here we are." The girl returns with a plastic tray full of bursts of two or three lashes, spider-legs bunched into a single knot at one end. She sets out tweezers and a little dish of clear goo that smells like an industrial cleaning product, then swivels me away from the mirror to face her. She grabs a cotton pad and starts to wipe off all of my eye makeup. "Have to start with a clean slate," she says. "The glue won't stick if you've already got mascara and other stuff on there."

I take a quick peek when she's done, and feel panicky when I see the circles under my eyes, concealer-free, exposed in public.

"Now, you might feel a slight stinging sensation, because of the glue," she says as she begins to shellac my lids with the goo. "But not to worry, it isn't harmful."

At first I don't feel anything, but as she continues to attach three, then four knots of lashes, I feel a slight tingle that gradually increases to an uncomfortable stinging. The glue settles onto the perimeter of my eyelid; the discomfort elevates to a raging burn.

Think about something besides the burn, I tell myself. My mind wanders back to the diary segment Maria sent me last week. Since I read it, Báthory's been appearing in my dreams. Last night I dreamt she was at the supermarket in the produce section, dressed all in white, platinum hair tied back in tight braids, diamond chandelier earrings. She was standing in front of the strawberries and I was afraid to pick up a carton.

"Try not to squint your eye so much," the salesgirl says. I attempt to keep my glue-ravaged lids closed and as still as possible. She starts attaching the lashes on my other eye, and the discomfort there seems more bearable, maybe because I'm expecting it.

"Ah, you are here!" says a voice a few feet away. "I run out of my best lipstick, so I come early to do some shopping, and here I find you!"

"Maria?"

"Please try to stay still," says the girl. "Almost done," she says with forced cheeriness.

"This is not so usual for her," I hear Maria say to the girl. "It is good, she is trying for a new look."

I hear Maria sniff. "Dani, you also have some new perfume? You are a bit earthy."

"Okay, you can open your eyes." The girl spins the chair around towards the mirror. "Just don't touch them until about half-one, and you'll be right."

I lift my lids and see my naked eyes, lashes dark and feline. Like I belong in a mascara commercial. The dark circles below my eyes cancel out the fantasy.

"Very nice, Dani," says Maria. "I always did like your eyes. But you look quite tired, dear."

Chapter Six

I met Maria at a conference called "Blood Crimes: Histories of the Deviant" at the University of Vienna. The conference wasn't a big academic draw; more than a third of the presenters were "independent" scholars or, as Carl referred to them, "mere hobbyists." I was at the welcome wine and cheese, cornered by a librarian from Düsseldorf who was trying to talk to me about Charles Manson (I think), despite my insistence that *"ich spreche nicht Deutsch."* Over his shoulder, I saw a woman at the hors d'oeuvres table, loading her little plate with a hill of green olives. She had long hair, dyed that vibrant shade of red found on drugstore shelves in Eastern Europe. She noticed me staring and walked over. Her long black skirt rustled as she moved, and light spun off the string of amethysts at her neck.

"I am Maria," she announced, and kissed me on the cheek. She turned to the librarian, said something in German, and he walked away. "I see you have met Dedrick. I sent him to get us some wine, and the queue is quite long right now." She spoke with an accent I couldn't place.

"Thank you. I mean—"

"No need to pretend, it was plain he was boring you.

Olive?" I took one from the plate she offered me. "And you are?" she asked just as I put the olive in my mouth.

"Danica," I mumbled.

"A Slovak name," Maria said. "You have ties there?"

"No, I think my mother just liked it. Probably heard it on a soap opera."

She said nothing and looked away, as if she were searching for an excuse to leave. "Are you giving a paper here?" I asked.

"Oh, no, I had some meetings in town and a few of my colleagues suggested I stop by this conference."

"What field are you in?"

"Archival, curatorial. My main research focus is Erszébet Báthory."

"Really?"

Maria smiled and stepped close to me. "Ah, you know about the Blood Countess?"

"Of course. She is . . ."

"Thrilling? Yes."

"Have you heard about that murder in England? The man who was supposedly obsessed with Báthory?" I asked her. Foster had committed his crime just the week before; all the English news reports I'd watched in my hotel room were covering it.

"Shocking, isn't it?" She smiled. "This reception, it dwindles. Shall we go elsewhere?"

Over glasses of Märzen lager, Maria told me about her visits to Čachtice, Báthory's castle. She had found pottery shards and pot handles at the ruin, and she thought these artifacts might complement the records and transcripts from the trial of Báthory's servants, carried out in Bratislava in 1611.

"This evidence, it supports some of the testimony, especially from her manservant Fizcko. Have you read the transcripts, Danica?"

"Not really. I've heard them mentioned in books about her, though."

"Ah, yes. Fizcko, he reported many of the ways they tortured the girls. Do you know that they poured pots of water over the girls in the snow? Once the girls were almost frozen stiff, ice statues, but not quite yet dead, the Countess would order the pot handles to be heated up in the fire, then pressed on the girls' hands, backs, bellies. The searing handle would brand the girls' flesh." She paused here, took a sip of her beer.

I'd never met someone so enthusiastic about Báthory. I watched her drink her beer and waited for her to continue about her research. Her passion for Báthory was almost tangible. When she spoke, even in the dull light of the pub she was radiant.

"And Danica, will you incorporate Báthory into your research? This terrible crime in England, the criminal, he would be an interesting subject for a psychologist, yes?"

I laughed. "I suppose. Though there's no way I'd ever get to work with him. I'm still a grad student."

"So?" Maria stared at me for a moment, blinked exaggeratedly a few times, her blue eyes fringed with thick lashes. "You finish your program, you go do what you want, work where you want."

I laughed again. "That's a nice thought. But it's not that simple."

"Of course it could be that simple. It is like Báthory's diaries."

"I didn't know she kept diaries." The bartender came by

and I ordered us another round. I felt Maria and I could talk all night.

"It is rumoured. We do not know where yet, but if they have survived I will find them." She said this with complete conviction. "Danica, you are staying in Vienna for how long?"

"A couple more days," I said.

"Then you should see Čachtice!" she said. "We will go tomorrow, by train."

The next morning, I waited for Maria in the Südbahnhof. Commuters and travellers swept through the doors and moved to and from the platforms. I was sitting on a hard metal bench by Platform Two, holding my ticket to Čachtice. I kept scanning the crowd. Our train was due to leave in six minutes. She'd show up, I told myself.

The train was standing at the platform, and I guessed the announcements over the loudspeakers were saying that it was about to leave. Maria still wasn't there. I debated: should I wait, hope she'll turn up later? But the way Maria had described the journey to the castle, it sounded easy. Take the train to Bratislava, then to Nové Mesto nad Váhom, connect with the train to Čachtice, see the ruin, come back. The trains ran until midnight, so I had lots of time to make the return trip. I checked my bag: camera, wallet, phrasebook/map. Passport snugged away in my pants pocket. I stepped onto the metal steps of the train, found my way into a second-class car and took a seat. I felt slighted, and disappointed that Maria hadn't shown up. But I'd find Báthory's castle on my own.

The train pulled into Nové Mesto nad Váhom at eleven sixteen; I had four minutes to make the train to Čachtice. I stepped down from the car and crossed over a set of tracks to the station. It was bustling—four sets of tracks came through this stop, and people were filing on and off the platforms at a quick pace. My ticket said the train to Čachtice would leave from Platform One. No trains to Čachtice were listed on the board, but there was a one-car train sitting on the track at Platform One. I stopped someone in a blue uniform and asked, "Čachtice?"

He nodded, "*Áno*," and I climbed up the rusted steps.

The car had bench seats and was half full, some mothers with little children, a few men. They all stared at me as I got on board. I was glad to see an empty bench at the end of the car. I slid in and sat next to the window so that I could see the station sign when the train approached Čachtice. The sun beat through the windows and heated the car like a greenhouse. The air was humid, heavy with the acrid smell of sweaty bodies. I held my ticket in the palm of my hand. I checked it twice; the sweat from my palm soaked the edges of the paper. According to the schedule, the ride would take eight minutes.

Two men boarded the train and sat beside me. They were in their mid-twenties, wearing dusty jeans, heavy workboots. They stared at me, then whispered to each other. The man closest said something to me in Slovak. I shook my head, said "*Anglický*" and pointed to my phrasebook. The two looked at each other, laughed, then continued to stare.

The train started to move, iron wheels clanging against the track. As we picked up speed, the car rocked from side to side. It was a mild movement, but twice the men pretended to be swayed by the motion and slid down the bench. At the next opportunity, one of them careened into me. He feigned he was powerless to prevent his thigh pressing against mine. I flipped through my phrasebook, at a loss for how to string together a sentence that conveyed the sentiment "get away from me."

I settled for *Prepáčte mi,* which meant "excuse me." The two men laughed. The train started to slow down, and I looked out the window, happy to see *Čachtice* written in three-foot-tall white letters on the upcoming station.

I shoved my phrasebook into my bag and stood up as the train came to a stop. I said *"Prepáčte mi"* again, loudly, tromped over the feet of my two seatmates and into the aisle. A girl, maybe five years old, was sitting on the edge of a bench. She smiled at me. I waved as I walked by, but her mother pulled her close, whispered something to her and stared back at me, lips tight.

I was the only person to disembark. The small train started up again and disappeared down the tracks into the hills. I breathed in the warm, sage-tinged air, happy to be out of the stench of the car. Then I looked at Čachtice station.

All the windows were closed and white boards were nailed in an X across each one. I had planned to buy my return ticket from the station; now I was abandoned amid rolling green hills and wheat fields. No town, no people in sight. Dragonflies flitted among the wheat stalks and the smattering of wildflowers growing between the tracks; their wings shone purple, green, silver under the noon sun. It was picturesque, but didn't help to assuage my panic at being stranded on the edge of the Carpathian mountains.

I walked around the station. There was a throbbing, rotting smell and the buzz of a fly swarm. By the side of the abandoned building lay a mess of bones, ripped fur, dirt stained with blood. Deer. Its head, gnawed on by something—Carpathian wolves?—was almost severed from the rags of its body. The kill site looked at least a couple of days old. Maggots writhed in one of the deer's half-ravaged eyeballs. I ran past the carrion towards the gravel road behind the station.

The road ran parallel to the rail tracks for about six hundred feet, then curved and disappeared behind the hills in either direction. There were no signs, no cars. To my right, I spotted what looked like a gravel quarry, about a hundred and fifty feet down the road. It was surrounded by a barbed-wire fence, with a small plywood shed outside. I dug out my Lonely Planet, cobbled together a rudimentary greeting for whomever I might meet at the shed and walked towards it.

As I neared the quarry, two Dobermans ran around the corner of a parked dump truck. They lunged against the wire fence that cordoned off the quarry, their claws and teeth snapping, woody breath humid on my bare arm, droplets of their saliva landing on my skin. I skittered back, tried to talk to them, but each word I uttered made them bark louder. I ran past them, towards the shed at the end of the fence. I hoped the owner was more friendly than the dogs.

A man stepped out as I approached the door. He was about forty years old, maybe older, and wore overalls with dusty work boots. He slouched against the door frame and scratched his ear, raised his bushy eyebrows and didn't smile at me.

I slowed down. He chewed on a toothpick and gave me a once-over. A few seconds later, he shouted something to the dogs. They backed off, but kept pacing the length of the fence.

I waved at him and moved closer. "*Dobrý deň,*" I said, "*Kde je hrad?*" This was supposed to mean "where is castle" in Slovak, but the man looked confused. I tried again, but this time opened my phrasebook and pointed out the word *hrad* on the page.

"*Ah, hrad!*" he said, his voice gruff. He drew the outline of a castle in the air.

"*Hrad!*" I said and smiled. He looked perplexed. I looked over my shoulders; the dogs had stopped pacing and were sitting as close as they could to the shed, panting.

Maria had made it sound like it was no problem: get off the train and boom, there'd be the castle. Nothing about a smelly train, lecherous seatmates, a maggot-filled carcass, an abandoned station in the middle of nowhere. I'd be lucky not to be eaten by half-crazed dogs, let alone actually find the castle and somehow catch a train back without a ticket.

The man spat on the ground. He pointed down the road, then walked two fingers across his left palm. I nodded, thanked him and started walking. The dogs jumped against the fence as I passed, another cacophony of barks and growls.

The road was straight for about a mile and then curved around the hill. By the time I reached the curve, I regretted wearing my jeans; the denim felt like thermal long johns in the summer heat. I walked faster, anxious to get to the town, a building, water, someplace out of the sun. I berated myself for not being prepared for the hike, not researching more thoroughly how to get to the village from the station. But Maria had promised we'd go together, she'd be my guide, that she'd been there "of course, many times before." I wondered exactly how many times she'd trekked along a rural Slovakian road for miles in thirty-degree heat.

I pushed on, bombarded by grasshoppers each time I stepped on the thick tufts of grass that rimmed the edge of the ditch. Most of the hoppers pinged off my jeans, but some leapt higher, the barbs of their legs and beady heads rough against my bare arms, my face. I was ready to cry from the heat, from the frustration, when I finally reached the end of the curve and saw there was only another mile at the most before the road turned to asphalt. The road passed through a graveyard, then into a town ahead. I hoped it was Čachtice.

I slowed down when I reached the graveyard. The hardtop road split the field of graves in two. Rows of graves nearest the road were simple slabs of stone, weathered black, a lace of moss inhabiting the cracks. About a third of the stones had bright flowers on them, or white candles, unlit, encased in clear glass globes. A raven landed on one of the slabs and cawed repeatedly.

I was almost through the graves and at the edge of town when a loud, tinny voice came from a speaker that was strapped to the top of a telephone pole in the ditch. The voice spoke urgently, almost a yell, in Slovak. It was repeating the same phrase over and over. I looked around for any security cameras, any watchmen. Was the voice talking to me? My throat was dry and I gripped my purse strap, my hand soaked with sweat. I walked back a ways, looked, turned, looked. Thought about going back to the station. Then the voice stopped and the speaker started broadcasting accordion polka music. I was disoriented, and had to take a minute to calm down and get my bearings among the graves.

I was nearer to the town than the station, so I continued through the graveyard, under a stone archway and into the village proper while the music kept blaring through the speakers. A large white delivery truck sped towards me and kicked up stones. I scurried up the steps of the building beside me, a church, to escape the spray of pebbles. The church cast a shadow, so I sat on the shaded steps, wiped the sweat from my face with the bottom of my T-shirt and spied on the truck. The polka music played on.

The truck parked in the town square. People emerged from all directions and congregated at the back of the vehicle, then the rear door slid up. Each person carried a cotton or burlap sack; the man at the back of the truck was taking people's money and handing them vegetables. The polka music stopped for a minute, another broadcast in Slovak rang out, then more music. Danica, you are ridiculous, I told myself, scared by a produce truck and a polka recording.

As I headed to the square, I passed people who were carrying sacks of vegetables; they stepped far out of my path, whispered to their friends. I was as conspicuous as if I'd been walking through town in a gold lamé prom dress. I averted my eyes when I passed by them, felt like I was intruding.

The town museum was just off the square. I climbed the crumbling concrete stairs to the entrance and pulled on the hot, wrought-iron handles of the wooden double doors. Locked. A small paper note was taped to the pale stone wall beside the door. A few words in Slovak, and a time: 13:00. It was 12:30.

I went back down the stairs to the street and stood in the mottled shade of a poplar tree, trying to decide what to do. I fished my compact out of my purse and popped it open. My hair was sticky and wet along the hairline, and my cheeks were bright pink. I tried to dab some powder on my nose, but my face kept perspiring, turning the powder into a wet beige film. My thin T-shirt was damp and stuck to me like papier mâché. I gave up on the compact and decided to look for a place to get a soda.

I found a pub in the square, just a few yards down from the museum. Over the entrance gate was a wooden cut-out of a woman's head, with what was supposed to be, I guessed, Báthory's picture painted on it. Below the head, a sign read *Alžbeta Báthory*. Her name in Slovak. Dense vines, green with small white flowers, twined around the tall gate. The place was tacky, but lush. Cooler than standing under the half shade of a tree. I pushed the gate door open a little; several plastic tables and chairs were set up on a cobblestone courtyard.

"Danica!" Maria stood up from a table. "You did come by

yourself!" She hurried over to the gate and led me inside. "I called this morning, Dani, but there was no answer in your hotel room. You are not upset, are you?" She motioned towards the chair across from hers.

"What happened?" I said. I didn't sit down.

"Oh, it was one of those things. You know. I got up this morning and Dedrick was in the lobby. He is an old friend of my ex-husband, he offered me his car for the day. I thought it would be so much nicer for us to drive here than take the train. Air conditioning, you know. But by the time I called, you were gone."

The waiter came over, and Maria said a few words to him in Slovak. "I just ordered you a Topvar. You cannot drink anything else in this heat." The table she had chosen was dead centre in the yard, no umbrella, no shade from the vine-covered gate. She took off her broad-brimmed sunhat and fanned me with it. "Sit, sit, Dani. Your face, it is so red. Rest." The midday light made Maria's hair look almost maroon.

"You made it sound so easy to get here by train," I said. I sat down. She had tried to call, after all. "I was a bit worried when I saw that the station here was boarded up. And there was no town in sight."

"Oh, that. I suppose it slipped my mind." The waiter came back and set a very large bottle of beer in front of me. I attempted to thank him in Slovak. He smiled and gave me a nod.

"See," Maria continued, "there are villagers only out here, no one who would hurt you. I knew you would find the town. I thought it might even be a bit of fun for you, an adventure, no?" She took off her dark sunglasses and arched her eyebrows. "And the weather, it is lovely. No rain to spoil a walk, yes?"

I drank a few sips from the cold Topvar. I could feel the flush fading from my cheeks. "I see the museum opens in half an hour," I said.

"Yes, we will start there."

"And the castle?"

"Dani, of course." She smiled.

I smiled back. It was impossible not to forgive her.

After the beer, we headed to the museum. An Austrian tour group was ahead of us, and they had just started to filter out of the foyer into a large hall through a pair of arched wooden doors. As the crowd left, I noticed a display of several large photos, bride-and-groom couples standing in front of an old castle tower or a crumbling arch, wild bluebells and poppies springing up from the dusty grounds of the ruins. One of the larger photos was displayed on an easel, and there was a stack of business cards on the right-hand side of the easel's ledge. "Maria," I said, "are those wedding photos taken at this castle—Báthory's castle?"

She swivelled around me, hand on my shoulder. "Ah, those photos. Yes. This display is larger than the last time I came. Everyone wants the fairy-tale background."

"But why would they want their wedding pictures taken in a place where so many awful things happened?"

"That part, they do not have to mention," said Maria. "Look at them. If you did not know, all you would see are wedding photos, brides and grooms in front of an old castle. They want a pretty picture, and they do not worry about the past."

The first room of the museum smelled like mouldy boxes of newspaper. Immediately, I noticed Báthory's portrait, hung prominently on one of the faded robin's egg blue walls. I had seen reprints of it in books, but it was larger, more vibrantly coloured than I had pictured it. She was ornately dressed, with a very pale face. Her eyebrows were thin and highly arched over round, heavy-lidded eyes. She wore a stiff, almost platter-like white collar, which sloped high around the back of her head and extended into a straight edge over her breast. A thick rope of pearls encircled her neck, looped over her collar and down the centre of the turquoise corseted bodice of her dress. Her thin white arms were visible through the light gossamer sleeves, which were gathered tight at the wrists with a band of turquoise velvet studded with rubies. Her right hand rested delicately on a pillow-lined window ledge. But her left hand firmly clasped a red-and-white zigzagged shield. Her fingers curled over the front as if they were atrophied around the metal.

"Her portrait," I said. The paint looked vibrant, as if it had been done relatively recently, but the portrait style was of a much earlier era.

"Ah, yes." Maria stood straighter and stepped towards the painting. "But that is not original, of course. That is by a contemporary artist in Bratislava, a copy. The original portrait, it was stolen from this museum years ago."

"Who took it?" I asked.

"That is still a mystery. Perhaps someone local, some teenagers looking for mischief."

Apart from the portrait, the room contained an antique chair, a few pastoral paintings that resembled the surrounding landscape, and a glass display cabinet that housed a hollow vessel made from a lizard leg, with a wooden top placed askew across the opening.

"Are all of these things relics of the countess?"

"Well," said Maria, "they are meant to be. At least, the

way they are arranged here suggests this is true. But I do not believe they have the documentation to prove it is so."

"Where are these things from, then?"

"Oh, they are quite possibly from the castle, or from Erszébet's manor house, which used to stand in town. But other nobles, other generations, used those grounds also. Come," she said, putting her arm around my shoulder, "the rest of the museum is more professional, more documentation. In another room, they have letters signed by Báthory."

Maria hurried me through two more rooms. As we went farther into the museum, the rooms became smaller, the air mustier.

"Wait," I said to Maria, trying not to give in to her constant tugging on my arm, "I want to look at these rooms, too."

"Dani, these things are of no consequence," she responded, pausing for just a moment. "These things may be from the castle, but I have been here before, I have talked to the curator, if you can call her that—they are all just knick-knacks. Some villagers found them in an old trunk and sold them here, it is likely. Dani, trust me." She stepped to face me squarely. "I will show you the real things."

I followed her into the last room in the museum. "Now, this is authentic," said Maria pointing to a block of stone. "They have it documented here, definitely from the ruins of Čachtice castle. And over here," she gestures to a black-and-white framed print of a tall man with dark hair and a heavy beard, wearing a long black tunic. "Her husband, Ferenc. He was a very successful warrior—they called him Hungary's Black Knight. Fought the Turks incessantly. Still, he took Elizabeth's last name when they married, because her family was more illustrious."

"I remember reading about that. I was surprised she kept her name."

"Yes, yes, and her children, too; it was very common. Pass down the most powerful name," said Maria, leading me along the wall. "And here, a letter from him to Elizabeth."

It was written on a thick parchment paper. "It looks well-preserved," I said. The paper was still almost white, and the only visible mark was a thick crease down the centre that the frame did not quite flatten out. I moved closer and tried to decipher the writing in the low light.

Maria laughed. "I am sure you will not get anywhere, squinting away at it like that. It is in Hungarian. It says nothing very interesting. He is away with the soldiers, he asks after what has been happening at the estate in Sárvár."

Another framed print, a reproduction of a painting, hung beside Ferenc's picture. It was a torture scene: winter, in a castle courtyard. At one end, Báthory was seated in a throne, dressed in layers of thick robes, and again wore a stiff white collar around her neck. In front of her, several women writhed, naked, in the snow. A crew of black-robed, white-hooded men were grabbing another naked girl, who dug her heels into the snow and resisted their attempts to throw her down. Several figures, all dressed in dark clothing, watched from the side of the courtyard, and an old, kerchiefed woman threw a wash-bucket of water over the supine bodies.

"This," said Maria, "is important. It is by a Hungarian artist, nineteenth-century, István Csók." She pointed to the signature in the corner. "It is a portrayal of the ice-torture I told you of. In winter, she had the girls stripped bare. They poured water over them until they froze, like statues."

One of the women lying on the snow looked lifeless; another's eyes were rolled back and she was straining her head upwards, gasping; another was sitting on her haunches, looking upward as well, seeking some salvation that presumably never came. The countess reclined leisurely, with a contented half smile.

"Now," said Maria, briskly, "we go to the castle."

Maria led me to the edge of the village and took me down a narrow paved road that led into thick deciduous forest. The canopy of leaves shaded the asphalt and cut the heat. After a couple of miles, the pavement stopped and the path turned into a steeper, ragged dirt trail that meandered among a more open area of brush and tall grasses. Dust and grass stains dirtied my sneakers.

"Are you sure this is the right road?" I asked.

"Just a little farther now," said Maria.

The sun was still relentless, the mid-afternoon air heavy with the smell of tilled earth and sage. "Maria," I said, "why did you start researching Báthory?"

"The question would be more, I think, why someone would not. She was so . . . human. Only a few people have the power she did, to do exactly what she wanted. What would others do, if they had that chance as well?" She glanced back. "And you, why are you interested?"

A wasp flew out of the bush and began to circle me. "Well, she definitely is disturbing, but immediately attractive. I don't know."

"You do not know? But you are here, climbing a mountain to see her ruin. You must know," said Maria, walking faster.

I didn't immediately reply. I was drawn to Maria, excited to be around her. But I wasn't sure if I should confide in her my fascination with the destructive extreme, my fixation on Báthory's story.

Finally I said, "I'm intrigued by her ruthlessness. She pursued beauty as a visceral experience. She's like a reverse fairy tale."

Maria stopped and turned to face me. Despite the sun and our pace, she was barely flushed. "I understand. But, Danica. She was not a fairy tale. She lived. Here." She stomped her foot lightly, then continued up the slope.

We tromped on for a few minutes and then came upon a sign, the first one posted along the path. It read *Čachtichý Hradny Vrch*, and a paragraph of Slovak ran below it. Below the sign, there was a photo of Báthory's portrait, with *Museum Čachtice* written across the top.

"They must get lots of tourists," I said.

"They are trying. Not so many now. Austrians, Germans, mainly."

The slope was getting steeper, and we slowed our pace. Under my shirt, my bra was soaked with sweat and chafed against my skin. "But this village, it is one of the only places associated with Báthory that advertises the link," continued Maria. "Her castle at Sárvár, her former home in Vienna, even Beckov, just down the river from here, they all try to ignore her. They have nothing in their museums, or in the literature on the ruins, that mentions her."

"But why?" I panted. "Wouldn't they want to promote it, get the tourist revenue?"

Maria let out a light laugh, then a sigh. "Things are not, or at least were not, all about the money. Báthory was hated and feared among the peasants, and at the end ostracized by the Hungarian nobility. It is still not popular to speak of the Blood Countess in some areas."

Maria slowed her pace and slid her small hand around my

waist, undeterred by my sweaty torso. "But Čachtice, it is different. It is good you are here, Dani." She wiped a trickle of sweat from my temple. Her fingers were cool, her touch light. "In ten years here, it will be as commercialized as it is in Transylvania, Wallachia. Buses full with tourists, with cameras around their necks, overrunning the sites. Like the tours to Bran and Peleş." She pulled her arm away from my waist and picked up her pace again, despite the incline and the heat. "You will see how Čachtice is now, no commercialism."

The path reached the top of the hill and flattened out, a grassed-over furrow that seemed to lead nowhere. We kept walking for a few minutes. Then the ruins of the castle rose into view, two tall towers and formidable stone walls. Because the structure was positioned on land slightly lower than the path, we couldn't see it until we were about twenty feet away. The walls were about fifteen feet high, made of grey, now-crumbling stones. The two turrets, kitty-corner from each other, rose three times higher than the walls. The tops of both towers had caved in. The larger tower was missing a wide seam of stones, top to bottom, as if an enormous vulture had gutted it with a talon.

Maria led me through the winding, crumbling walls. She kept hold of my hand as we picked our way through half-buried steps and remnants of firepits. "From the local teenagers," she said. "This is a place they gather."

"A hangout?" I asked. "Čachtice isn't preserved as a historical site?"

"There are many castles in these mountains, Dani. There is not money or interest enough to preserve them all. Here." We stopped in front of the tallest tower, stepped inside through the cleft of missing stones. Maria pointed out where the masonry patterns indicated a door, a staircase, a floor. "This," she pointed twenty feet up, "would have been the middle of the tower. Probably the royal chamber, for the lady. Where she would have died."

A thick scattering of poppies, with a few pansies and blue-bells, carpeted the ground where we stood. I wondered how many people's blood had fertilized the soil. The red petals frilled like petticoats, each a girl cut, spilled.

We walked through the flowers, farther into the ruins. Maria stepped ahead under a dilapidated archway made from crush-ingly heavy stones. The mortar that held the rocks together was cracked, half of it chipped away. A crow landed, took off from the top and loosed a smattering of pebbles. I hesitated.

Maria was on the other side. She turned back to me. "You come all this way to be halted by some little stones? You are not serious, Dani." Her hair shone, ruby waves against her mustard gold sundress. She looked at the rocks. Each lens of her dark sunglasses reflected a curved, contorted image of the arch. "It will not fall. Stepping through, it is hardly a risk." She took three steps towards me, extended her hand underneath the stones. I held her hand and jumped through.

Chapter Seven

After I pay for my spider lashes, Maria and I go for lunch. She leads me through a series of quick lefts, rights, down a side street, and finally we're at the vegetarian place she's picked. We walk down a creaky set of stairs, order at the counter, then take the only table left—a two-foot-square surface made out of plywood. Maria tells me to hold our place while she goes back to correct her smoothie order. While she's gone, I pop open my compact and smear some concealer under my eyes, careful not to touch the lashes.

"There, I caught them before they put in the lychees," says Maria, wiggling between the table and a pew-like bench bolted against the wall. She sits and shrugs off her electric blue plaid coat, flips her blonde waves behind her shoulders. "They just do not go with the raspberries, I think."

"A tragedy averted."

"Dani, now you are teasing me." She smiles. "Have you been here before?" She knows I haven't.

"No. It's small."

A man bumps my chair on his way to the next table, set not quite a foot away from ours.

"Part of the charm, you will see."

"I'm sure I will." I have to shout over the whirr of a blender.

"You are always so serious." She leans in closer. "So," she says, "the section I emailed?"

"Mmm. Interesting."

"Interesting?" she repeats. "You see, finally, some of Báthory's diaries and that is all you have to say?"

"It's the beginning of a good story," I say. "Maybe that's all it was." I keep my eyes on her face for any reaction. All she does is smile again, a carbon copy of the one she gave me thirty seconds earlier.

"Well, it is true, perhaps she did embellish things. Perhaps she fabricated the entire document. We cannot know for certain. But it is her writings, her words. Is that not what you wanted to see?"

"Her words?" I fold my hands together, place them on the plywood tabletop. "Do you have any documentation, any proof of your supposed discovery?"

"I see." Another smile. "You doubt me."

"I do." I feel satisfied saying this to her. She's quiet for a moment.

"Dani," she finally says, "you know my interest in Báthory, it is genuine. To forge these documents, what benefit would it be to me?"

She has a point. It would be a huge risk for her career if she faked recovering the diary. But I wouldn't put it past her to give me a highly stylized version of the truth.

"Well, then, as a professional archivist and curator, I am sure you have the necessary evidence to authenticate your discovery. So, to start, you can tell me how you found the originals," I say.

"Dani, you are so impatient. Yes, I will tell you the whole story."

"You mentioned something about Szeged?" I know this is a city in the south of Hungary, but while we were collaborating Maria had never described it as important to the search.

"Number eighty-seven! Eighty-seven!" yells a deep voice from behind the counter.

"Oh, now, that is us," says Maria. She digs in her purse, pulls out a piece of paper and pushes it across the rough wooden tabletop towards me. She stands up and taps the paper a couple of times. "Look at this."

"EIGHTY-SEVEN," the voice hollers again, louder.

"Oh, I am coming. So impatient," she says, striding off.

I look at the paper. It's a handbill, purple with a thick white border and a logo for an art gallery in the top right corner. It reads *Honey, Torture. A film and performance installation by Erszébet Báthory.* The opening reception is in two weeks, and I realize part of the Fantasy and Disaster festival that Henry and a few other people from his residency have been preparing for too.

"I am so sorry. Can you excuse me?" Over my shoulder I hear Maria making her way through the crowd.

"There." She leans around, one arm on either side of me, and sets down our tray. "Their salads are divine. And this will be the best moussaka you have had." She wiggles back into her seat.

"We'll see," I say, setting down the flyer and picking up my cutlery.

She pulls her smoothie and her salad bowl towards her, and I shift my plate in front of me. "So, you will come," she says, nodding to the paper.

"Is this by the Dutch artist, like the show in Budapest?"

"The one who has changed her name to Báthory, yes. But this one, you will like. It is her solo show."

I'm curious, but the last time Maria and I went to a performance the evening ended badly. "So, you're going?"

"Of course. Edward, he is reviewing several of the openings that night."

I'm quiet for a moment, then say, "Henry is showing that night."

"Your artist? In the festival?" Maria says in a singsong voice. "Which gallery? What is the name of the show? Is he working with anyone?" She rat-a-tats me with questions and immediately I regret mentioning it at all.

"I can't remember."

"Well, you must look it up," she says. "Really, such luck. And also come with me, and Edward, to the Báthory show." She takes a delicate sip from her smoothie. "Besides, for your work, it would be good. Seeing that man all of the time. Báthory was his muse, yes?"

I blow on a forkful of my moussaka. "I think they overheated this."

"For the case with Foster." She sips again, ladylike, her big eyes locked on me for a reaction.

The moussaka's still steaming, but I try a bite anyway, then have to take a drink of ice water to cool the burn in my mouth. Maria keeps looking at me expectantly. Part of me wants to confide in her, to share the rush of my first interview with him. I also want to keep Foster to myself, like she's kept the diaries. In the end, though, it matters very little what I want; as his clinician there's not a lot I can divulge, not without getting into some messy moral and legal issues.

"There are rules about confidentiality," I finally say. "You know that."

"I suppose. But you have mentioned him before."

"Not while I was his clinician."

She smiles and I realize I've admitted to her that I have contact with him.

"The diaries," I say. "You were going to explain to me how you found them."

"Yes, that. But I am telling you very much, Danica." She shuffles her plate over, puts her elbow on the table and rests her chin on her upturned palm. "I would like to hear about your work as well."

"How polite of you." I give her a close-lipped smile. "But really, I insist. So, the archives?"

"Yes, fine." Maria takes her elbow off the table, leans back in her chair. "A few months after you left, the Báthory boxes came to the archives. I searched. It took many days." She spears a tomato with her fork, takes a bite.

"And you found the diary in those boxes? Just like that, when no one else had before?"

She takes another bite of the tomato, then another drink of her smoothie. "No, I did not find them there. It was more complicated."

I am so frustrated by the pace of her storytelling that I want to dump the rest of her smoothie in her lap. "Then where did you find them?"

"Dani, you are impatient. Is it your new job? You are very stressed? It is not good for you."

"The diaries?"

"Yes, yes. I did not find them in the boxes at the archives. There is much material attached to the Báthory family. They were large, their dynasty—is that the word?—their titles and land were passed down for many years. But you know this. So, many letters, many documents, about estates, about inheritances. But not many personal papers, correspondences. I sent the boxes back. I spoke with the archival staff, with some of my other colleagues, I considered the research I had conducted already on Báthory. And then I had an idea!" Maria joyously clasps her hands together.

"Which was?"

"Čachtice, you know, it is not located in modern Hungary. The boundaries, they are much different now. Even where Báthory was born in Transylvania,that is part of Romania now. She had the house in Vienna, the castle at Sárvár in Hungary. She was in what is now many countries. Her papers, I thought, they could be anywhere. The National Archives is not the only possibility. So I began to look at university archives. I asked in Budapest, but nothing. Then I had a little contract with the House of Terror, the new museum about the dictatorial regimes in Hungary. I suggested, I think, that you visit it—did you go there?"

"No. So, you had the contract, and?"

"There was a reception. I met Professor Orbán." She twirls her wrist in the air, a *ta-da* kind of flourish. "She is based at the university in Szeged. It is said it is the best university in Hungary. More known for the medical school, but—"

I cut her off. "And how did this help you find the diaries?"

"Ah, you cannot wait for the whole story! Fine, the shorter version. I went to visit her at Szeged. She is a young professor—she reminded me of you, Dani, really, very pretty, very smart—and so she introduced me to some of her colleagues, I met the librarian in charge of the rare books and manuscripts, we discussed some things. They had holdings about the Báthory family, many things."

"And the diaries were in the collections? Just sitting there? Nobody else had bothered to check, to report them before?"

"Ah, no, it was not so easy, Danica! The diaries, they were not in the catalogued collections. After some time, the librarian, he began to appreciate my devotion to my subject, my respect for Báthory. He allowed me to search the uncatalogued manuscripts, the material they have not filed or identified, the ones they do not allow the students, the public to view. And," Maria twirls her wrist in the air again, "she was there."

"That was lucky for you." Maria's story seemed plausible. But she hadn't told me much that I could fact-check or verify. "And what does this manuscript look like? Where is it now?"

"The librarian, Polanyi, we have made an arrangement. He agreed, he will hold the manuscript, will not catalogue or tell any other researchers it is there, until I have made secure my deal with a publisher. He will be mentioned in the book, of course." She says this last sentence in a hushed, serious tone, her doll eyes wide. The offer of acknowledgement seems like a very small token of thanks, but I've noticed that Maria often gets away with arrangements like this. She could make you feel like your short end of the stick was a bejewelled scepter. "And I have a few photos. I can show you, but you must promise me, you will keep it confidential."

"Photos?"

"It is not the usual practice for the university to allow photographs of the uncatalogued material. But Polanyi, he said for me, a small exception. He allowed me to take a few, and I will return to take more when I have finished the translations."

"How far along are you?"

"You have not told me—how did you like the section I sent you?"

"It was . . . compelling. If it is true, as you say."

"More compelling than Foster?"

I let the question linger. If she is telling the truth, she's sharing the diaries, even offering to show me the confidential proof. She's trusting me. I consider giving her some harmless piece of information, maybe something that could be found on public record. Like the length of his sentence, a detail from the trial. Anyone could check into that, it wouldn't be confidential.

But before I think of something, she says, "Edward tells me Foster is getting a new lawyer."

What? "Where did he hear that?" It had to be another empty rumour.

"Oh, it is the talk, a story the newspaper is working on, for next week. Foster, he is a celebrity. Everything connected to him, they write about."

"Well, I haven't heard anything about it." I say this in a way that implies Edward and his supposed sources are speculative hacks. "What else . . . I mean, are they planning any other articles?"

"It is possible. Foster, he is popular, there is much talk about him. I will keep a watch for you."

I nod and almost feel for some reason that I should thank her, though I'm unsure why.

"Dani, I wonder if you could do me a favour. For the book."

She's going to ask me back on the project. We started looking for the diaries together, and she wants to ask me back, to work together.

"I speak to you as a colleague," she says. "We have common interests."

"Yes. I have always valued that connection." After a month of reports and papers at Stowmoor I'm very ready for her to ask me back in. I want to be involved in something glossy, something more glamorous, more public, than shuffling through the gates of Stowmoor every day.

She smiles, sets down her cutlery, leans back and pushes a few stray tendrils of blonde behind her ears. "I would like a visitor pass. To interview Foster."

"You're joking."

"Dani, I am not. You can get me a pass."

"Maria," I say loudly. The man at the next table swivels his head in our direction. "Maria," I say again, almost in a whisper, "you can't magically get a pass to someplace like Stowmoor."

"Dani, I do not mean to offend. I know, it is a difficult thing." She touches my knee under the table. "That is why I ask for your help."

"Why do you want to see him?" I think about pushing her hand off my knee. I don't move.

"It is for an interview, for the book. He can speak to me for research if he agrees, yes?"

"It's more complicated than that." Much more complicated. Aside from the legalities of such an interview, I cringe to think of the lecture I would get if I even brought up the idea with Sloane.

"Yes, his visitor list, I imagine it would be restricted. But you could arrange something, for me?"

I move my leg away from her hand. "I can't help you get a pass. Even if you somehow got one, I'm not sure you could publish any part of a conversation."

"Dani, not everything has to be official. Besides, I would like to meet him for my personal interest. Is that so odd?"

"So this is all about satisfying curiosity?" I try to sound authoritative, but I come off as sarcastic.

"Isn't everything?" She shrugs her shoulders, as if we'd been talking about trying a new nail colour.

She's potentially found the diaries and now she wants me to risk my job to satisfy her whim of getting an interview with

Foster. No invitation to work with her, to be involved on the project we'd originally thought of together. But she insists: *We're colleagues.* I don't think so.

I stand, bump the lopsided table, jostle my glass. Water slops onto the plywood, soaks the *Honey, Torture* flyer Maria had pushed towards me earlier. "Sorry, Maria, I have to go." I give a few curt excuses and stomp up the rickety steps to the congested street.

"Dani," she calls after me, "I'll be in touch."

Her suggestion that I help get her a visitor's pass is ridiculous. Though I can't say part of me wouldn't love to see those two in a room together. She thinks she can just flit into a forensic hospital, charm Foster, and he'll be her docile pet, tell her everything, and she can write it down in a perfect little story.

She's delusional. I've never assessed Maria, clinically. But it's possible she could be diagnosed with some disordered tendencies, histrionic, narcissistic. She needs to be constantly at the centre of attention, to create drama. Everything is a game to her, entertainment, even the idea of hearing about a murder right from the killer. But she would be in over her head with Foster. I would love to see her flounder.

Chapter Eight

He pulled the silver Audi sedan into the dockside parking lot. "They're unloading already," he said, and pointed to a large freighter at the end of the wharf. Workers ferreted among the orange and black cargo containers. Some held clipboards and Styrofoam cups of coffee. A forklift driver scooped three stacked boxes, taxied them to the other side of the dock, went back for more. Lifted, carried, set, lifted.

For a moment they sat and watched. His passenger opened her red alligator clutch, pulled out a brush and ran it through her long, dark hair. She turned the rear-view mirror towards herself and dabbed on some lip gloss. "Shall we?"

He turned the mirror back to its original position and checked his dark hair before he stepped out of the car. He pulled his brown leather gloves over his manicured hands and surveyed the wharf. "There." He pointed at a man with beige coveralls and a brown hat. Steel grey beard, late forties. They started towards him. She buttoned her long dress coat and effortlessly dodged rubble, though she wore heels. He put his sleeve over his nose and tried not to breathe in the docklands stink, to remain untainted by the grime. They stood at the bow of the boat.

Finally the worker saw them and asked, "You two here for

that delivery? You don't waste time. Just came in an hour ago."

They didn't say hello. The younger man drew his sleeve away from his face, reached in his coat pocket and handed the older man a plain white envelope. "Where is it?" he asked.

"This the entire payment?" The worker riffled through the bills in the envelope.

"It's all there. Where is it?"

The worker looked at the man, then the woman. She was beautiful. Young, not even twenty-five, he thought. She was taller than both the men and kicked impatiently at the ground with one of her high-heeled feet.

He tucked the envelope inside his coveralls. "Must be quite important, then?"

Neither of them even smiled. They stared at him until he said, "All right, no small talk." He adjusted his hat. "This way."

They walked to a small office shack. The walls were corrugated steel, the floor plywood. The small windows were fogged with grease and condensation. Mouse droppings lined the window ledge.

"And how long has it been in here?" the woman said. "It shouldn't be in humidity like this."

"I told you," said the worker, "it just got in an hour ago."

The flat rectangular parcel leaned against the wall, underneath the ledge with the droppings. The young man put a hand on his companion's arm. "I know," he whispered to her. "Conditions of transport are variable." He plucked the package from the mess.

"Right, if you need to use my services again, just give me a bell." The older man patted the envelope in his pocket. "Pleasure doing business with you."

They drove towards her flat in the East End and unloaded the parcel from the car.

"We can't keep moving it, not with conditions like that," she said as she opened her door. "It's four hundred years old. You can't have it tossed in a dirty old shed."

"I know," he said. "It's becoming dangerous. But it's tradition. Ritual."

"Which is why it should be shipped by a professional company," she said as they walked inside. The walls were dusty pink, and a bouquet of lilies filled a crystal vase on the small table beside the doorway. She threw her keys on the table and they clattered against the vase.

"You know we can't. Suggest it if you like, but it won't work. You know it's crucial we arrange . . . less obvious modes of transport."

"It's just, what if something happened to it?" She pointed to a spot against the wall, across from the daybed. "Put it there."

He set down the painting and freed it of its dirty cardboard outer casing and the bubble wrap inside. She hovered as he removed each layer. "It would be safer to leave it in storage," she said. But after he opened a final layer of paper and she saw it again, she understood why it was worth the risk, the impracticality.

It was the physical connection. They needed to see it, to touch it. Báthory was once in the same room as this canvas. Looked at it, breathed on it with a pant of anticipation or of indulgence, with thoughts of a servant just killed or about to be. The wet paint covering pale canvas like a girl's blood on her skin.

He touched the heavy gilded frame, the wood cool against his tanned skin. He knew each brushstroke of her square, lace-trimmed collar, the turquoise cuffs tight against her wrists at the end of gossamer bell sleeves. Hair pulled back from her face with a tight cap of jewels. Báthory's lips and eyes relaxed, not a smile, not a frown.

They would hang it later. For now, it commanded the space in the small, lily-scented flat.

From her wine rack she pulled a bottle of Egri Bikavér. She unwrapped the foil at the neck, dug in the screw. Turned, turned, pulled. She poured them each a glass of the deep red wine. They sipped and attended on the Countess.

Chapter Nine

Every morning on my way to work, I pass by an angel outside the front gate of Stowmoor. The statue sits a hundred yards in front of the regal-looking archway and high brick walls of the institution. She probably used to be white stone; now, dirty grey veins run down her dress and through her wings, which she holds over her head, half-spread. She is mottled and worn. But beautiful in spite of, maybe because of, this decay. I wonder whom she's there for; the patients walled inside never see her. Maybe she's there for us, the people who pass in and out of the gates every day.

This Monday morning, I hustle past the angel and give her only a cursory glance. I'm scheduled to do the second interview with Foster this afternoon. But first I have a meeting with Abbas and Sloane, to consult with them about my initial report. I dig through my purse for my ID and string it around my neck. I say hi to Trudi, who works the main entrance most mornings. She buzzes me through the first gate. It clangs shut behind me and I hurry down the dark grey hallway, the heels of my boots slipping on the concrete epoxy floor. I pass through another set of gates, get my mail from Kelly and make it to my office two minutes early.

We must be on time on Mondays. Mondays, they test the alarm at ten o'clock. Any early morning interviews or sessions must finish before nine forty-five. Then all patients are taken back to their rooms and accounted for. Guards and orderlies stand by the doors, and we all wait for the alarm to start. The sound is similar to a WWII air-raid siren. But it's not as loud inside as you might think. It's meant to project outside, to let the three towns surrounding Stowmoor know that someone has escaped. All of the schools have lockdown plans in case of a security breach.

As substantial as the security seems, there have been problems inside the hospital. Throughout my grad school training I interned and volunteered at several hospitals and forensic facilities. I thought that horror movies exaggerated the bleakness of prisons, the unsettling atmosphere of an insane asylum. But they aren't that far off. Stowmoor is every cliché you can imagine. Bleak, cold, colossal. The facility was built in 1863, part of the boom of asylums that sprang up in Victorian England. Since then, modern wiring and updates in plumbing have been graphed onto the place. But there are holes. The buildings are too old and large to be fitted with an automatic lock system that connects with the fire alarm. So Health and Safety decreed that to avoid loss of life in the case of a fire, guards must manually lock and unlock the gates. Nothing has happened since I've been here, but I've heard about past incidents. Patients have gotten through the gates and onto the grounds or the sports fields. A group of male sex offenders assaulted two female patients on the football field last year. After the press picked up the story and started reporting on the archaic security at the hospital, the administration decided to stop housing women at Stowmoor. But they didn't change the security system.

The most infamous "incident" involved Robert Maudsely. He and a partner invited another patient into an empty room. Maudsely barricaded them all inside and he and his partner tortured the third man for nine hours. Maudsely held the mutilated body against the window in the door so the guards could see. When security got into the room they found the victim's skull cracked open, part of his brain missing and a spoon dug into his cranium.

But that was thirty years ago. Now Stowmoor has the Paddock.

The Paddock is where they house the patients termed Dangerous with Severe Personality Disorder, the most violent criminals at Stowmoor. Foster stays there. The Paddock sits just behind the main building, a short walk across a well-manicured lawn. A guard staffs the front gate; another patrols the back door. But as we're told when we begin work here, even though some convicted criminals live at Stowmoor, we are a hospital, not a prison. The people here are patients, not inmates; their quarters are called siderooms, not cells. The Paddock has security, but it is still a hospital building with plenty of traffic in and out. Laundry service and supply deliveries come and go through the underground cargo bay. It's much like any other building on the grounds, except all of the patients housed there have been deemed DSPD. But it sounds good, doesn't it? The Paddock. Safe, secure. Don't worry, we're keeping the worst of the worst in the Paddock. Like everything else, it's a lot about semantics and paperwork.

It's hard not to constantly check the clock during the minutes leading up to the alarm. I try to focus on my latest intake report. This patient is a candidate to move to a lower-security part of the facility. Three years ago, high on crystal meth, he shot two people while he was robbing a Tesco Express. He's been through addiction counselling and has consistently shown remorse for and insights about his actions. We see a lot of cases like this one. He's not a psychopath, not irreversibly antisocial. He grew up in an environment that normalized abuse and crime. He made several bad choices. At nineteen, in a twenty-minute period, he made several acutely bad decisions that ensured he'd be in custody for the rest of his life. I interviewed him for thirty minutes, and now I'm writing a document that will determine whether he gets to move or not. I almost finish before the alarm goes off.

At ten thirty, I meet with Dr. Abbas and Dr. Sloane in Abbas's office.

"Danica, sit down," Dr. Abbas says. He waves in the general direction of a chair but doesn't look up from the document he's reading. "Good work with the first round of the assessment," he says, as he hands a copy of Foster's file to Dr. Sloane. She flips through it, barely glancing at the pages.

"Hmmm, yes, I read this last week when you filed it. Fairly competent," says Sloane.

"Thank you," I say, leafing through my own copy of the report. "So, for today, I was planning to discuss remorse, responsibility, the efficacy of any of the rehabilitation therapies he's been engaged in since he's been a patient here."

"You got the memo, then?" asks Abbas. "Yes, today it's a standard interview-type assessment."

"Great, I'll get going." I stand up to leave.

"A moment, Dr. Winston?" Sloane stands up. "You are aware, I assume, of the significant media interest in Foster's case." She stands directly in front of me, leans one of her French-manicured hands on an office chair. "And you know, last year during his annual report, there was a resurgence of this coverage. Mostly in the more disreputable publications."

"Yes. It's a sensational case."

"I do hope you're not swayed by anything you read in the media, Danica." She crosses her arms over her chest, sniffs slightly. "As I assume it's entirely probable you read those . . . stories."

I cross my arms too. "I take the initiative to inform myself about all aspects of Mr. Foster's case, in order to be the most effective clinician possible for his needs."

Sloane clears her throat, steps behind the desk with Abbas. "Danica, your job is to focus on Mr. Foster in a clinical setting. You cannot be distracted by hearsay and sensationalism. You are not a detective or a journalist. You are a psychologist."

I'm not sure what I've done to trigger this lecture. "Of course. It's just—"

Abbas taps his pen on the desk a few times. "I think," he says, "Dr. Sloane is possibly trying to prepare you . . . I was going to wait until things were more certain, but . . ."

I take a couple of steps towards the desk.

"It seems that Mr. Foster may retain new legal counsel."

"I see." Maria's information was right. I keep my expression neutral, try not to look surprised. "Well, I'll certainly cooperate with his new counsel if I can."

"This means," continues Abbas, "that there is likely to be, again, a resurgence in media interest in Foster. This solicitor has hinted . . . he has suggested he might . . ."

Sloane straightens the cuffs of her blouse. "He's given some indication that he wants to facilitate moving Foster to a lower-security facility, that he may pursue some of the more far-flung theories presented at the outset of the original trial, perpetuated by the media." She picks up her notebook from the desk, looks for a moment at Abbas's tropical-fish-themed mouse pad, the silver-framed photo of his three teenaged daughters. "Specifically, about Foster being influenced, having help. As I said, you must remain professional. Objective."

"Of course." My curiosity is piqued by the possibility of a new lawyer. His current one is a solid defence solicitor who is well respected.

"Perhaps you can sit down for a moment, Danica." Sloane opens her notebook. I pick a chair.

"I've looked over your fellowship proposal, some of your past work," she says. "I've noticed you appear to be sympathetic towards theories that suggest an individual's behaviours can be significantly, unduly, influenced by others. That you support the theories surrounding brainwashing, mind control."

"I do not believe I've ever used the term *brainwashing*."

"Hmm. You've expressed an interest in researching the relationship of and influence of organized groups on an individual's violent actions."

"That's not an uncommon tenet in research on violent behaviour."

"But as you must be aware, many of your colleagues, many of your *established* colleagues, would caution you on that front. I am sure you are familiar with the debates surrounding this issue."

I see what she's going on about. There's a significant professional divide between the idea that an individual is responsible for his or her actions, completely and absolutely, and the idea that someone can be unduly influenced, or "brainwashed" (though that term is rarely used in clinical circles). There's contention about claims that American prisoners of war in Korea experienced "brainwashing," that followers of Manson were subject to a sort of mind control or that the high-commitment, extreme working habits of Enron employees were the product of a corporate cult mentality. Some researchers back the idea that mind control or cultic influence renders an individual less responsible, perhaps not at all responsible, for his or her actions.

"I am aware of that," I tell Sloane.

"I think what Dr. Sloane is perhaps cautioning you about, Danica, is to focus on your role as a clinician in this case," says Abbas. "Don't get caught up in the glitz surrounding Foster's new legal counsel or any stories you may see in the news."

At least Abbas is partially addressing their actual concern. The concept of influence has legal ramifications. If the idea of mind control and organized group influence on individuals becomes widely accepted, then those individuals may not be criminally accountable for what they do. Which could lead to people like Foster receiving lesser sentences, or possibly not being convicted at all.

"I will of course conduct my interviews with Mr. Foster in a professional way. I will, as you say, Dr. Sloane, remember that I am a psychologist, and I will not concern myself with Mr. Foster's legal situation." Until this point, I hadn't fully considered that my clinical approach could acutely influence Foster's sentence.

"Right." Sloane snaps her notebook closed. "You've been allowed on this case because of the aims of your fellowship, to gain experience in your areas of specialization. We've handled Mr. Foster's case very well here, and I trust you will uphold that level of care." She crosses her arms again and doesn't smile. I'm surprised how much this situation needles her.

"Danica, I'm sure the interview today will go well." Abbas walks around the desk, opens the door. "Remember, we're

here if you have any concerns at all." He smiles and pats me on
the shoulder as I walk out of the office.

As soon as I get back to my office I google the news reports from
Foster's trial. I read most of them at the time, but since then I've
been more focused on his case studies and the history of his stay
in Stowmoor than the rise of his infamy in the media.

There are hundreds of articles. And at least fifty from almost
a year ago, the anniversary of his admittance to Stowmoor. I
understand the interest: a middle-class, intelligent young man,
with a career and education, obsessed with an Elizabethan-era
Hungarian countess's crimes, ritually murders a pretty school-
girl. It's the plot every crime show wishes it had written; plus,
it really happened. Foster has become a criminal celebrity.
He's mostly feared, hated, and his name has become shorthand
for the worst possible consequence for women walking home
alone. His fixation on Báthory makes him aberrant and, in the
narratives of some publications, glamorous. He has fans: ones
who concoct theories to promote his innocence; others who
revel in, love him for, his guilt. But whether people support
him or abhor him, the most popular and controversial theme
to emerge from Foster's media coverage is the idea that he may
have had assistance—physical, monetary or both—in the com-
mission of the crime.

No conclusive DNA evidence, or evidence of any sort, placed
anyone but Foster at the crime scene. There are reports of
Foster's alleged correspondence with other people who idolized
Báthory, and allegations that he had amassed a large and diverse
collection of films and books on the Blood Countess. Many stories stress that the branding, the dagger and the biting indicate

that the murder was ritualistic in nature. But the articles that alleged Foster was part of a team of perpetrators mostly died off in the first few weeks after his arrest. At trial his lawyer did not pursue the possibility. He also downplayed the ritualistic aspects of the murder.

I close my browser and turn to Foster's chart. I organize my notes. As I told Sloane, I'm a professional.

"Good afternoon, Mr. Foster."

"It's very nice to see you again, Dr. Winston." He adjusts his tortoiseshell glasses, nods. "Very nice. A pleasure."

"I'm here today to continue our interview from last time, to ask you a few more questions, see how you're doing." I flip open the file, pull out my pens and get my notebook ready. I try to look at him just enough, not too much. I take a deep breath and remind myself that he is the subject. I am the interviewer, the authority. I look up and he's still staring at me. The frames of his glasses look like tiger's eye quartz; they shine gold, then a darker mahogany each time he moves his head under the fluorescent bulbs.

"I am at your command. Lovely earrings you have on today."

My hand jumps to my earlobe. I feel the smooth amber beads strung on silver sleeper hoops.

"They really pick up the tones in your hair. Quite chic, really." He smiles, folds his hands and rests them on the table.

I look at his pale, freckled skin and the closely trimmed fingernails. I try to imagine those hands grabbing a small, thin shoulder. Searing the skin, using a blade. I know the description of the crime. I know the person sitting here committed the act. But I can't immediately, viscerally, marry this too-polite man to that murder. "Let's get started," I say.

"With pleasure." He smiles, unclasps his hands and turns his palms towards me.

I ask him about his time in Stowmoor, if his outlook on his crime has changed since he's been here, if he feels remorse about his victim. He gives fairly routine responses. Yes, he feels he's used his time here to reflect on his actions. Yes, he realizes he caused harm to another person. That what he did was not acceptable to society. He understands that his actions hurt not only the victim, but also caused emotional hurt for the victim's family.

He's saying everything he's supposed to say. Once people have been in the system for a while, they know what psychologists and parole boards want to hear. I flip through my notes. It's possible that offenders can be sincere. But they can also be very good liars.

"Everything in order, Dr. Winston?" he asks softly. "I hope I've given you enough for your report."

"A few more questions," I say. "Do you accept full responsibility for your actions?"

He hesitates, a second, two. "I do," he says, looking down at the table.

"Why the hesitation? Are you confused on this point?"

"No confusion." He looks up and to the right, starts swaying a bit in his chair.

"So, to be clear: you accept responsibility for killing your victim, for the events leading up to and including the murder?"

"I am responsible for carrying out actions that resulted in the murder of that girl, yes."

"Carrying out?" His ambiguity seems deliberate. "But do you take responsibility for your intent to end the life of your victim?"

"I knew . . . it was . . ." He trails off.

"Yes? Please continue." I'm barely breathing. There could be something else here. Something even Sloane has missed these past two years.

"I didn't care so much if she died. I knew she would. It was going to be part of it. But it was about watching her, then catching her. Then it was about the skin and her blood. Like . . ." Again, he stops talking, looks down at the table.

The blood. I close my notebook. In the back of my mind, I hear Sloane's lecture about focusing on my role, not playing detective. But he's given me an opening. "Let's talk about Báthory."

He's speechless for half a minute. "No one has asked me about her for a while."

"Is she something you still think about?"

"Some*one*. She's someone, Dr. Winston."

"How do you think about her?"

"*How* do I think? Isn't that what you're supposed to tell me, with all your questions and charts?"

Bill knocks on the door, peers through the wire-reinforced window. I'm running close to time; there's another interview scheduled for this room after Foster. Keeping to schedule is highly valued. But I signal that I need five more minutes.

"In what light do you think about her? In connection to your feelings of remorse for your actions?" I ask.

"I've missed talking about her, Dr. Winston. They haven't encouraged it much since I got here. It's all about reflection, diffusion of violent thoughts, playing angry drum-filled songs at the music therapist's to channel my angst." He leans back and smirks.

It's not technically true that he's been discouraged to speak about her. His chart shows that he began mentioning her less and less and then not at all. His therapists have noted this as a positive sign of increased mental well-being.

"You could have raised the subject with someone," I say. "If she's still on your mind."

"We both know it's best for me not to raise much of my own volition."

"Why do you say that?"

He laughs, looks away from me. "Haven't I answered all your questions nicely?"

Bill knocks on the door again, more urgently. He brings his wrist to the window and taps his watch, holds up his index finger. I have one minute.

"Not as nicely as I would like."

"What will you give me to be nicer to you?"

"Do you miss talking about her? You used to talk about her to others?"

"Of course. There are many people who find her fascinating."

I hear the key turn, the door creak. "Dr. Winston," says Bill, "Dr. Abbas and Dr. Latha are waiting for the room."

"Thank you, Bill." In my mind, I curse them, their patient and Stowmoor's ridiculously restrictive schedules. "We're just finishing up." He nods and shuts the door.

I turn back to Foster and stare for a moment at his blue-grey eyes. He folds his freckled hands together, puts them on the table and leans forward. "You find her fascinating, don't you, Dr. Winston? It comes across, in your article. In the way you ask me questions. You should ask me more."

This time, I look down at the table. I flip through my notebook, click the pen in, out, in. I don't know what to write. A host of questions whirrs through my mind. I want to ask him everything. But I'm apprehensive. Maybe a little afraid.

"We're out of time for today, Mr. Foster. We'll continue our assessment at a future appointment."

"Out of time, out of time for today," he parrots.

I stand up. Bill opens the door and two orderlies come and escort Foster around the table, towards the door. He adjusts his glasses, gives me a polite nod as he goes by. "A pleasure, Dr. Winston. I look forward to our future appointment." The orderlies walk him down the hall.

"At least he's respectful, that one," says Bill. Another set of orderlies escorts in the next patient. Jana Latha, an assistant psychologist, and Abbas are waiting outside. Abbas sends Jana in with the file and hangs back to talk to me.

"Danica, that seems to have gone well. He seems to be responding to you politely, as a professional."

"Yes, I think so." I shuffle my notes, avoid looking at him.

"But you must watch your time. It can put everyone's schedules off if you go over the limit."

"I know, it's just—"

"You're still getting used to the system here, I know. I look forward to reading the report." He turns to walk into the room.

"Dr. Abbas?"

"Hmm?"

"I need to schedule another interview with Foster. I did have a bit of trouble pacing the interview and missed some key points you outlined in the memo." I'm taking a risk by telling him that I didn't finish the agenda on time. But I need to speak to Foster again. "Also, near the end of our interview, he mentioned Báthory, the woman with whom he was obsessed, whose crimes he initially posited he was recreating." I say this as authoritatively as possible; this admission is even more of a risk. I know it would set off an avalanche of disapproval from Sloane. But with Abbas, I think it's a better strategy to reveal at least part of the truth.

"Well." Abbas scratches his beard. "I'd have to look over his case file for the specifics, but I don't believe he's brought that up for some time. We have done some therapy with him regarding his obsessions . . . perhaps it hasn't been as effective as we'd initially perceived, or perhaps he's regressed."

"Possible. I think it's in the interest of the patient to assess more specifically his levels of obsession in general and to investigate the level of possible idolization of violent, anti-social figures. It is a possible display of maladaptive tendencies that should be examined for the report." I say this in my most measured, assured clinician voice.

Abbas takes a deep breath, scratches again. "Agreed. Have Kelly schedule you a brief appointment with him for next week. But, Danica," he turns to face me fully. "Only assess his levels of obsession in regard to this issue. Don't push him farther. As we said, this is a sensational case, and I don't blame you for being intrigued by it. But we must remember our roles, stick to form. We don't want to undo any progress he's made here."

"I agree completely," I say, while thinking about how I can talk Kelly into scheduling me for more than a half-hour slot.

He pats my shoulder. "Very good, Danica."

He walks into the room and sits beside Jana, across from the patient. Bill shuts the door.

I try to keep my footsteps at an even pace, but I feel as exhilarated as the first time I spoke to Foster, and again I want to run, to skip down the hall. I'm half nervous, half excited that I'll get to see Foster again. What does he mean when he says there were many people to speak to about Báthory? I almost want to thank Sloane for what her lecture has prodded me to think about further.

Back in my office, I start my report on Foster, but I can't focus. All I can think of is Báthory, Foster's obsession, his possible cohorts. Maria would salivate over this possibility, this information. I daydream about the book she's proposing. What if we combined her discovery of the diaries with chapters of mine about Foster? It could never happen, of course. It would be almost impossible to write about Foster, as I know him now, without breaking confidentiality regulations. Though, if he agreed, I could interview him not as a clinician, but with the intent of researching the book. He might agree to it. He knows he's a celebrity. He ripped out my article from the journal. Maybe he'd want me to write about him.

I stop my thoughts there, chastise myself for even fantasizing about promoting the fame of a murderer. For my personal, vain, purposes. If Maria knew I entertained these sort of thoughts . . . I think she would be intrigued. I consider teasing her, dropping hints that I would never follow up on, batting her hopes about like she's done mine.

I haven't checked my email since this morning; I open my inbox, hope to see her there. Maybe she's heard more about the new lawyer. She did say she'd be in touch.

I breathe deeply. A message.

Dani,

These few pages may catch your eye. Do let me know what you think.

x, M.

P.S. The opening is next Thursday, in case you have forgotten.

Maybe it's serendipity. The attachment is titled "Elizabeth."

Chapter Ten

Sárvár, January 14, 1601

I do hope he did not suffer long. If it was the same disease he wrote of in his letter to me last spring, he would not have known much. When at his worst, he told me, he could not remember what he was like; the doctors reported that he was cold yet sweating, unable to walk, unconscious most of the day; and later they told him that in those brief times when he had been awake, his eyeballs had rolled to and fro in their sockets and he could not form any words, only mumblings. I know he wished to die on the battlefield, but there he was always victorious. It was the unseen, this illness, that broke the body of my Black Knight.

At least now I can move from this puny estate, and away from Ursula. She should be long dead, but still she lives, feeble and useless. Though she manages to bark out her commands, her insipid requests. "Where is my grandson? He must spend more time with me." As if I would poison him, as if I don't pay for a tutor to tend to him all day. At night, her decrepit hacking rings through the halls and echoes in the drawing room, so if I wish to escape her invalid's clamour, I must sit in the library, with the books she has bound all in the same plain brown leather, in the ragged chairs she refuses to replace. She has deemed it sufficient for there to be just a braided rug on the floor, the kind the chambermaids make out of rags. I believe she thinks if she flaunts the Nadaskys' poverty and simplicity, it will make their nobility seem all the stronger by comparison. This is passing foolishness, the thoughts of a deranged old woman.

I wish for her to suffer greatly with this illness. I remember when I was a girl, seven or eight, when I was with my family at Ecsed, before Ursula grabbed my life by the scruff and arranged my marriage to Ferenc. A band of gypsies had come through our village, and a constable in the service of my father had caught one of them for selling his daughter to the Turks. They came to visit my father to let him, the ruling lord, decide how this man should be dealt with. My father told them to take the man to the stables. I overheard and asked for leave from my tutor to go and play on the estate. I hid behind the stables and watched as one of our boys led an old grey mare into the yard. The gypsy was yelling that he was innocent, and straining against the constable's men who held him, but as he struggled, a purse full of money fell from his belt. He would not explain to my father where he got the money, and my father did not care to give him another chance. He told the men to beat the gypsy until he was limp, and to tie him up. Then he gave a nod to the stable boy. The boy produced a long, sharp blade, and slit the mare's neck in one strong motion. Blood swelled from the slash, painting a dark bib on her grey-haired chest. The horse stumbled, took two steps forward and fell. The boy rolled her onto her side, then slit her belly open, sternum to tail. Her entrails spilled out, dark, snakey tubes, and her limbs twitched and kicked. The men dragged the beaten gypsy over to the dying horse and stuffed him inside her belly. They left his head outside the wound, cradled on the escaped intestines. Then the stable boy took a needle and twine, and stitched the belly closed. The gypsy's head still stuck out, just under the horse's tail. His hair was now slick with slime and dung that had leaked out of the severed bowels.

I watched this scene and felt that hard, sick knot in my stomach. I had watched my father discipline our servants before, and I had seen the authorities beating peasants for one thing or another when we rode in our carriage through the village. But the extremity of this, to sew a live man into a dying animal to rot and fester, was something I had never witnessed. The men, and my father, laughed at the gypsy, then walked away. The gypsy's eyes welled up, and he let out a howl once he understood they meant to leave him trapped inside the body of the horse. My father and the men looked back briefly, and then only laughed harder.

I stayed hidden for a few minutes, until the men had gone and the stable boy went to groom one of the other horses. I edged closer. The sun was warm, and everything smelt like hot iron, like slaughter. Flies buzzed around the horse's spilled blood, the crack of the wound, the dung in the gypsy's hair. The knot in my stomach became harder, and for a moment I thought I might vomit. I turned around, collected myself, then looked back. The gypsy's head was lolling around, and even though he was bound, he was trying to wiggle free, his futile movements muted by the heavy flesh of the corpse. This time, I saw it: it did look funny. He looked like a tiny, ugly doll struggling to burst from the wreckage of that old mare. I giggled. After all, he did sell his daughter to the Turks.

The gypsy lived through the next day. The day after, from my window, I could see a few of the stable boys lugging the grey rotting mess out of the yard.

I wish a death like this on Ursula. Except she should be stuffed into a cow. I would stitch her into the gutted animal myself.

There's a knock at my door. "Heading to the staff room for lunch?" It's Jana. Her fishbowl office is in this corridor too, a couple of doors down from mine. She's holding up a brown paper bag.

"Uh, yeah." I close the attachment. "I'll meet you there. Have to finish something up." I'm preoccupied with images of dead horses and feces.

"Right, then, see you in a few."

I know Báthory's story. But somehow I had hoped that as a little girl she might at least have thought about helping the gypsy. I look at the tuna sandwich I shoved in my briefcase this morning, half-squished in its zip-lock baggie. I leave it there and walk away from my desk.

Chapter Eleven

It's Thursday night and I'm on my way to the gallery openings. Henry's been excited about the Fantasy and Disaster festival for weeks. He's been at the gallery all day setting up his show, *Le Paradis Rouge.* I'm a few blocks away from the venue for *Honey, Torture* when Maria texts me: *At Orange Palm. Show to die for. U must come.*

I've been thinking about the horse and the gypsy and the girl countess all week, wishing Maria could translate the diaries and send me instalments at a faster rate. The more I think about it, and the more I read, the less I suspect that Maria is fabricating these entries. She's eccentric and sometimes deluded about what she's entitled to in life, but her story about how she found them sounds authentic. She's been trying to find them since we met two years ago—why would she suddenly fake their discovery?

I text her back: *Will stop in.*

I told Henry I'd be at his gallery, the Wynick, by seven. The Orange Palm is just a few blocks from Henry's show, but it's already six fifteen so I'll have to hurry. He hates when I'm late. I pass some graffiti, *Art Is My Hustle,* spray-painted in stencilled block letters on the sidewalk. I pick up my pace.

The Orange Palm is tiny, with a small foyer that leads into one main gallery space. The foyer is half full of people; everyone has an edgy haircut, or very cool boots, or dull metallic, chunky jewellery. A small chocolate fondue fountain sits in one corner, ringed with strawberries and blood orange slices. There are also two open wine bottles and an assortment of glasses, none that match, some pre-filled with red wine.

I scan the room but I don't see Maria. I pick up a glass of wine and am just dipping a strawberry under the fountain when a very polite English voice says, "Excuse me, Dani?" I pull the strawberry out of the cascading chocolate and see a tall, dark-haired man in a well-tailored suit. Edward.

"Oh, hi!" I say. I drip chocolate onto my blush open-toed pumps.

"Here you go." He holds a serviette under the fruit.

"Thanks." I put my wine and the strawberry on the table and bend down to wipe the chocolate off my shoes. "Nice to see you," I say, looking up at him. "You're reviewing this opening?"

"Yes." He holds out a hand to help me back up. "I'm stopping by the White Cube, too, of course, and I'm meant to go to the Wynick, as well. Maria says your boyfriend has an installation there, yes?"

So Maria did tell him about Henry's show. "Oh, yes, he does. Are you planning to review it?" Henry was nervous he wouldn't be mentioned in any reviews at all.

"Quite possibly. There's a lot of work going up tonight, but Maria was adamant that Henry is quite the new talent."

Maria's never seen any of Henry's work. "Well, it's generous of her to put in a good word for him," I say. "So, this installation," I gesture towards the entrance to the inner part of the gallery, feeling somewhat uncomfortable discussing Maria's endorsement of Henry's show, "have you seen it already?"

"Mmm," he nods, "just been through it. Quite a striking mess. But it's a bit theatrical for me. Maria is still inside."

"Must be a real spectacle to hold Maria's attention."

"Truly," says Edward, and leans one hand against the table. He picks up an orange slice, then looks at me. "She was hoping you'd stop by tonight. Go on in—don't let me hold you up."

I take my wine, but abandon the strawberry on the table. The curatorial statement near the entrance reads:

"Honey, Torture." Performance, film and light installation. Artist Erszébet Báthory, formally Sanne Brill (b. 1967), legally changed her name in 1992 in homage to the Hungarian Countess Erszébet Báthory (1560–1614), who tortured and killed over six hundred of her servant girls. She often bathed in her victims' blood as part of a beauty ritual designed to preserve her youth. The Countess's famed "honey torture" involved coating a naked girl in honey and making her stand in the woods for a day. The honey attracted various pests, and the girl would eventually die from excessive insect bites and exposure.

The room is small and dark. There's a projector near the entrance; a knot of people cluster around it and stare at the image it casts on a screen on the opposite wall. The film shows the back of a young woman. She is standing in a forest of evergreen and deciduous trees. She is naked, coated in a clear, sticky-looking liquid. Her brown hair hangs around her shoulders in clumps. The camera circles around her, zooms in. The girl has welts all over her skin. Flies, bees and beetles are mired in the honey.

Besides the glow of the film, the corners of the room are lit with red spotlights. A trail of white rocks and pale, dry leaves snakes from the projector to the far wall; the trail spirals like a cockled snail and the rocks glow, illuminated by a black light. Most of the people in the room are crowding behind the projector, keeping a distance between themselves and the image on the screen. I bump into random limbs as I weave through the crowd to the front. Someone's skin feels like a rough stucco wall against my bare forearm; I smell sandalwood cologne, baby powder deodorant, patchouli oil, the scents mixing in the stuffy, warm air. Someone steps on my left toe, the shoe I dripped the chocolate on. The pair is probably ruined.

An arm wraps around my waist and I'm enveloped in gardenia perfume.

"Danica, this way." The arm releases and a hand rakes down my right arm, grabs my hand. It's Maria. The stones in her rings are askew and dig into my skin. She pulls me farther into the room until we're in the middle of the crowd. "Watch," she says.

What I see makes me grip Maria's hand hard, despite her rough jewels. The camera circles to the woman's face. It is distorted and full of bites: her eyelids are puffy as marshmallows and her lips look as if she's had repeated injections of collagen. Strands of honey-slick hair slither down her breasts. The camera zooms out slowly; the flesh by the nipples is bitten and bleeding. Little tributaries of blood branch from the wounds, follow the curve under her breasts and flow down her welt-covered stomach. The carcasses of deer flies and wasps fleck her abdomen. The blood runs into the woman's pubic hair, which houses a seething mess of yellow jackets. A rat gnaws her left ankle. The figure is so distorted it's hard to tell if she's a human model or a mannequin dressed for the project.

"So real, isn't it, Dani?" whispers Maria.

"That's a live woman?" I drop her hand and hear loud, steady footsteps approaching from the far end of the room. The crowd murmurs.

"It is her." Maria hisses directly in my ear, her breath humid on my skin. She tries to grab my hand again. Her long nails cage my wrist.

The artist impersonating Báthory steps out from the dark periphery of the room into the black light. She is wearing a dress similar to the one in the picture I saw at Čachtice: an embroidered corset, tight at the waist, with a long, flowing skirt of lace. The sleeves are gossamer and gather at the wrist into an embroidered cuff. A square collar, trimmed with ivory lace, sits on top of her shoulders. A heavy choker of pearls wraps around her neck, and a silver, filigreed headpiece holds back her platinum hair. Her skin is pale, almost blue-white. Her eyebrows are plucked in a broad, thin arch; her lips are stained dark red and slightly pursed. She's luminous under the black light, her skin phosphorescent. She walks the spiral path while the film of the tortured woman continues to play.

"Such a likeness," says Maria. She's transfixed, her eyes nailed to the artist as she walks in a wide circle in front of the video projection. Maria adjusts her grip on my wrist, presses her nails into my skin one by one. She's in awe, or jealous, or both.

The artist does look very much like the pictures of Báthory, and the film of the honey torture is startling. My stomach keels over as the camera sweeps the swollen, insect-ridden body, and I want to look away. But I keep watching, notice that the close-ups become more frequent and linger. I can see that the flies aren't real, the rat is plastic. The woman doesn't breathe; she isn't alive. A plastic mannequin. The images become benign. It's the work of a skilled mimic, a sterile recycling of Báthory's violence, Báthory's legend. The artist finishes her parade, steps away from the cockled swirl of white stones and walks slowly to the dark corner and into a back room. The train of her costume gets caught when she closes the door; she tugs at the material and pulls it free, snaps the door shut. What would happen if I put this impersonator in a room with Foster? Would they be impressed with each other, or would she recoil at the extremity of his obsession, he at the superficiality of hers?

Maria stares at the dark corner the "Countess" disappeared into. I can't believe she's so enthralled by this performance; I expected she'd think it was trite, that the wax girl was unconvincing. But it has always been hard for me to predict what will attract Maria's interest. She's rarely consistent.

"I'll see you outside," I say to Maria.

"Oh, you cannot go yet—she will return."

"I have to go. And I'm out of wine," I say, and begin to weave through the other spectators in the direction of the door.

"Dani, we'll get wine later," she calls after me. "You are not supposed to bring it in here, anyway."

I pretend I don't hear her, head out of the room and onto the street.

I arrive at the Wynick just after seven. It's a bigger gallery, with two separate exhibition spaces on either side of the foyer. Henry's pacing near the entrance to his installation, beside a table laden with half-carved wheels of brie, slabs of Gouda, crackers and wine.

"Hey." He gives me a quick kiss. "You're a little late."

"Yeah, but guess what? I stopped by the Orange Palm—"

"Why did you stop there?" He plays with his dirty blond hair, fluffs up what he calls his ironic faux comb-over. It's a bit much, but I don't say anything. He's particular about his hair.

"There's a reviewer from the *Guardian* coming to see your show."

"What? How do you know?"

"He told me, at the Orange Palm."

"Who is he? How do you know him?"

"His name is Edward, friend of a friend. She knew about your show and told him, something like that." I pause for breath. "Kind of a long story. Anyway, he's coming!"

Henry puts his arm around my waist, pulls me in and kisses the top of my head with a loud smack. "You're amazing." He finishes the last of his wine, takes a step back and holds out his arms. "How do I look? Good enough for the *Guardian?*" He sets down his glass and rubs his palms against his tight dark jeans.

I straighten the lapels of his slate blazer, adjust the ragged black scarf he's taken to wearing a lot lately. "Yes. Fabulous." And he does, he looks like the beautiful hipster boys who wear skinny pants and carry guitar cases down Spring Garden Road.

He smiles, scans the crowd over my head. "I've got a few people to talk to," he says. "Go check out the show. And you should go see Andreas's sculptures, too," he motions to the exhibition space across from his. "I'll catch you in a bit?"

I smile and nod, and he begins to wander into the crowd. He turns back, winks and says, "Hey, tiger lily, make sure you sit in the throne!"

. . .

HOLLY LUHNING 98

Henry had explained *Le Paradis Rouge* to me beforehand, but I wasn't sure what to expect. I knew it involved the throne, and also some recordings of Henry reading the backs of cereal boxes and the directions on shampoo bottles. "It's a self-conscious, simultaneous questioning and embodiment of post-ironic re-enchantment," he said.

I walk in. The throne is in the centre of the room, surrounded by a two-foot-wide violet moat. A lime green plank spans the moat on the right-hand side. The walls of the room are lined with tall trees covered in yellow and pink hibiscus blossoms, and there is a hammock suspended between two of the trees near the back of the room. Wreaths of flowers and leaves hang from the wires that stick out from the throne; strings of white and purple blossoms cascade over the thick red arms. The throne looks fleshy and dressed up for a carnival parade. The light is low, and alternating spotlights of orange and pink bleed in and out. On a soundtrack, Henry's voice plays slow and distorted, "Laaattheerr, Riiinnssse, Reeepeeat," mixed with birds chirping peacefully, punctuated by an occasional louder cry, like an angry macaw or a mating peacock. I pause near the hammock; the entire garish setting charms, yet alienates me. I feel claustrophobic, like I'm in a parallel Alice in Wonderland world.

Someone taps me on the shoulder.

"Dani, you were so fast, leaving the other show."

I turn. Maria makes a sweeping gesture towards the whole room. "So, this here, this is your Henry's show? For this you rushed away?"

Her hair is in a messy twist and studded with sparkly pins. A pink spotlight shines on her, and the rhinestones shimmer.

"Oh," I say, "you finally tore yourself away from the Báthory artist?"

But Maria doesn't answer me. She's looking across the room, where Henry and Edward have just entered. Henry's gesturing at the throne and smiling, and Edward is nodding, writing down notes and waving his photographer over.

"So that is your Henry," says Maria. "Tall. Very nice. Looks like he is the star tonight." She steps past me and strides towards the men.

"Henry," I hear Edward say, "can I get you by the throne?"

Maria puts her arm around Edward's waist, and he looks at her and smiles. Her dress is purple satin, spaghetti straps holding up a fitted bodice, skirt flaring out and falling mid-calf. She's wearing a long necklace of crystal beads, and the heavy rings that pinched my skin earlier.

She holds her hand out to Henry. "I am Danica's friend, Maria. Surely you have heard of me?"

Henry takes her hand, doesn't mention I've never spoken of her.

"And you ask for people to sit in this throne, yes?" Maria unwraps herself from Edward and crosses the plank. She rests one hand on the arm of the throne and puts the other on her hip. She is completely blocking the photographer's shot.

"Can you move for a minute, love?" the photographer asks, impatiently shifting his weight from foot to foot.

"But if it is meant to be used, you must have a model in your chair," she says to the three men and climbs into the seat of the throne. "Edward, what do you think?"

The purple of her dress is lush against the deep red wax. Maria crosses her legs, grips the black wires that emerge from the ends of the arms. Even though she's being completely inappropriate, I can't deny that she looks like she belongs up there, a perfect monarch. For a moment, Edward looks annoyed, but then his face softens and he smiles.

"Brilliant. Let's use it," says Edward, and the photographer starts snapping. Maria looks at the camera and curls into the seat, like the throne was made especially for her.

Chapter Twelve

Six months after Vienna and Čachtice, I saw Maria again. I was in Toronto; Carl had brought me and another of his grad students to the national Congress for the Humanities and Social Sciences. Carl was staying at the Royal York, but Shannon and I were relegated to a shared room at the Econolodge.

I was at an evening reception, talking to Dr. MacIvor, a prof from Mount Saint Vincent whom Carl often derided for her use of qualitative research. He called her a "storytime" specialist.

"Dani!" called someone behind me. "So good to see you!"

It was Maria.

"Your name, I saw it in the program." She slid her hand onto my arm and kissed me once on each cheek. "I hoped I would find you here."

She was wearing a black wrap sweater over a long deep green dress. A square diamond solitaire punctuated each earlobe, and a matching floating diamond pendant rested on her lightly freckled décolleté. The red waves of her hair fell loose over her shoulders. Maria was beautiful whenever you saw her; now, materializing without warning, she seemed sublime.

I didn't say anything, just stood there, stunned to see her. Maria introduced herself to Dr. MacIvor and said, "Oh, I must steal Dani away for a moment—there are some colleagues of mine who would like to meet her." I managed to say a polite goodbye to MacIvor and followed Maria across the room. She pulled me into an alcove by the coat check.

"There, now, I have freed you," she said. "Next, our coats." She rummaged in her purse, a large, black beaded clutch, for her coat check ticket.

"Uh, I don't think I should really leave yet," I said. "I was fine back there, really."

"Dani, this is *me*. You do not have to pretend. Ah—" She held up her ticket, triumphantly. "Now, where is yours?" She put one hand on her hip and held out the other, palm up.

"Why are you even here? How did you find me?"

"A meeting, darling, it is always the case, yes? Some archivists, curators, strengthening connections between North America and Europe, la la la—you know how it is."

"But—"

"Dani, I know you cannot really want to stay here in this boring place. There is a whole city out there. I have friends waiting for us."

I looked back at the reception. Dwindling mounds of cubed cheese on tables, people knotted into small clusters. I heard Carl half-talking, half-shouting about his upcoming book. Smatterings of conversations about funding and research projects.

I pulled my ticket out of my pocket and placed it in Maria's palm.

Outside, Maria stopped the next cab and we piled into the back seat.

"Where are we going?" I asked.

"C Lounge." She pulled out her phone and sent a text. "There," she said, "I've told them we are on our way. Now," she looked at me, "we must fix you up. Take off that business jacket."

I peeled off my blazer and let Maria assess my cobalt blue collared blouse.

"Under your shirt, you have another, a little one, with the straps?" She drew her finger over my shoulder, miming spaghetti straps.

"Uh, well, it's kind of a tank top camisole thing . . . it's just a—"

"What colour?" she demanded.

"Um, black."

"Good. Take this off," she tugged on my shirt collar, "and take your lovely hair down."

I shook my hair out of its ponytail and looked out the cab window to try to see where we were going. Halifax bars rarely had a dress code beyond any old shirt with jeans.

"Here," Maria pulled a blue scarf out of her purse. "Tie this in your hair. Like this."

With Maria's accent, I heard, "You are making it *buon-chi* . . . like *theeeis* . . ." I felt like I was on one of TLC's upscale makeover shows, where famous European stylists bestow their magical touch on some poor, tragically unfashionable girl they rescue from the mall. I felt Maria wrap, tug and tie the scarf, then finger-comb and fluff my hair.

"Much better," she said. "Just, wait . . ." She handed me a lipstick and mirror. "Put on a bit of colour."

I followed her instructions and applied the brick red colour to my lips. I checked out my hair in the mirror. The scarf was wrapped and sleek against my hairline, and my hair tumbled perfectly down my back. "Thank you," I smiled and handed the makeup back to Maria.

"Just one more thing." Maria unfastened her necklace. The pendant sparkled like fairy dust floating in the air between us. She leaned in and put it around my neck.

"Maria, that's yours!" I said. "And I'm sure those are not rhinestones."

She laughed. "You are right. But I know you will take good care of them tonight."

Maria passed me the mirror again. "You see! Beautiful." She stroked the back of my head.

I touched the diamonds at my throat, then double-checked the clasp.

"We are almost there," said Maria. "Put that shirt into your satchel. You can leave that jacket and everything at our table. Ah, tonight will be so much fun. I am glad I found you." She smiled. "Ready? We are here."

Outside, there was a small mob of people clustered at the front of a club. A silver SUV stretch limousine was idling to the side of the building, and a black one drove by and parked a few feet away. The driver got out and opened the back door; a stream of girls in miniskirts and sparkly heels piled out, strode through the mob and up the stairs to the door. A woman in a full-length white fur coat ticked off her clipboard, and a tall, broad-shouldered man in a leather jacket opened the door and ushered them in.

"I don't know if I'm really dressed well enough for this place," I said, looking down at my plain dress pants and clunky shoes.

"Do not worry, Dani," said Maria, taking my hand. She weaved us through the crowd to the perimeter of the roped-off area in front of the club. Everyone was trying to get the attention of the woman in the fur coat, who stood on the first step, clipboard in hand, scanning the crowd. I perched on my tiptoes and tried to peer into the club's windows, but they were blurred out by a sheet of running water, a waterfall trapped between the double-paned glass.

"Perfect," I heard Maria say. She yanked on my hand. The bouncer unhooked the rope and ushered us through.

Inside, chaises and zebra-print bucket chairs were arranged in clusters near the long, colourful bar. Bodies stomped and swayed on the dance floor. A crowd huddled near the DJ booth in the far corner.

"Milo!" Maria exclaimed, kissing him on both cheeks.

"At last," he said. "We're all over there," he gestured behind him. He looked at me. "And *who* is *this*?" The way he said it seemed very fake and made me feel conspicuous.

"I have told you about Danica," said Maria.

"Ah, yes." He stared at me. "Beautiful." I lowered my eyes and probably blushed. "Now, this way," he said as he put his arm around my shoulder and pulled me with him into the crowd.

We arrived at a string of silver tables ringed with shiny vinyl cube chairs. Milo led me to one of the tables, took my bag and jacket and motioned for me to sit down. Three other people were already at the table: a guy and two young women. The girls were exquisite. They reclined against the shiny white vinyl, tanned legs elegantly crossed, holding crystal glasses in their manicured hands. One was blonde; her hair was curled into a smooth fifties-style bob and adorned with a large crystal barrette. The other had short, dark hair and delicate, high cheekbones. She looked like a pixie.

"Sit down, Dani, sit down," said Maria in an excited, sing-songy voice. "Now, this is Darius." She waved at the man at the far side of the table. "Vee," she pointed at the pixie, "and Sylvia."

"Drinks?" said Milo. I noticed the bottles on the table—champagne, vodka and gin nested in silver buckets of ice and meltwater.

"Champagne," said Maria. "Dani?"

"I'll have, um, gin. Is there tonic?" Milo nodded and poured me a drink. He handed it to me and Maria clinked her flute against my glass.

"So good you can be here, Dani."

"Yes," said Milo, "Maria has told us all about you." He touched my arm.

"Oh, I'm—" I looked away from his green eyes and willed myself not to blush again. The bass from the dance floor made the liquid ripple in my glass. I tried to think of something to say that wouldn't sound trite or stupid, but only came up with "happy to be here."

Vee put her hand on my knee. "So, Maria tells us you're a psychologist?"

"I'm still studying. I'm in the middle of my Ph.D."

"So, do you get to talk to a lot of, you know, really crazy people? In institutions? Or is it more like people sit down in an office and tell you about their problems with their kids and husband and things like that?" She took a sip of her drink and looked at me expectantly with her dark brown eyes.

"It depends on where you end up working." I wasn't sure how much detail she wanted to hear, whether I should mention that we don't usually use the word *crazy* to describe patients. People often think practising psychology is much more exciting than it actually is. They don't want to hear about long research studies and paperwork. "What kind of work do you do?"

"I'm an actress. Well, working on being one, full-time, you know?" She put down her drink. "Anyway. You must get asked psychology questions all the time. It's just that I'm always trying to collect information about people, what they do, why they do it—to help with different characters, audition strategies, you know."

"Vee, she is very dedicated," said Maria. She reached across me and brushed aside a wisp of pixie hair from Vee's forehead. "Working on her craft, all of the time." Vee leaned into Maria's touch and smiled. "And of course you should ask Dani. She is brilliant." Maria turned towards me. "At the conference reception, when I asked one of the delegates about you, he said your paper this morning was excellent."

The conference reception seemed like a dull speck, even though we'd left it less than an hour ago. "What? Who were you talking to?" I asked.

"According to Maria, word is you're very talented." Milo said as he refilled my drink.

Did Maria fabricate this stuff? I hadn't thought anyone noticed me or my paper at the conference. I usually felt like a permanent shadow of Carl's.

"Dani, you look so surprised. Do not be so modest." Maria curled her hand tighter around my waist.

"Didja see me out there, ladies?" A man with a physique like a boxer roared to the table from the dance floor. He leaned forward and kissed Vee and Sylvia on the cheek. "You're both looking more beautiful than before, if that is possible."

Despite his bulk, he lithely stepped over Sylvia and plopped himself between Darius and Milo on one of the white vinyl chairs. "I need some refreshment," he said and downed a shot of vodka. The top few buttons of his dress shirt were undone and sweat beaded on his forehead. He slammed the glass on

the silver table and almost leapt out of the chair when he saw
Maria sitting across from him.

"When did you get here? I can't believe I didn't see you!"
His voice was louder and faster than the music.

"Not so long ago," said Maria.

"Oh, yeah? And your friend," he got up and gave me a
slight bow, took my hand and kissed it, "is this the young lady
named Danica you told us about?"

"Um, yes?" I said. I looked at Maria.

"This is Kent," she said. "He is always livening up our parties."

"You can count on it," he said. He turned back to me. "Love
the red hair. You've got a glamorous wood sprite sorta thing
going on."

"Wood sprite?" Was he making fun of me?

"Totally. All ethereal, otherworldly. Gorgeous." He poured
himself another shot, then clinked my glass. "Milo, top up the
ladies' drinks."

For the next couple of hours Kent kept everyone's drinks
filled. I danced with the girls and listened to Milo's travel stories, but I kept an eye on Maria. She was my anchor in this
surge of well-dressed people and hypnotic bass-beat thrum.
Kent was trying to get the girls and me back on the dance floor
when Maria linked her arm through mine and whispered in
my ear.

"Let's go outside."

"Outside? It's January."

"That is not a problem." She pushed me gently out of the
booth. "You must excuse us," she said to Kent, "Dani and I, we
must get some air."

"All right," I said. "I'll get my coat."

"No need." We started to walk towards an exit. There was a

girl behind a counter, doling out plush jackets to people going out the door, hanging them up for people coming in. She gave men grey, women white. I took a coat and stepped outside.

Maria's heels clacked on the wooden boardwalk that led around the building. I followed the sound, pulling the white fluff of the coat around myself and peering down to find the end of the zipper. The clacking stopped and I walked smack into Maria's shoulder.

"Careful, Dani," she said. "Here." She straightened the coat on my shoulders, led my hands to the slide of the zipper.

"Need some help, ladies?" A tall man, grey jacket on, beer in hand, approached us.

"I do not think you can be of assistance," said Maria. She took my hand. "This way," she said, leading me away from the man. When we had walked a few paces, she whispered in my ear, "Two redheads, I suppose we should expect such attention. We make a nice pair, yes?"

I smiled noncommittally, aware of her hand warm against mine. "To the bar," she said, and we began walking across the immense deck.

The deck, surrounded by a tall wooden fence, had a rectangular raised pool in the centre. The pool was filled with pieces of glass that looked like ice cubes, and a streak of flames, fuelled by thin black pipes of natural gas, ran lengthwise down the middle. At each corner, there was a pillar heaped with cubes of polished glass and topped with a gas flame. We walked around the pool. Pulses of warmth from the fire hit us intermittently as we made our way towards the bar.

"Two lemon drops," said Maria to the bartender. The bar was carved out of ice. Maria ran her finger along the smooth top of the bar and then pushed a sugar-rimmed shot glass of vodka, with a wedge of lemon perched on top, towards me.

Neck arched, she drank her shot, sucked on the lemon. Maria watched as I copied her. "Now," she said, "let us sit."

I followed her to the far side of the flaming ice pool, to a row of queen-size beds, each draped with a fluffy polar bear blanket and surrounded by silver crystal bead curtains. A faux bear head hung over their feet. Maria motioned towards a bouncer, who came over and led us to an open bed.

Maria stretched herself over the fur and crooked one leg slightly over the other. Her head rested on her palm, her elbow sank into the bed. She twirled her nails through the fur in front of her. "Sit down, Dani."

Through the sparkly beads, I could see a couple on the bed to my right. They were laughing, the woman trying not to spill her martini. Beyond her, through another set of beads, four or five women were strewn on a further bed, drinks in their hands. They didn't pay us any attention. Even the bouncer had stepped back, blending into his post by the edge of the pool.

I sat. My feet were still on the ground, but my body swivelled towards the middle, towards Maria. Her coat slipped off one shoulder. She fanned her emerald skirt over her legs, deep green falling over the polar snow.

"So. You are glad I rescued you from that reception? You have had fun?"

"Totally." I could feel a brief wave of heat from the fire in the pool, and the bed buzzed, just slightly, with the bass from inside the club. I picked my feet off the ground, turned my hips to mirror Maria's pose, and let my coat fall off my shoulders too.

"I am glad. I have made up for making you take the train to Čachtice alone?" Maria tousled her hair, dark red waves falling against her lightly freckled arm. Her wrists and earlobes glittered crystal and silver, almost as bright as the curtains, the white-white beds, the fire-lit ice. My body vibrated from dancing, from the lemon drop, and I couldn't remember the last time I'd had as much fun as tonight.

"Distant memory." I said.

She smiled. "Well. I am glad. And you liked my friends?"

"Yeah, they're really nice. Interesting. How do you know them? Do they all live here?"

"Oh, I have many friends. You know, I travel frequently. We will all have to meet up again sometime."

I took this last sentence as a throwaway, the polite "I'll call you" that never happens. After tomorrow it was back to Halifax, the lab, my dissertation.

She sat up, leaned forward slightly. "Is Carl taking you to the conference in Prague in the summer?"

"The CEACPS conference? Why, are you going?" Maybe she really did mean for us to meet again.

"No, no. My archival work is not *that* interdisciplinary. I have some acquaintances that spoke about it, that is all."

"Oh," I said. "He hasn't decided if he's taking me or Shannon, his other grad student. But one of us will have to go, to make sure his PowerPoint works, and all that stuff."

"Perhaps there are some benefits to having such a needy supervisor?" she said. "If he picks you, maybe you could arrange a few days afterwards to visit me in Budapest? It is a short plane ride, or you could even take the train, if you want some scenery."

"Really?"

"Budapest is such a beautiful city, right on the Danube, you know. You would stay with me. There are many things to see. I would show you."

A few days in Budapest, in Maria's world, would make a

week of running after Carl tolerable. "I'll see if I can talk him into taking me," I said.

She looked over my shoulder, then back towards the bar. "Dani, it looks like this place is closing soon."

"What? It's past two already?" I had to be up at six, to meet Carl at seven and make sure the computer and projector were set up to his exact specifications in the conference room for his eight o'clock presentation.

"You do not have an early morning?"

"I do. I have things to do for Carl. And if I want him to take me to Prague, I better be on top of things tomorrow morning." I sat up.

"It is a pity," said Maria, running her hand down my arm. "We have not had enough time together. We have not traded stories about our research. What are your plans when you finish at Halifax next year? You are still interested in Báthory, in the English murder?"

"Well, yes, but . . ." I didn't want to tell her the dull truth that lately I'd only been working on my dissertation and trying to keep up with Carl's demands. "It's nice to take a break from thinking about research, actually." I leaned towards her, touched the fur of her jacket sleeve.

"Of course. The girls, Milo, we will all be going to Milo's loft. You cannot join us?"

I was pretty sure that Milo's loft would be much more fun than going back to the Econolodge and getting up at the crack of dawn to attend to Carl. But I had seen Carl extremely angry once or twice, and even a glamorous after-party wasn't worth it.

"Then it will keep until Budapest. But before you go, I must not forget—"

She put her arms around me, slid them up my back, under

my hair, to the nape of my neck. She leaned in, and her halter grazed the black cotton of my tank top. I wasn't sure what she was about to do, and I sat very still, barely breathing.

Her fingers found the clasp of the necklace. She kissed my cheek, warm, slowly, as she unfastened the silver catch. I felt the stones fall away from my throat; until then, I hadn't been aware of their weight on my skin.

"My diamonds," she said, pulling away. Light spun off the gems as she held them between us. "They looked stunning on you."

Chapter Thirteen

It's finally Friday, the day of my third interview with Foster. Kelly only slotted me in for a half-hour—I think Sloane denied me the hour because she wants the room at three—but I'll work those thirty minutes, I'll get him talking again. My desk is strewn with all of my notes from his file. I read over my report from the last interview, even though I know it by heart; I've gone over it dozens of times, before and after I filed a copy with Abbas. I spent days writing it, agonizing over everything: which words to use, how to come across as professional and detached for my audience of Sloane and Abbas, how at the same time to capture every detail Foster gave me.

I put the report down and turn to my other papers. I've made some charts. One is a timeline: I went through Foster's entire file from the moment he was admitted into Stowmoor and noted when Báthory was mentioned in his therapy or assessment reports. I made a red star if the clinician brought her up, a blue star if he brought her up. Two years, eight blue stars, six red. Almost all of them within the first year and a half. Then nothing until now. One red star. Me.

I also have a pie chart that breaks down the themes of Foster's therapies and assessments. Focus on understanding that his crime was antisocial: yellow. On the realization that he has caused harm to others: pink. On the importance of feelings of remorse: orange. On the reduction of violent tendencies: purple. On obsessive actions or tendencies: green. On level of positive engagement with staff and fellow patients: blue.

The pie is largely pink and orange and yellow. A bit of blue. Relatively small slivers of green and purple. He's had the greatest exposure to therapies concerning his responsibility for and remorse for the crime. Granted, these are two major tenets of rehabilitation therapies. But it also means he's had a great deal of opportunity to learn what the clinicians want to hear on this subject, what we interpret as "positive" answers that reflect progress. We've taught him how to lie to us.

I begin work on a bar chart to track Foster's references to outside friends, support groups or influential individuals (besides his obsession with Báthory). Aside from my interview with him last week, he hasn't made a single reference of this kind since he came to Stowmoor, but if I start from when he was arrested, and if I use newspaper and magazine articles as sources, I've got some material to work with. I can hear Sloane's tirade about the dangers of hearsay and imagine her horror that I'd even consider those reports as sources. And she's right. It's complete speculation. I have a hunch, informed by my own fixation on Báthory and her diaries, largely unsubstantiated media reports and Foster's ambiguous mention of people who share his interests. It's poor clinical practice.

There are footsteps down the hall. I shuffle the charts under some paper just as Sloane walks within view of my fishbowl window. She's smiling, the corners of her brown eyes tilted up, a bit crinkled. The smile looks genuine. A tall blond man in a suit walks beside her.

"Of course, we have things set up so you can see him straight away," she says to the man.

"Excellent. I'm glad to see things run efficiently here. And with such discretion. Important with a client who has the potential to attract much public interest."

I stare at my computer screen, pretend I'm reading email. Out of the corner of my eye, I see Sloane glance towards my fishbowl, then turn her focus back to the man.

"Yes. Well," she tucks a stray wisp of hair behind her ear. "I can see we're both committed to providing Mr. Foster with the very best psychological and legal care."

It's a struggle to keep my eyes on the screen. They're just past my window when an email comes through from Dr. Abbas. It's to all staff working on Foster's case. We're advised that Foster has retained new legal counsel, a Mr. B. Lewison. In the coming weeks, Mr. Lewison may request to meet with personnel working with Foster. Abbas also reiterates Stowmoor's confidentiality guidelines for clinicians and other hospital staff.

I fight the desire to follow Sloane, press my ear to her office door while she speaks to Lewison, while he meets with Foster.

I've got three hours before my interview with Foster. I pull out my charts, go over my notes repeatedly. I try to write up another assessment that's late, but I can't focus. I check my email every two minutes, hoping for a distraction. Hoping for a message from Maria. There's nothing. I haven't heard from her since the opening. No more diaries, no suggestion of lunch. My fingers twitch over the keyboard; I want to write her a message that hints at my interview; I want her to know I'll soon be in the same room as him. Instead, I log out of my email and struggle with the late report.

. . .

I slide into the chair across from Foster, set my file and pens down on the stainless steel table between us. "Good afternoon, Mr. Foster," I say, as I open my notepad.

"Dr. Win-ston," he says slowly. "I've been expecting you."

I ignore his attempt at a joke. "I trust you've been well. I have a few—"

"Questions for me?" He smiles. "Somehow I expected that. I hope they're sufficiently interesting today. And yes, I've been well, thanks for asking. Very well."

"Good to hear. I want to pick up on some themes that came up in our last interview."

"Oh?" He raises his eyebrows. "Well, by all means."

"You said that you still think about Báthory. Do you think about her often?"

"Define often." He digs some dirt from under his fingernail, flicks the speck to the floor.

"I mean, do you currently have any thoughts about Báthory, or maybe about another person, event or idea, thoughts that take up a lot of your time." My tone is calm, measured.

"So, you're asking me if I think about things throughout the day?" Another dig, flick from his fingernail.

"Do you think about a specific person, event or idea to the extent that you are fixated on a particular thought? And if so, does this fixation pervade and perhaps influence your day-to-day routine?"

"My day-to-day routine? Jam-packed as it is. I can hardly keep up."

"Mr. Foster, we're conducting this interview to complete your assessment. It would be to your benefit to take my questions seriously."

"Hmm, yes, but I do. So, do I have fixated thoughts?" He

drops his hands into his lap. For the first time since I've sat down, he looks straight at me. I think he's almost smiling. "It's a good question," he continues. "And what about you? Have you spent any time thinking about Báthory since our last meeting, Dr. Winston?"

I pause. But I ignore the question and keep going. "You mentioned, in our last meeting, that you missed speaking about her to others. Am I paraphrasing your statements accurately?"

"As best I can remember. You've probably kept a better record of what I said, doctor."

Again, I ignore his comment. "Do you still feel this way, right now?"

"I think about her, yes. Though you're the second person today to ask me about her. So I do in theory miss speaking about her to others, but you're helping to alleviate that lack."

"Who else did you speak to about her today?"

"Oh, I'm not sure . . . the client-lawyer confidentiality thing, I'm not sure how much I can say."

"So, you discussed her with your lawyer."

"Oops. Cat's out of the bag."

"What does talking about her do for you? How does it satisfy you?"

"Dr. Winston. You know how beautiful she was, don't you? How pure? She was focused. She didn't shirk what she was; she took her privilege as an opportunity to bloom."

"To bloom? Into what?"

"Dr. Winston," he says, as if I'm a child who's failed to grasp an equation on a blackboard. "Into the perfect manifestation of what she was."

I can feel him waiting for me to ask what she was, exactly. Instead, I say, "Before you came here, did you have anyone in particular with whom you discussed her?"

"*With whom* I discussed her? Why so formal, Danica? We're beyond all that stuffiness, aren't we?"

How does he know my first name? He must have overheard Abbas or Sloane.

"I got it from the article," he says. "Your name. That's what you were wondering, right?"

I tap my pen on my notebook. "Please answer the question."

"I had friends. That's a healthy thing, right, to have friends? You psychologists encourage it?"

"Who were these friends?"

"They were peers *with whom* I spent time." He smiles. "Isn't that who friends usually are?"

"How did you meet them?"

"We had interests in common. These are very predictable questions." He fake-yawns.

"Did these friends know about the murder?"

"Did they know? The whole of England knew."

"Did they know of your intent?"

He turns his palms up towards me. "My intent was their intent."

Is this another joke, or is he admitting something? "Can you elaborate? These people also want to commit, or have committed, similar acts?"

"No. They're more . . . they're . . ."

I realize I'm leaning forward, elbows on the table. I'm chewing on my lip. "They're, uh, they are what?" I sit up straight, jot a few words in my notebook.

"It's complicated. I miss them. They understood." He looks down, holds the sides of his head with his hands.

I write down every word. And then he holds his head up, winks and laughs.

"Hypothetically, Dr. Winston, wouldn't it be good for me if I admitted I was influenced? Had help? I've heard," he hits the table with his palms a couple of times, "that it could work in my favour. Legally, you know." He raises his eyebrows.

"Hypothetically, it would not be good for you to lie to one of your health care professionals. Especially while she's trying to do an assessment. Lying would not reflect well on you at all."

"Are you accusing me of lying?"

"Aren't you?" I say sharply. I take a breath, employ my calm voice again. "Look, we're on the same side here," I say. "It's in your best interests to—"

"Ooh, you sound angry. Have I annoyed you?"

"Not at all." I manage to keep using my professional voice. "Perhaps we've covered enough ground for today." I start to gather my things.

"Hypothetically, what if I wasn't lying? What if—"

"You gave information about your accomplices? That's a legal matter. You should take that up with your new solicitor." I stand to go, push in my chair.

"Thank you, I will. I already have. But that wasn't what I was going to say, Danica."

I turn back. "It's Dr. Winston."

"Yes, as you like. I was going to say, hypothetically, that if I had accomplices, they would still be out there. Still meeting with each other." He waves his hand in the direction of the front door of Stowmoor. "They would, I am sure," he leans back and scans my legs, torso, finally stares at my face, "like to know about you."

I look at the steady red light of the surveillance camera, think what a disaster it would be if Sloane or Abbas ever used the security footage to observe my interview skills.

I've failed at furthering the assessment, I've failed at finding out anything about his thoughts regarding Báthory. Foster's laughing at his ability to bat me around, to have me bite into whatever piece of information, whether true or false, he throws at me.

I knock on the door and Bill lets me out. As I walk down the hall, I hear Foster yell after me, "A pleasure as always, Dr. Winston." His taunt stops my breath, a crushing weight on my chest. Don't let him scare you, I tell myself. Or make you angry. Think clearly. If other people were involved, why wouldn't he have brought this up before, at his trial, during his assessments, his therapies? He's likely only saying these things now because of his new lawyer's influence. He must be lying.

But why would he do it in such an antagonistic way? He could be bored. Or maybe he is telling the truth. Half-truths, anyway.

"How did it go this afternoon with Foster?" Abbas asks, after I run into him in the hall.

"I'm not sure it went well," I say, searching for the most opaque terms I can use without confessing it was a total waste of time. "He was not as cooperative as in past interviews."

"I see," says Abbas. "Don't be so perturbed, Danica. You look like someone's just stolen your bicycle."

"I'm not sure I'll have much new material to add to my report."

"That's how it goes sometimes. You have to learn not to take it personally."

"Right."

He awkwardly pats my shoulder. "There are many reasons why an interview might not go well. It needn't reflect on your abilities as a professional. Patients are not predictable. They have good moods, bad moods. Foster's had a long day, met a new solicitor, and—"

"Danica!" Kelly rushes down the hall, intercepts us a few feet from my office door. "We've been waiting for you."

"I was in an interview. It was in the schedule."

"I know, but it's urgent. We think you must have misfiled a chart—we can't find it. It belongs to the patient Dr. Sloane is set to interview at three. His last name is—"

"Kroesen." Sloane strides down the hallway. Her rubber-soled heels make a dull thud on the concrete tiles. She shoos Kelly away. "The file is missing, Danica, and we think you were the last person to handle the chart. The hard copy is missing from central files. The digital copy hasn't been updated. Can you shed any light on this?"

"The Kroesen file?" I mentally scan my roster of patient files and reports. No Kroesen. I glance at the few paper memos on my desk, which I sometimes take a day or so to get to. Did I miss something there? Was there an email I didn't get? "I'm sorry, Dr. Sloane, I'm not sure that I—"

"You're not sure? You're not sure if you lost a patient's file?" She squares her hips towards me, takes a step forward.

"What's the matter here?" Abbas asks Sloane.

I turn away from her and unlock my office door. "Why don't we discuss it in here? I can take a look at my files, but I'm quite sure I wasn't assigned to that patient."

She walks in and leans against my desk. Abbas follows. "Look," Sloane says, clearly still annoyed, but more restrained, "I'll get Kelly to reschedule the interview until tomorrow. But please look into it as soon as possible."

"We'll sort this out, not to worry," says Abbas. "Kelly can search again. Danica will keep looking here, too, I'm sure."

He steps out of my office into the hallway and Sloane moves to join him. She leans in as she passes me. "Interesting chart, Danica," she half-whispers, half-growls in my ear. I glance at my desk; I've left a copy of my Foster bar chart by the printer. Her shiny teak ponytail brushes my shoulder as she sweeps by, sidles up to Abbas. He makes placatory hand gestures. She shakes her head.

I set Foster's file on my desk, try to relax my shoulders. Swing my door shut, pull down the blinds. Under the buzzing fluorescent light, I close the filing cabinet and sit down. Kroesen. I flip through the memos I ignored. Nothing. I have no memory, no record that I was ever involved with that file. But of course Sloane would go out of her way to accuse me of messing up, and in front of Abbas and everyone. I shove the memos to a corner of my desk; it doesn't matter if I know what's going on or file everything perfectly. Sloane will never accept me as a colleague.

I pull up my pie chart, the timeline, delete them all. All my preparation for today was a waste of time. To keep my mind off Foster, I go through my files one more time to try to find the Kroesen file, even though I'm almost positive I was never responsible for it.

The more clinical work I do, the more I know that I got into this profession for the wrong reasons. When I started studying psychology, it was out of prurient curiosity. I could take classes where I learned about bizarre patient histories, deviant behaviour, violent criminals. I took every abnormal and forensic psych class I could. The case studies we read, the theories we learned, seemed dynamic, even glamorous.

And I did very well in those classes. I started to listen to my classmates, my TAs, everyone who told me I was so talented, that I could be so successful. So I kept studying, went to graduate school for clinical psych. Started working with Carl, winning grants, publishing articles. And when I began to hate all the paperwork, to realize I didn't even really like being a clinician, I kept listening to everyone who told me I had such potential, had already come this far. When I actually started *doing* therapy, clinical work—I knew I wasn't drawn to it. It was dreary, repetitive work, usually carried out in small, dank rooms in outdated mental health facilities. I asked the same questions, in the same way, over and over. There was nothing glamorous about it.

I had a professor who once said being a clinical psychologist was a calling, like the priesthood. Everyone in class nodded enthusiastically, believing, or pretending to believe, that they thought the same thing, that they had all heard a call. I nodded too, even though I knew I was a fake. But I kept on the path. I thought it would get better at some stage, that I'd start to be better. After this interview today, I know I'm not. I accomplished nothing of clinical worth in that interview. I tried to indulge my own interests and failed even at that; now I'm confused, slightly paranoid and, for the first time, a bit frightened.

Chapter Fourteen

"Just arrived. I'm heading in now." He pushed against the glass door with his shoulder, the phone to his ear in one hand and a long carrier tube in the other.

"Yes, I checked it. Exactly what we ordered," he said to the person on the other end. ". . . Yes, she is. I'm lending her the car on Wednesday to pick him up."

He stepped into the elevator and pressed the button for the sixth floor. ". . . I know she is. She's just worried about it, but it's fine, it's at her place now . . . All right." The door opened. "I'll be there soon." He flipped the phone shut.

"Excuse me," he said to the receptionist. "Can you see that Mr. Lewison gets this parcel?" He set the tube on her desk.

"Who is it from?"

"He'll know what it's regarding." The man tucked his phone into his suit pocket, then returned to the elevator and descended to the lobby.

It was nine p.m. and finally the firm was quiet, the receptionists had gone home, phones were dead in their cradles. He stepped into his office, closed the thick oak door. The parcel was by the door, a two-and-a-half-foot-long tube with a silver plastic cap on one end. A white ribbon tied around it. A deep-red card with black cursive writing: For the office. An addition to your collection. To a prosperous beginning.

He leaned the tube against one of the floor-to-ceiling bookcases that lined the walls. Hung his blazer on the back of the leather-upholstered desk chair. He tossed the card on the shiny walnut desk, grabbed the decanter of sherry with his big, pale hand and poured some of the liquid into a lead-crystal glass. He held the glass to the lamp, watched the crystal pattern split the warm light into seven colours against the backdrop of dark sherry. Cross and olive. His doctor warned him about lead seeping into his drinks, but who could sip from a plain glass? Besides, he craved a little lead. There should be more lead, more dirt, more risk in this world, he thought.

At the funeral, he'd known right away that they would bring him risk. He was acquainted with almost everyone else at his father's wake except these people. Yet they had the air of being important, of having known something intimate about the deceased. They stayed knotted in a corner, sipping wine, professional mourners in their expensively tailored suits, black dresses.

"We knew your father well," said one of the men, shaking Lewison's hand. "A real pillar for our organization."

"He was integral," said one of the women. She held his thick hand between her two slim, soft ones. "Such a loss."

He surveyed the small group. They seemed aware of each other's movements, statements. They were a unit, a swarm of gorgeous black beetles. His father had had many interesting clients, but he'd never mentioned anyone like these people.

"Yes, thank you. I'm taking over a number of my father's clients. If I can be of service . . ." He handed the woman his card.

She tucked it inside her small black purse and snapped the clasp shut.

They had money. Some from sources he would need to keep anonymous, some from sources that were anonymous even to him. Only a few people knew where it all really came from, but he was getting closer; he would prove himself further, and then he would know. He'd manage the spreadsheets, keep the accounts offshore, keep them off the financial grid. Soon he'd be integral.

They paid well, but that wasn't what excited him. They had history, heft, a purpose. And now he did too. Theirs was a noble sort of blood sport.

His shelves were filled with books about war, dynasties, invasions, occupations. He'd been collecting them since he graduated with his law degree, almost twenty years ago. On his walls hung maps of the Persian Achaemenid Empire, the Han Empire, the Roman Empire and the great Mongol Empire. The maps were sentinels of the office, watching over him as he worked, as he conquered, controlled, won.

He picked up a pair of scissors and sliced the white ribbon, then wedged one of the metal blades between the cap and the tube and popped it open. He slid a thick scroll of parchment out of the tube and unrolled it. Another map: the Ottoman Empire during the late 1500s. Suleyman's Turks pushing west, the Hungarians pushing back. And on this map, certain castles marked in black calligraphy: Ecsed, Beckov, Sárvár, Čachtice. The manor house in Vienna. Her birthplace in Transylvania. A geography of Báthory, where she lived, where she killed.

The castles, the houses, dotted the border of Ottoman/Hungarian control. She lived amid constant threats of conflict and invasion. But instead of succumbing to fear, of acquiescing to helplessness and uncertainty, she built her own empire on the threshold of precarious boundaries.

He stood back and stared at the new map. He would do more than his father. He would keep the money hidden, but he'd also move ahead with their other legal issue, as they'd put it last night over drinks. There was no denying it would be a challenge. Even if he called in every favour he was owed, it might take years to obtain parole. There was no guarantee he could make any improvement on Foster's behalf, and also, it was a risk to be publicly, officially tied to him. But he knew a couple of people inside Stowmoor who could be useful. He sipped sherry from his lead crystal. He'd make some calls tomorrow.

Chapter Fifteen

I'm too late to make the five o'clock train and have to take the 5:45. This wouldn't usually be a problem, but I'm supposed to be ready to leave for a party with Henry at 7:30, and at this rate I'll only just make it home by then. I sent him a text before I got on the tube at Ealing Broadway, but I've had no reception since.

I step onto the Shepherd's Bush platform at 7:20, race up the left-hand side of the seemingly never-ending escalator, pass the park and breathlessly turn the latch on our door at 7:35. Henry is on the phone, pacing the room.

"She just walked in," he says into the receiver as he gives me a *where the hell were you* look. I mouth the words *I'm sorry*. "Yeah, ten minutes is great," he says. "We'll be out front."

He hangs up and interrupts my stream of explanations. "It doesn't matter right now. Wilson is coming to pick us up in, like, ten minutes."

"I thought we were going on the tube."

"He just called and he's on his way. I want some time with him before the party to hear what he thought about the review."

The review. It's been up on our fridge for the past week.

Every time I go to get a nectarine or a piece of cheese I have to see the photo of Maria curled up in the throne.

"And they might use me for a feature—Edward stopped by my studio today. Your friend Maria was with him too."

"Maria?" What was she doing dropping in on Henry?

"Yeah. Anyway, Wilson's going to be here any minute, so . . ."

Wilson is the director of Henry's residency program and he lives on the fringes of Notting Hill. That puts him about seven minutes away by car if he left right after Henry hung up the phone.

"All right, all right," I say, dropping my shoulder bag and flinging my coat over the kitchen table.

"Don't flip out," says Henry. "Go in what you're wearing, just throw on a sweater or something."

I am wearing a navy pantsuit, which clearly is not suitable for a Friday-night party. Henry appreciates the finished product when I spend an hour dressing to go out, but can never understand that without said hour the results will not be the same. I kick off my shoes and wiggle out of my pants as I head towards the bathroom. I pull my hair out of the day's ponytail and look in the mirror. My makeup is faded. I have dark circles under my eyes and there is a large, unflattering kink in my hair from the tight elastic.

"Hey, toots, about five minutes!"

"I *know*."

No time to hide the kink with curls or plug in the straight iron. I grab another elastic to scrape my hair into messy pigtails and hope I can pass off any dishevelment as intentional boho-chic. Then I dig through the closet for one of my standby dresses: the baby blue faux-satin one, spaghetti straps, empire waist.

"I'm going out front to catch Wilson, but you've got to hurry."

I hear the door click shut, and my first reaction is to take my time and make him wait. But I remember that I was the one who was late, that this means a lot to Henry and he might be a bit nervous, all of those things that reasonable people should remind themselves of in this sort of situation. And I want to ask him about Maria's visit before Wilson shows up. So I throw on the dress and grab a string of gold plastic beads that's sitting on top of the dresser instead of searching for my amber pendant. I shovel a handful of cosmetics into my purse and make it to the street just as Wilson's black Yaris hatchback slides to a stop in front of us.

"Hey," says Henry, opening the passenger door. Grime music pulses from the car stereo. "Thanks for the lift. You remember Dani?"

Wilson is about forty-five, with spiked, streaked hair and flashy gold hoop earrings. Henry said he was one of *the* up-and-coming London painters in the nineties. I wave hi and start to crawl into the back seat.

"You can have the front if you'd rather," says Henry. Wilson echoes the comment.

"No, I'm fine back here," I say, settling into the corner. "You guys have stuff to catch up on." I start to examine what I swiped into my purse: concealer and a compact, which is promising, some pink and blue glittery eyeshadow, which is less so, and some lip-plumping gloss I got last week and haven't even opened yet. I sit back, pop open the compact and listen for any mention of Maria.

Wilson starts the car from second gear, and we shoot into the street just ahead of a sedan. He builds speed until the engine is roaring, then pops it into third. "So, Henry," he says, "quite a coup with the *Guardian* review last week. They really took a fancy to you."

"Yeah, I'm pretty happy. Edward Grant, the reviewer, stopped by the studio today."

"Reaallly," says Wilson, drawing out the word. "Has his eye on you for a feature in *Time Out,* maybe?"

"Sounds like it, but you never know."

"But it's a good sign. The review spent a lot of time on you—I'm sure Andreas is right ticked that they only gave him a few lines."

"Well, I don't know," says Henry. I can only partly see his face, but he's smiling. He and Andreas have studios close to one another and have gone out for drinks several times, but Henry hasn't said much about him this past week.

"And who was that bird they photographed in your throne?" says Wilson. "She's quite a looker."

I sit forward to hear better and lean my hand, which holds a long gold tube of undereye concealer, against the back of Wilson's seat. We're coming up to a roundabout, and Wilson stops short to avoid merging into the side of a black Mercedes. I'm pitched forward and almost poke myself in the eye with the tube.

"Bloody hell," says Wilson, as he makes a second, smoother attempt to enter the roundabout. "Just to wake you up, that was," he laughs.

I survey my reflection in the tiny disc of the compact. I have a blobby line of concealer under one eye, mid-cheekbone to temple. Anemic linebacker style.

"No worries," I say, redirecting as much of the concealer as I can onto the dark circles under my eyes, patting it in gently with my right ring finger. He doesn't look in the rear-view mirror for my reflection but instead turns back to Henry.

"What were we talking about? Andreas? He's green as a pea over that review, I'll wager."

Wilson keeps prattling on about Andreas and several other people I've never met, but whose names I think Henry's mentioned before, and by context I guess that they have spots in the residency as well. I learn that Wilson fancies Tabitha and Meredith, that Nicola barely scraped into the program and was originally tenth on a waiting list but the spot opened up so last-minute no one else would take it, and if he weren't program director and hadn't moral standards he'd be sleeping with her, because she's a stunner. Wilson is the guy who will be encouraging everyone to down tequila shots by eleven, telling a story about some sort of tragic, tortured event in his life to two pretty girls by midnight, and by one in the morning, after a litre of red wine and a few vodka shots, will be wearing some sort of improvised headgear and proposing a game of strip something or other.

I make it sound like Wilson is annoying, middle-aged and smarmy. And he is, but really I enjoy going to Henry's parties. Compared to some of the functions—*parties* would be misleading—that I've had to attend, Henry's parties are giddy carnivals. I remember one painful evening last year in grad school, hosted by Shannon, my contest-entering-obsessed, depressive office mate. She gave out *written* invitations four weeks beforehand, sent emails to follow up and made reminder phone calls two days before the event. To keep peace in the office, I had to go. When Henry and I arrived at her house, she led us downstairs to a circle of folding chairs (probably set up since the one-week-prior mark) and a wobbly card table pushed against the far wall set with a bowl of Bits 'n' Bites, a plate of Rice Krispie squares, stacks of Styrofoam cups and two-litre bottles of Dr. Pepper and diet cola. Carl and her husband were the only other people so far, and they sat on the far side of the folding-chair circle, away from her barking puppy, which she had put in its kennel under the snack table. At Henry's parties, people actually wanted to enjoy themselves. And people like Wilson made it hard not to.

I'm done with the makeup, my eyelids now dusted with pink glitter and my lips tingling and numb from the lip-plumper. I'm not sure how much longer it will take to drive to this place in Shoreditch but I want to know what happened with Maria and Edward at Henry's studio today. I lean forward a little more, and when Wilson pauses to take a breath in the middle of a diatribe on the incestuousness of art reviewing in London, I dare to break in, going for an obvious question.

"So, Wilson," I say, "is Henry's review in the *Guardian* really significant, in terms of recognition from other artists?" Henry turns his head, slightly surprised that I'm asking a question he knows I know the answer to.

"Dear, as I said, it will turn them green."

"I thought the photo they ran with the review was really, um, provocative," I say. Another look from Henry.

"Yes, right, that woman in the throne." He turns back to Henry. "She's right fit. Do you know her, or did she just turn up randomly?"

"Actually, she's a friend of Dani's," says Henry.

"Reaallly," says Wilson, again drawing out the word. "Is she a colleague?"

"Um, well, she's not a psychologist, but I guess I met her through work. At a conference. She does archival and curatorial work. From Budapest. She's here doing some stuff for the London Museum."

"Has she been in town long? What's her name?"

"Uh, Maria," I say. "I think she's been here a little while. As long as us, anyway."

"Does she go to openings much? If she's in need of an escort to another opening or anything," he starts digging around in the tray under the car stereo, "you should give her my card. Just let me find it." He whips both hands back onto the wheel to switch lanes, then digs around again.

Henry laughs and claps a hand on Wilson's shoulder. "Good thinking," he says, "but I think she's already seeing someone. Isn't that right?"

"Yeah, she's dating Edward Grant. They seem pretty tight." I keep an eye on Wilson's reflection in the rear-view mirror.

"*She's* dating *Grant!*" Wilson's eyebrows arch up, up, up. "I see, I see." He glances at Henry. "That's working out well for you. Hang on to this one," Wilson jabs his thumb backwards. He shifts his eyes to me in the mirror. "Looks and connections—can't ask for more."

We arrive at a renovated brick warehouse in Shoreditch. Henry's chatting with Wilson and leaves me to climb out of the back seat. We all head to a door in an alley that opens to a flight of stairs. Henry lingers a few steps behind Wilson. "What were all those questions in the car about?" he says in a low voice. The dim yellow light of the stairwell stains both of us a dark gold.

Before I can say anything, Wilson pushes the door open and a flood of music and conversation spills out from the party. "Come on, you two!" He leans into the open doorway and motions for us to step inside.

"Henry!" Two girls rush up to him as soon as we walk in. "We haven't seen you since the review came out!" says one. "Brilliant, just brilliant," says the other.

"He's our new star," says Wilson, slapping Henry's shoulder.

"Drinks?" I nod and Wilson heads deeper into the party. The two girls prattle on about Henry's show. He smiles and laughs with them. Finally, he turns to me. "This is Tabitha and Meredith. They're in my program."

"Hi, I'm Dani."

"Here we go," Wilson's back, hands Henry and me a bottle of Newcastle each. "Are we still talking about our Henry's review?"

"It's just so exciting," says Tabitha. "Makes the program look great, too."

"That it does." Wilson takes a long swig of his beer. "How did it go? '*Le Paradis Rouge* embodies the frantic extreme of the carnivalesque.' Genius." He clinks his bottle against Henry's.

"The frantic extreme," repeats Meredith. "Gorgeous."

"Genius *is* extreme, of course," coos Tabitha.

Henry smiles, tilts the bottle to his lips.

Chapter Sixteen

Henry rolls out of bed and heads to the kitchen. He's up early to make his Saturday morning class. I sit up, groggy from the late night. He flips on the coffee grinder.

"Want to check that?" Henry yells over the whirr and points at the flashing red light on our answering machine. I bury my head in the pillow until he's finished grinding, then shuffle over and hit play.

Maria's voice wafts out of the tinny speaker. "Danica, Henry. It is Maria. I am wondering if you are free on Sunday. The notice is short, I know, but Edward has tickets for the Bourgeois exhibit at the Tate. And, Danica, there is an email I sent for you tonight. Call me. *Viszlát!*"

Henry must have given Maria our home number.

"Hey, that sounds good," says Henry. "I've been meaning to get to that show." He goes into the bathroom, starts brushing his teeth. "Give her a call and tell her we'll meet them," he shouts over the running water.

"Really? You don't think it's too short notice?" The thought of Maria and Henry becoming friends seems like putting salt on ice cream.

"Why, what else have you got planned?" He comes out of

the bathroom, pulls a navy blue T-shirt over his lean torso. "Sounds like a nice afternoon."

"Because you want to hang out with Edward?"

"What? They seem like nice people. Why wouldn't you want us to hang out with your friends? They're way more interesting than the people I met at your staff thing."

"That party was fine. They were fine." He's referring to the dinner party Jana invited us to our first week here. We ate casserole on TV tables and made awkward conversation with people from Jana's horticulture club.

"Are you serious? We were home by ten thirty." He pours coffee into his travel mug, grabs his keys. "Hey," he says, pulling one of my stray red hairs off his T-shirt, "do you know you've left hairs all over the bathroom counter? There's a bunch in the sink—they look like little red worms," he says as he shrugs on his jacket.

"Uh, okay, what am I supposed to do about that? I have hair and I brush it and some comes out."

"Relax, tiger lily. I'm just saying, living with you, I'm noticing you shed a lot."

"Thanks for noticing. Really romantic."

"So tell Maria we're on for tomorrow." He gives me a quick kiss goodbye and he's out the door.

I try to fall back asleep, but I feel uneasy about Maria and Henry's burgeoning friendship. Will she confide in him, tell him about her work, the diaries? In the bathroom, I grab a piece of toilet paper, dampen it and wipe the strands of my hair from the sink and counter. I drop the tissue into the garbage, pour a cup of coffee and play Maria's message again. She sounds friendly. I play it one more time, listen to her intonation when she says our names, her tone when she mentions the short notice. Maybe she's sincere.

And the email. Has she heard more Foster stories through Edward? I turn on my laptop.

Dani,

We should see each other soon. We have not met since the openings!
For you, another instalment.

x, M.

Sárvár, December 15, 1601
At last, some respite, some gleam of intrigue in this drab little castle. It seems a long time has passed since Ursula finally died, yet for another month I must pretend to be sombre and in mourning. At least she is in the grave, though she manages to make me miserable still. But this week I have met with good fortune: I have made the acquaintance of Anna Darvulia. And she promises great things.

Helena Jo met her at the marketplace, and they entered into a discussion about where to find the best nettles, and then how best to keep a household's laundry-women in line. Helena brought her back here, thinking I might like to add her to my entourage.

I have interviewed her several times. She is one of those things you never knew you needed, but, once discovered, do not know how you did without. She has a wide knowledge of herbs, poisons and cures. She has travelled across the continent, learning from high court physicians, barber-surgeons, gypsies, even witches. She has distilled the effective treatments from all the wives' tales, knows what really benefits ailing bodies. And then last night, she delighted me further.

It was just before seven, and we were in the salon, sipping a cordial before supper. I was already suitably impressed with her medicinal knowledge, and although she is not a beauty, there was an efficiency in the way she presented herself—chestnut hair pulled back into a firm, elegantly swirled bun, her clothing plain, but made from a beautiful, solid muslin—that I could respect. She is no maiden, but she has an energy in her countenance that is strong, almost virile. I tested her.

I remarked that I often dread this time of day.

She asked me if what I dreaded was the darkness, which is almost perpetual this time of year. She barely moved as she spoke, and stared straight at me, turning her crystal goblet slowly, methodically between her fingers. It seemed, almost, that she wanted to know something about me. But she was patient, and played the part I cast for her.

I told her it wasn't the darkness, but that my seamstresses are supposed to finish their day's work by seven, precisely. And at seven, I must go and check on them. Immediately, she said it was dreadful that the lady of the house must perform such a task herself, and that my seamstresses must be very lazy, insolent girls if they need to be hounded so much.

I agreed that it was rather offensive. I sipped the last of the dark maroon liquid in my goblet. I told her that I have found that it is best to take a firm hand with these girls, and that sometimes I bring Helena or Dorca along, but it is me they fear the most. I set down my glass and returned her look.

She requested if she could accompany me this evening and share some techniques I might find pleasing.

She was astounding with my girls. When we walked in, the silly slatterns were talking, and by the large pile of garments by the door, it was clear that they were not done their work. Darvulia singled out the small-breasted, tall one, I think she is called Tania. She walked over to Tania's chair and soundly slapped her across the face. The girl started blubbering immediately.

Darvulia shook the girl by the shoulders and asked her why she dared to talk while there was still work to do. Tania started to make excuses, said something about Helena dropping off a fresh batch of sewing only a half-hour ago, but Darvulia slapped her again and again, until her nose bled and she was silent.

Then Darvulia threaded the girl's darning needle. She motioned for me to come over and told me to hold the girl's head. Then she stuck the needle down through the girl's upper lip and guided it out through her lower. The girl screamed, and Darvulia hit her again, this time hard on the head, to stun her still. The girl quieted, and Darvulia continued to sew. In just a few moments she had caged the mouth with dark blue thread. The girl's face was a swollen mess of bruises. Blood seeped from the needle punctures that rimmed her lips.

I laughed and smiled. I would have been delighted just at this act, but she had more to show me. One of the girls, a new one, I don't know her name, only that she is short and a bit chubby, starting whimpering, then gasping repeatedly, like a hysteric. Darvulia looked to me, said that my girls were snivellers, and that she could quiet them.

I nodded and she moved towards the girl, grabbed her by the hair, dragged her away from her table and pulled her towards the stove where the flatirons were heating. The girl continued to scream. Darvulia picked up an iron and shoved the hot triangle into the girl's nose and face. The girl made an unintelligible noise, her mouth first blocked, then transformed from orifice to wound by the searing metal. Her nose, which was piggish to begin with, seemed to melt under the pointed tip of the iron, and the flesh, then the bone of her jaw sank in. I could hear the muscle and fat bubble, and the room smelled of burnt meat. The girl eventually fainted, and Darvulia pulled the iron away, dropped the body on the floor. The face was ravaged; the eyes were intact, but the nose, mouth and jaw were a raw, simmering wound.

After supper, I asked Darvulia to stay for some Tokaji. I told her how pleased I was with how she handled my seamstresses. And I told her what I had discovered, with the blood and my skin. She did not blink once. Instead, she put down her glass of wine and put her hand on my forearm. She said that if I would allow it, we could do much of this work together.

She is to move into the castle and join my entourage at the end of this week.

The lips threaded shut, the iron melting the girl's mouth. The images of Darvulia torturing the seamstresses consume me, make my anxieties about Henry and Maria's friendship seem small as a hangnail. I think of Foster's evasions. I imagine him in his sideroom with his little pile of books and magazines.

What would he tell me in exchange for a look at a copy of Báthory's diaries?

I need to get the rest from her, to know if they are authentic. Maybe it's best to be friendly. I dial her number.

"Darling," she says, "so wonderful to hear from you. My email, you received it?"

"Yes." I want to ask if I can come over right now and look at the photos, the proof that they're real. "Very compelling."

"I thought you would like it. I am very glad. And you and Henry, you are coming to the Tate tomorrow?"

The way she says it sounds like she assumes there's no way we wouldn't. It almost makes me want to tell her no. But I try to sound cheerful and force myself to say, "Um, yeah, I think we can."

"Good, good," she says. "We have hardly seen each other lately. It will be so wonderful for all of us to go out, do something fun."

"Yes, sure." It's true, I haven't seen her since the opening, even though she's been almost omnipresent: the emails, diaries, studio visits with Henry. She's too much in my life, but only as a phantom; I haven't been alone with her in weeks.

"So, did you see your Henry's review last week?" she asks.

"Yes. It's clipped out and posted on our fridge. Nice photo." I can't keep the sarcasm from creeping in.

"Yes," says Maria, "Edward said the paper was very pleased with it. Much good feedback, from readers."

"That's nice." I pause and restrain myself from asking if Edward has heard anything else Foster-related around the newsroom.

"And Henry, he is pleased?"

"Of course."

"Did he mention, Edward and I, we visited with him yesterday, at his studio."

"Yes, he mentioned you were very friendly."

"Ah, well. He is very kind. So, we shall all meet tomorrow, two o'clock?"

Again, she seems sincere. Maybe she is in her own spontaneous and eccentric way. Maybe, as Henry said, she's the most interesting friend I have.

Chapter Seventeen

We file onto Millennium Bridge and merge with the pedestrians pouring across the Thames. Henry's in a good mood this afternoon. We're walking slowly, watching boats on the river. I reach to hold his hand. He looks at me, smiles and puts his arm around my shoulder, pulls me in synch with his step, his hipbone brushing my waist. We stop halfway across and lean against the railing. "You look nice today, peach delight," he says. "Pretty dress." He runs his hand down the side of my skirt, holds me close.

Things feel easy together, how they used to feel all the time before we moved. It's just been a period of adjustment, I tell myself. The new city, new flat. The new job that's a lot more complicated than I anticipated.

We hadn't been dating long when I decided to move here with him. We were in his studio and he was smoothing strips of plaster-soaked cotton around my left leg. Six inches above my kneecap, the brush of his fingers against my inner thigh tickled.

"I told you, stay still." He didn't look up and continued to wrap.

"I'm trying."

"Just relax. Have more wine."

In my right hand I held a cup half full of shiraz. I took a sip, careful not to wiggle too much.

It was February. Two months before Henry's graduating show. We were in his studio and I was a model for his final project. He had piles of plaster casts of body parts scattered around the room. Hands in one corner, a few backs in another. Four chests, two female, rested by the door; three torsos and a male pelvis lay nearby. I sat in the middle of the room on a folding chair in my bluebell-print panties. My leg was propped up on a plastic milk crate, knee bent at a thirty-degree angle.

"That's better," he said. "Don't I take care of my models?"

His head was down, focused on the plaster. He wrapped the damp cotton farther up my leg. The cloudy plaster water bled off the material, inched towards my hipbone and blotted out the faint café-au-lait birthmark on my inner thigh. I watched the top of Henry's head as he wrapped, his severe widow's peak, an occasional flash of the half-hoop earrings that looked like fangs in his lobes. He stopped wrapping the plaster a few inches from my panties. Finally he looked at me, a half smile, his gold-brown eyes crinkling at the corners.

"Think you can stay still while it dries, princess?"

"I'm a professional." I said. "We models suffer for art."

"That's the way I like it." He stood up and ran his hand up the right side of my abdomen, his hands still wet from the plaster, threatening to tickle me.

"Hey!" I shouted.

"Just kidding, relax." He crossed to the other side of the room, grabbed a few rags and started to clean his hands. His green T-shirt, littered with white smudges, was a half size too small for his tall, lean frame.

"Only the most dedicated model could maintain her composure in such a challenging environment," I said.

He dropped the rags, poured himself a glass of wine from the box he kept on the shelf beside his books. "Well, then," he said, pulling up another milk crate and sitting down beside me, "I'll have to keep you around. Not that you're going anywhere right now." He motioned to my leg.

Henry had been accepted to the residency in London the previous week. We'd gone for pints of Moosehead the afternoon he received the news. But for me the celebration was tinged with anxiety. We hadn't discussed what would happen between us when he left in the fall. We'd been dating five months. I was due to defend my dissertation in the spring and I was applying for a few jobs, but I didn't really know yet what I was doing after graduation. Ever since the letter came, Henry had been talking about nothing but London.

I drank the rest of my wine. "You'll never find a better model in London."

He laughed. "Really, it's a pretty big city." He stood up, took my plastic cup and refilled it from the box.

"Yeah, but, I mean . . ."

"What?" He handed me the cup and sat back on the milk crate.

"It's just, you know." I wanted him to say, *No one could be better than you, I'll miss you terribly, would you come with me?*

"Know what?" He leaned back, tilted his head down and stared. His eyes were close-set, wolfish. When he stared at me like that, I felt exposed, a stray kitten. I didn't know what to say.

I squirmed.

"Stay still—it's not quite set yet," he said.

I wanted to leave, but his almost-dry cast kept me captive. Underneath, my skin was starting to itch.

Henry stood up. "London's going to be amazing. The program, the city. Everything. So much more going on there." He moved behind me and put an arm around my shoulder. He started smoothing my hair.

I didn't want to lose him to this move, yes. But I also felt jealous. He was moving to an exciting city to pursue an opportunity, a discipline he was passionate about. I pictured what the year ahead held for me: stacks of job applications, intense interviews, grant proposals, laborious research studies. No adventure. No risk. Since he'd received the news, I'd been daydreaming of going to London too. I'd pictured myself working at Stowmoor, where I knew Foster was serving his sentence. I imagined starting an exciting, important new job at one of the biggest forensic hospitals in Europe and working on my dream case.

"You're quiet," he said, kissing the top of my head. "Five more minutes and we'll cut you loose from this thing."

"Henry, what if I came with you?"

When Henry and I hit the south end of the bridge, we walk around the outside of the Tate Modern and down the concrete ramp to the huge, factory-like entrance. Henry drops his arm; we weave between families pushing strollers and green-haired teenagers sporting ripped black fishnets.

I see Maria waiting for us at the base of the ramp; she spots us and starts to wave. Her hair is loose and looks almost white against her bright red wool coat.

"Henry! Dani! Over here!" she says, hopping up and down.

I can't help but smile a little. I look at Henry and he's full-on grinning. "Good to see you!" he says, as we approach Maria. She embraces him and kisses him on each cheek.

"And Dani!" She hugs me as well, gives me the two kisses, and then keeps hold of my hand. "It is so wonderful that you could make it, with the short notice. We will all have such a wonderful day."

"Where's Edward?" I ask.

"He is sliding." She points up. Henry and I crane our necks towards the ceiling and see a criss-cross network of Plexiglas slides in the middle of the building. There's an entrance to a slide on each floor, and the tubes corkscrew down to the ground floor. We see bodies jetting through the transparent slides, people spat out, a little dizzy, at the bottom.

"It is an exhibition, see?" Maria hands us a leaflet that explains the piece, *Test Site,* by Carsten Höller. It says sliding is supposed to inflict "voluptuous panic on an otherwise lucid mind."

"Is Edward reviewing this or something?" I ask.

"No," Maria laughs, "I do not think so. He wants just to slide. Ah, there, he is at the bottom now!" She points again.

Edward picks himself up from the end of one of the Plexiglas chutes.

"That's good fun, yeah?" says Edward, putting his arm around Maria's waist. "Hello, hello," he says and shakes our hands. "Nice to see you again. So, are any of you going to give it a go?"

"With these shoes, I do not think so," says Maria, pointing to her heeled Mary Janes. "But I am glad you had fun."

"I might give it a go," says Henry.

"You boys," Maria laughs. "Let us see the exhibit first. Here, already we have the tickets." She hands us one each.

"Thanks, but you didn't have to get them," I say.

"It was really no trouble," says Edward. "Shows are free for members, so that covers us, and I always get comp tickets. I'm happy to see them go to use."

"Shall we go?" Maria links her arm with mine, and the men pair up ahead of us.

The Louise Bourgeois exhibit is not very crowded. I hear Edward and Henry art-speaking ahead of us: "Her work really didn't get sufficient critical attention until later in her career, and it's hard to say which movement can really claim her"; "Really, I think she resisted categorization, both organically and intentionally . . ."

Maria is silent. She reads the pamphlet about the retrospective and breaks away to look at the works. I'm floating around the gallery, trying to focus on the paintings, but I've got one ear open to eavesdrop on Henry and Edward, and one eye on Maria. I feel outside of their little group. It's probably something I've constructed in my head, but still I worry I'm being purposefully excluded.

I've been standing in front of the same painting for five minutes: it's a long, rectangular piece, the canvas coated with a dark grey wash, a tall, blocky skyscraper in the background and a woman's naked body from the waist down, legs splayed, in the foreground. I've managed to register the title, one of the *Femme Maison* series, but the rest of the blurb is lost on me. What would I say about this piece if Edward asked me? Maria and Henry would have brilliant commentaries, and I would probably stutter or relate it back to some outdated, boring inkblot theory I learned about in third-year undergrad.

I see Edward and Henry move into the next room. Maria hovers near the doorway. She's studying a caged sculpture.

"Like it?" I ask. I scan the curatorial statement: it's a scale marble sculpture of the artist's childhood home, enclosed in a cage, meant to symbolize the trauma of her childhood.

"*Like* is perhaps not the right word," she says. "Very skilled— the detail, the house, amazing. Simple, yet so precise." She still doesn't look at me; her eyes fix firmly on the piece. She starts to walk around it; I follow. She makes a full circle and seems ready to move on to the next room. I try to get her attention again.

"Do you think Henry and Edward are having a good time?" I whisper. Through the archway, I see that they are already halfway down the next gallery.

"Hmm?" She looks at me, seemingly startled from a reverie.

"Henry and Edward?"

"What about them? Look, already, they are there. Probably they are talking shop, as you say."

They are engrossed in an animated conversation, presumably about the sculptures in front of them. Edward gestures, Henry nods; then they reverse the actions.

Maria puts her hand on the small of my back, leans towards my ear. "Dani, they are fine. They are in their element. Do not worry."

"I'm not worrying, I just want to be sure that everyone is having a good time."

"But are you? You are distracted. Here." I follow her to a line of totem-like sculptures displayed in the next room. "Just be still. Just look. Experience this. You do not have to think, just feel what you feel."

She says this in the kind of tone we are supposed to use for patients who get stuck on the literal details of questionnaires. Except, in contrast to my fake-calm voice, hers sounds sincere.

Like she cares, like she knows for certain that she's leading me towards some new and special place.

I try it. By the fourth room, I even stop looking at the pamphlet to see if my reaction to the spider-nest-vortex sculpture matches what's been written by the curator. I feel a relaxation, a freedom from judgment. I walk into the sixth room, lost in my thoughts. I'm drawn to one of the sculptures; it's called *Avenza Revisited*. The name means nothing to me, and for the first time I don't worry that it doesn't. Instead, I focus on the piece: a blobby plaster creature, with egg-sac type bubbles on the top. Languid streams of plaster extend from the bottom and settle into fleshy ribbons on the floor. Entrails, a sliced abdomen, guts spilled. Like Báthory's diaries.

The next room contains installations staged within cages. I lose Maria in a series of larger pieces, miniature rooms, boudoirs filled with sculptures of limbs, red stuffed animals, pillows on beds. Cages containing textiles, old clothes, a white woollen peacoat with *the cold of anxiety is very real* painted on the back in red letters.

I step into the last room. Small sculptures, arranged on shelves behind glass, line two walls. I wander down one strip until I come to another *Femme Maison* piece. A Barbie doll encased in a brick of clay. Her face is embedded in the grey mass; only her blonde hair, her arms and her long legs stream free. A few cracks run up the side of the clay, like the doll tried to struggle against this smothering.

"I think Báthory, she would wish she had thought of that." Maria is to my left. I'm not sure how long she's been there.

I don't respond at first. Then I say, "But there would be no blood."

"True. But I think that was rather secondary. Something she could take. She craved it, wore it. It became hers."

"And how would she make something like this hers?"

For a moment she stands very close. I feel the hairs on my arm tingle, my skin aware of her proximity. I wait for her touch.

She walks out of the room.

I push open the doors and walk into the foyer and gift shop area. Maria and Edward are standing near the shop entrance, chatting over a stack of souvenir cards.

"There you are!" says Maria.

"You enjoyed the retrospective, then," says Edward.

"Yes," I say. "Very engaging." Suddenly I start to worry again about saying something clever about the art. Maybe *engaging* was too vapid. "And you?" I manage to ask back.

"Yes, yes, brilliant. The Tate does manage some wonderful shows, even though it is somewhat like a supermarket for art."

"Oh, do not be such a snob," says Maria.

Edward laughs, puts his arm around her shoulders and kisses her hair. "You are right, my darling. You always lighten me up."

I feel like he'd rather I weren't there. "Where's Henry?" I ask.

"Oh, he's having a go on the slide," he says. "Shall we meet him down there?"

"Sure," I say, and we all start walking towards the stairs.

"I will meet you there in a moment," says Maria, "I must stop at the loo. Go on, I will be a moment only."

Edward stares after her for a couple of seconds as she walks away, and almost runs me into the stair railing. "Oh, terribly sorry, Dani."

"No worries. Can't take your eyes off her?" I joke.

He stammers a bit. "I . . . I guess not." He's suddenly flushed. "I admit, I'm quite smitten. Besotted, really."

"That's sweet. So things are going well between you."

"They seem to be. I mean—they are, yes. Yes. It's only been a short while, but I hope things continue, become serious, do you know what I mean?"

The last phrase comes out all strung together, that unconscious *dya-nowot-I-mean* that punctuates some English teenagers' sentences. It's surprising to hear it from a suddenly stammering Edward. He must really be in love. I feel bad for him; Maria may care for Edward, but I'm not convinced she's serious about him.

"In any case," he says, clearing his throat, "how's work going? There's a lot of guys from the newsroom sniffing around for Stowmoor stories, about that terrible man."

"Yes. It's a sensational case. Sells papers, I guess. Maria told me there were lots of stories and rumours going around." I don't want to say too much. But I'm curious whether he knows about any new theories the reporters are putting together.

"Oh, definitely. Rumours. They're scrambling after any source they can get, anyone who has even a scrap of a comment."

"What are they looking for?"

"Last I heard, someone at the *Telegraph* had some sort of tip that Foster didn't act alone, that he has the support of an obsessive group behind him. But it's mostly hearsay. The more reputable papers wouldn't run a story like that, just based on anonymous tips, you know?"

"Right. That's quite a story."

"I'll say. Probably all rubbish, but imagine if it were true? Come on," he laughs, "what's your professional opinion?"

"Serious stuff, if it's true. If these other people exist, they'd probably be very dangerous." I'm careful to speak in the hypo-thetical, and I know Edward is just joking, but now I'm the one who's uncomfortable.

"So," I say as we reach the ground floor, "do you think we can spot Henry coming down one of these tubes?" We glance at the bodies sailing through the Plexiglas chutes. Then I see a flash of Henry's khaki jacket and dark blond hair whiz out of the longest slide. He stands up and I wave at him. He gives me the biggest smile I've seen from him in weeks.

On the walk back to the tube station, Henry says, "I'm glad we did that. You know, met up with them. They're both great. He's really nice, and Maria, I mean . . . there's no one like her."

"Yeah, I guess."

"What, what's the problem?"

"No, no," I smile and try to sound lighthearted. "It was great. I just meant I didn't have as much fun as you did, on the slide and everything."

"Oh." he gave me a quick shoulder squeeze. "You could have slid down, too, kitten."

"Maybe next time."

Chapter Eighteen

He walked through the Heathrow arrivals door, pulling his black wheelie suitcase with one hand, holding his briefcase and a large boutique bag in the other. The crowd waiting to meet travellers was sparse today, and he picked her out immediately, even though they had never met in person. Tall, with long, dark hair and olive skin. She was focused on her phone.

He parked his suitcase in front of her. "I believe you're my ride?"

She looked up. He surveyed her brown, almost black, eyes, fuchsia-slicked lips. Her long legs, white and silver python-skin boots. She lived up to his expectation that she would be uncommonly pretty.

"Yes," she said. "Lovely to meet you, finally." They leaned towards each other and kissed cheeks. She smelled like sandalwood and honey, and ran her hand down his shoulder and upper arm.

He followed her to the car.

"I'm to take you straight to the meeting," she said as she merged onto the motorway.

"So, no nap to get over my jet lag?"

"I'm afraid not. My instructions were explicit."

"Well, if those are the instructions. Of course."

"The thing is, it's all moving along fairly quickly." She saw him stifle a yawn. "We'll see about getting you a coffee."

"Great. So things are on schedule?"

"More or less. Almost everyone is here. The painting arrived a little while ago."

"Really? I've never seen it, you know, in person." He'd been involved in the cause for over a year, but had been outposted for most of that time.

"It's spectacular. It's stored it in my flat at the moment."

"Could I sneak a look?"

She shifted gears and accelerated the Audi past two cars, then veered into the left lane. "Do you have everything ready?"

He unzipped a compartment in his wallet and took out an SD camera card. "Right here."

He'd spent months abroad to get these photos. The town was small enough that people often left their car doors unlocked, made small talk in coffee shops about the weather, but still big enough for him to blend in. He'd researched three possibilities. There was a series of photos of a girl in an ice rink, fair hair peeking from her hockey helmet. Off-ice, lugging her equipment bag across the parking lot. Another girl, at the public library. He'd worn a ball cap and read a novel while he shot her, his small camera hidden under a few blank pages of loose-leaf. And what he thought was his best work: a half-dozen photos of the girl who bused dishes at a diner. The way her thin arms trembled under the weight of the dishes made her seem waif-like. Barely strong enough not to break under a fully loaded tray.

He felt an anxious flutter as he displayed the card in his palm. They'd all agreed the next project needed to be away from CCTV cameras, so he'd been sent to scout girls someplace more remote. But would they be able to get everything in place? "It seems so . . ."

"Impossible?"

"Complicated. But yes, maybe impossible." He slipped the card back into his wallet.

"We've made progress on that front. Very good progress." She turned off the motorway and started threading the car through narrow city streets. "You'll see. We're almost there."

"There's a solid plan, then?"

"I meant, we're almost here." She stopped the car in front of a tall building. Through the entranceway's glass doors he could see a white couch and high-backed chairs in the lobby. "But we're close on the plan, too. We have a new lawyer. They'll tell you. Ninth floor."

"You're not coming?"

"Sadly, I'm not. Car's on loan and they've set up other duties for me today." She looked in the rear-view mirror and checked her lipstick. She turned back to him. "You can text me later about the painting, if you like," she said as she petted his leather-clad shoulder again.

He got out, then reached in the back seat for the large cream boutique bag. The handles were tied with dark brown, curlicued ribbon. The bag sagged from the weight of the box inside.

"This is for you," he said and placed it on the passenger seat.

"What is it?"

"Sadly," he smiled at her, "I can't say." He shut the passenger door, took his suitcase from the trunk and walked into the building.

Chapter Nineteen

I'm ten minutes early, but the phone is ringing as I open the door to my office. I let it go to voicemail; technically, I'm not obligated to answer my phone before nine. As soon as the ringing stops, it starts again. I shut my door, hang up my coat, let this call go too. The phone is silent for thirty seconds and then rings again. I give in and pick up.

"Dr. Winston, Dr. Danica Winston?" asks an unfamiliar man's voice.

"Yes?"

"This is Tim Porter, from the *Sun*. I was wondering—"

"I'm not interested in a subscription, thanks."

"No, no, Dr. Winston, I was wondering if you'd care to comment further on the Foster case?"

Comment further? "I don't comment on any of Stowmoor's patients to the media."

As soon as I hang up, another ring. "This is Fiona Russell, from Sky Radio One," a smooth, broadcast-ready voice booms into my ear. "Can you share your thoughts on the type of people Martin Foster is thought to be associated with in regard to his criminal activities?"

The next call is from Kelly. "Danica, you're wanted in Abbas's office."

"Okay," I say quietly. This can't be good.

I knock on Dr. Abbas's door. It swings open immediately. Both Abbas and Sloane stand inside the office. They look extremely angry.

"Sit down, Danica," says Abbas. I sit in the uncomfortable wooden chair in front of his desk.

"This is unacceptable." Sloane throws a copy of the *Daily Press* in front of me. I read the huge headline: *FOSTER'S ACCOMPLICES?* Underneath in smaller font: *Ritual Killer Potentially Influenced by Murderous Cabal.* I scan the article. It's completely speculative and sensational. It's bad tabloid writing that presents Foster as a "possible" plaything, a victim of a larger criminal organization that "could potentially" exist. It says "sources claim" that Foster's new solicitor, Bryan Lewison, has evidence to prove that Foster was not solely responsible; the paper quotes him referring to his client's "misunderstood state of mind." Besides that, the article seems like just another rehashed version of all the half-fictionalized articles that were published when he was first arrested.

"Yes, very poor journalism," I say, unsure why she's showing this to me or how this relates to this morning's calls. "A 'cabal,' really? This is like all the other stories that have come out about him. All conjecture, meant to sell papers. Right?"

"But did those other articles have a quote from a Stowmoor psychologist who works with Foster?" Sloane hisses in my ear and stabs the article with her long, French-manicured fingernail.

I look again. Oh no. Please, no.

Foster's mental health team suggests that such an organization could not only contribute to Foster's desire
to kill again but also may be dangerous to the general
public. "If such people did exist, they would probably
be very dangerous," said Dr. Danica Winston, one of
Foster's psychologists at Stowmoor Hospital.

"I didn't, this isn't anything I said to them. I'd never talk
to the papers about any patient, about anything here." When
did I say that? This is very, very bad. "I take my responsibili-
ties seriously," I say. That quote . . . it sounds like what I said
to Edward this weekend. But would he really sell me out to a
trashy paper like the *Daily Press*? Is that even legal?

"Do you know what this looks like? Do you know how
unprofessional this makes us look?" Sloane is almost yelling.

"It's, it's not accurate, I didn't say . . ." How can I possibly explain this? I was speaking tangentially, speculatively,
about Foster's case. Nothing that anyone who'd read any of
the recent coverage mightn't say in passing. Did Maria know
about this?

"Well," says Abbas, "if they've completely made it up, we
can ask for a retraction, take legal action against them. But do
you know how they might have focused on your name and
that you work with Foster?"

"It's not . . . the words aren't exactly what I said, and it's . . .
it's completely taken out of context."

"So you did say this?" Sloane rips the paper out of my hand
and waves it around.

"Not exactly! And I didn't say it to that paper! This weekend, a friend, I was talking to a friend, he's a journalist, he
was asking me what I thought about all the new stories and
rumours about Foster. He said there was a rumour that Foster

was part of a Báthory-obsessed organization. We were just talking. I had no idea."

"You were 'just talking' to a journalist about a Stowmoor patient? And you didn't think that was a bad idea?" says Sloane.

"I wasn't thinking of him as a journalist. He's a friend, and—"

"You weren't thinking at all. How did he know you were assessing Foster? Is patient confidentiality a joke to you, something you might consider if it doesn't interfere too much with social conversations with your friends? What, is it your party trick, talking about our patients here?"

"I take Stowmoor seriously." As soon as I say it, I second-guess myself, wonder if I do take it seriously enough. I should never have said anything to Edward. I should have been more careful. I don't want to think about what all the seemingly minor admissions I've made to Maria could become in tabloid form.

"Danica, this situation seems to have resulted from a series of unfortunate circumstances," says Abbas. "It sounds like your comment was taken very much out of context, with much added conjecture, and I understand that you in no way intended for the *Press* to quote you on this matter. However," Abbas gently takes the crumpled paper out of Sloane's fist and smooths it out on his desk, "you must develop an understanding of the level of public interest, and media distortion, surrounding this case. You must also develop a greater respect for the rules regarding confidentiality at Stowmoor." He holds the headline in front of me again. "This reflects very, very poorly on us, regardless of your intent." He tilts his head down, scratches his scalp.

"I didn't mean to . . . I'm sorry." I'm trying to think of something helpful, something appropriate to say, while keeping my embarrassment and my anger under control. I'm mad at Edward for tattling on me to a tabloid, and I'm mad at myself for not considering that he would.

"You have made us look ridiculous," says Sloane, still yelling. "It's a disaster."

"Danica," says Abbas, "our public relations and legal teams are working on this. Dr. Sloane and I will see how things progress in the coming days and go from there. But as long as you're still working here, you must follow the confidentiality rules to the letter. Absolutely no contact with any sort of journalist."

"Of course, yes." I stand up. My legs feel weak and I hold on to the back of the chair as I turn towards the door.

I shut the door to my fishbowl office and close the blinds. The voicemail light on my phone blinks furiously. I ignore it and log into my email. There's a flood from reporters. One from Kelly saying they've changed my extension number and are no longer listing it in the staff directory.

I grab my mobile and text Maria: *I need to speak to you re today's Foster article.* Was the invitation to the Tate designed to get this quote from me? I thought Edward was just an art critic—why would he give any information about me to a tabloid?

Abbas and Sloane can't technically fire me; I'm here on an externally funded fellowship. But they could petition to have my fellowship revoked because I violated their confidentiality agreements. Or if they didn't go to that extreme, they could easily file a poor progress report on me, pull me off DSPD cases, increase my paperwork, make sure I spend the rest of my fellowship with the least possible contact with patients. End all contact with Foster.

A tinkle alerts me to a new email. I expect to find it's from another reporter, but it's from B. Lewison, Esq.: *Dr. Winston, I read the article today. Are you available to meet with me sometime this week?* I stare at the email. Then I delete it. Lewison wanting to meet with me can't be good news.

I look down at my Stowmoor ID. Right now, I have high security access. I can come and go in all the buildings, including the Paddock. But I'm in danger of losing this privilege if Sloane and Abbas decide the *Daily Press* debacle warrants punitive action.

This might be one of the few days I have left with access to Foster's schedule. I check and see that he's in the library. He's taking a correspondence class and receives one hour of monitored computer access per week.

He's at the far end of the table, nested in a flurry of notes and highlighted pages, a clean, blank notepad in front of him. The library is a cramped, low-ceilinged room. Unlike the bare concrete hallways, the floor is covered with ratty amber carpet. Rows of shelves jammed with paperbacks line the walls. An orderly leans against the blue metal door frame, thumbing a copy of *Grazia*. I wave at him and at the librarian seated behind the laminate-covered checkout desk. A pile of fresh newspapers sits on the counter; the librarian clicks away on his computer and barely glances at my ID as I walk past.

The fluorescent tubes flicker overhead. Dust coats an ancient magazine stand. Copies of *National Geographic* are clamped behind black wire, covers of pink sand beaches, peacocks, the Great Pyramid caught in the Venus flytrap doors of the rack. I walk quickly to the back of the room and sit across from Foster.

He looks up from his textbook. "Dr. Winston." He pushes his shaggy ginger fringe to the side. "Such a surprise."

"Mr. Foster." I look towards the door, anxious that Sloane might walk by. There's just the guard flipping through the glossy and the librarian fixated on the computer screen. "I have a few questions. Off the record," I say, quietly.

"Oh, yes? Happy to oblige. But first, I should thank you, Dr. Winston. You've made me even more famous!" He pulls a copy of today's *Daily Press* from under his notebook. "My new solicitor, he sent me a message about it this morning. It's handy that the library has subscriptions to all the *quality* papers."

"Mr. Foster, that quote was taken out of context. I know your lawyer is concerned about your confidentiality rights, but—"

"Concerned? No, no, Dr. Winston. I adore this sort of press. Not as weighty as an academic article, but it has its perks." He clasps his hands together gleefully. "Do you know I get fan mail? Well, my correspondence is of course strictly vetted in here, but some arrives care of my lawyer. I have the most interesting fans, truly."

"I see. And this pleases you?"

His smile is wide, almost manic. I feel a tug of panic and involuntarily lean back in my chair to put as much distance between us as I can. He pulls his chair closer to the table, to me. "Oh, it's wonderful. Now, you had a question, off the record? This sounds much more interesting than your regular interview questions."

There's a scraping sound from the front of the room. I jump before I realize it's just the librarian adjusting his chair. I clutch the ID strung around my neck. This might be my last chance ever to speak with him. He puts his elbows on the desk and cups his chin in his palms and keeps grinning.

"Is it true?" I ask. "Are you involved with a larger group?"

"Isn't it an exciting story? What did the paper call it today—a cabal? Ooh." He mimes a shiver. "That's absolutely brilliant. I wonder if they'll keep calling it that, or maybe they'll go back to *organization,* which I think is a little dull. I'd suggest *cult* as an alternative." He stretches his hand in front of him as if to frame a banner headline. His fingers are inches from my face. "How's this: *Foster Involved in Báthory-Obsessed Cult.* Intriguing, yes?"

I will myself not to flinch. "I didn't ask if it was a good story. Why are these theories coming out now? Is it true?"

"It's difficult to know why certain stories become popular in the media. There are many factors that contribute to something emerging from the zeitgeist." He holds up his textbook. It's titled *Cultural Studies: A Reader.* "I just read a chapter on zeitgeist for my cultural studies course. Fascinating, really."

What can I do to make him answer the question? The only possible leverage I have, the only thing he might trade on is if I tell him about Báthory's diaries.

"Maybe it's not about you," I say. "Maybe it's Báthory the public is interested in. I hear her diaries have been discovered. Might be published soon."

He drops the book on the table. It thuds against his notebook. "It *is* about me. It's about continuing the work of Báthory. That's what we do. That's what my fans are interested in."

"*We.* More than just you?"

He sits up straight and takes a deep breath. "Dr. Winston, I fear if I comment further I will jeopardize the mystique surrounding my story. Now, I have to get back to work. This assignment is due today, and it won't write itself." He flips open his textbook and begins to read.

"Mr. Foster?"

He underlines something, keeps reading as if I'm not in the room.

Later that afternoon, still no reply from Maria. I text her again: *Call me.* I go over everything in my head, the afternoon at the Tate, the pleasure Foster's deriving from his "fame," his vague comments today, the possible influence of his new lawyer. His self-centered response and seeming disinterest in the diaries. Still, I chastise myself for bringing them up; I should never have even considered encouraging a patient's obsessive traits. Part of me thinks I should be taken off the case, out of Stowmoor completely. I check my empty inbox and my texts repeatedly. I'm desperate for any news, from Abbas, from Maria.

By four o'clock I've finished the week's residual paperwork and reorganized my office. I've still heard nothing from anyone, unless you count an email from Kelly, who tells me she's moved all of my patient appointments to next week on Sloane's suggestion, in light of the "media troubles."

Henry's not home when I get in. I dump my shoulder bag by the door, step out of my shoes and chuck them in the closet. I wiggle out of my dress pants and blouse, put on a T-shirt and yoga pants, and flop in front of the TV. I pour myself an end-of-the-bad-day beer. Another hour later, I call Henry's mobile. No answer. I leave a message, make some tea and watch reruns. Half an hour later, I call again.

"Hello?" The line is crackly.

"Henry? Where are you?"

"Hey, tootsie."

"Where are you? Are you coming home for dinner?"

"Hey, yeah, I just—"

The line goes dead. I try again, and get a "This customer is not in service" message. Two minutes later my mobile beeps. Text from Henry: *On tube home.*

Twenty minutes after that he comes through the door. "Hey, pixie!" He scoops me into a bear hug and gives me a big kiss.

"Where were you?" I say.

"Out for drinks." He smiles and tousles my hair.

"Don't." I hold his hand still. "I've had a really bad day."

"Sorry to hear that, sweet pea." He half-hugs me, then opens the fridge. "Want a beer? Hey, there's only three left— did you drink one?"

"Um, yeah." I want to tell him all about the horrible meeting this morning, how confused I am about everything. "Do you want to go out for dinner or something?"

"Ooh, can't." He opens a beer, takes a few swigs. "I'm just going to grab a sandwich and run. I'm heading out for pints with Wilson and a couple of guys from the studio."

"I didn't know you had plans. Do you have to go?"

"Don't sound so down." He puts his arms around my waist from behind and attempts to lift me up. I know it's meant to be sweet, but it feels like an attempt at the Heimlich manoeuvre. "I'd ask you to come along, but you know, it's a guys' night. How about we go out tomorrow night?"

"I'd rather go out now," I say and wiggle around to face him once my feet are back on the ground. "Didn't you just come from beers with the guys?"

"Nope. With Maria. We went to a really cool place, near Old Street station."

"Maria?" I echo. I shrug his arms off me completely and take a few steps away. "Why?"

"Why? Well, she came by the studio." He sits down on the bed.

"With Edward? She and Edward came by?"

"No, just her. It was really nice of her, actually."

"But why did she come by? Why did she want to see you?" I start pacing in front of the bed. "Did you see the *Daily Press* article today?" I say frantically. "Did you see it?"

"What are you going on about? Why would I read that paper?"

"It's . . . it's part of my bad day. I said something to Edward about the Foster case, and it showed up in the *Daily Press* today. Why did Maria drop by? Did she say anything?"

"Look, you need to calm down. Have you asked Maria or Edward about this? I'm sure it's all a mix-up. He doesn't work for that paper—he's a *critic*. Don't get so worked up." Henry tips the beer to his lips.

"It turned into a huge deal at work. I think it might be really serious."

"Cherry blossom, you're kind of yelling. I think you should just chill and wait until you talk to Maria and Edward and ask them their side of the story." He finishes his beer and grabs his jacket. "I think I'm going to eat something at the pub, give you some alone time, you know."

"Henry."

He gathers up his bag and opens the door. "Really, take a bubble bath or something. You can't think straight when you're all crazy upset like this. I'll see you later." The lock clicks shut and he's gone.

I grab the pillows off the bed and throw them at the closed door. What the hell was he doing out with Maria? Why does she have time to stop in on him but not to return my texts?

I whip out my phone and send Maria a message: *Where r you? Call me now. Urgent.* Another message: *Vry urgent!*

I wait a few seconds. Nothing.

I sit on the couch and watch a reality program on the BBC about out-of-control teenage girls who are sent on a desert hike in Arizona to sort out their lives. By the end of the trail, their hair is in neat pigtails, their faces fresh and black-eyeliner-free, and they are all excited to see their moms and stop doing drugs. I wish someone would send me on a desert hike and I could emerge with my career magically intact, with Maria gone, along with her games, and a doting and sensitive Henry waiting for me at the end of the trail.

My phone chirps. I lunge for it. From Maria: *Just got your messages! Sent you an email. Be in touch soon.*

Chapter Twenty

I open Maria's message immediately.

> *Dani,*
>
> *I saw the tabloid. Terrible. Edward feels horrible. All of it, a misunderstanding.*
>
> *Will you come for tea, my place, Saturday? I will explain everything.*
>
> *Do not worry. No one pays attention to the tabloids. In case you need a bit of a cheer-up, here is another section for you.*
>
> *x, M.*

All of it a misunderstanding? Right. And she wants to explain, of course. I think of writing her back, telling her I'm not coming for tea on Saturday, not speaking to her ever again.

But as Henry said, shouldn't I hear her side of the story? Not that her story is going to make any difference to the fallout at work.

For now I don't reply. But I open the attachment.

Čachtice, March 6, 1603

I have always loved night in this castle. We have been so much happier here in Čachtice. The castle is a proper fortress, and far enough away from the town to give us some privacy. Still, I hear that ridiculous minister preaches against me every Sunday. But he is of no matter.

From one side of my chamber, the world is pitch black, only the lonely call of owls emerging from the darkness. On the other, the same darkness punctured with a light or two from Višňové, far down in the valley. The lights are pretty, but those Slovak townsfolk are stupid for burning lights this late. It is quiet in the castle now, and I can finally make note of my last session with Darvulia.

Fizcko pulled the carriage up to the house. Darvulia came out immediately and helped me down and into the house before any townsfolk could notice or approach me. They can be such a nuisance. Why should I do anything about their crops, their taxes, whatever is annoying them?

The house was plain inside, but had a large open area with the fire going strong on the south side, a sturdy table pushed against one wall, filled with jars and herbs and dried flowers. Darvulia uses the house as a storeroom for her tools. She had come back from the markets and collected fresh supplies.

She held my hand and led me over to the light of the fire. She examined my skin carefully, and I stood still, knowing she would be happy with what she saw.

She traced her fingers across my cheekbone, down my face and under my chin. Then she placed a hand on either side of my face, holding my head with both hands. Her skin was rough against mine, and her eyes, that dark blue, almost violet, were edged with deep crow's feet. I wondered once why Darvulia did not use her powers to preserve her own looks. Now I understand that my beauty gives her more pleasure than her own ever could.

She told me she had brought me a present. I followed her into a small kitchen and down a dark set of stairs.

The cellar was low and mostly earthen. The ceiling, made of thick wooden rafters that support the underside of the floor above, was just a few inches above my head. The room was damp and smelled of urine. Darvulia, one of her hands circled around my wrist, the other holding a candle, led me farther into the cellar. Then I sensed it, maybe heard it: a girl's breathing. She was scared. I'm sure Darvulia could feel my pulse quicken. We approached the back wall and Darvulia's candle spilled light on the girl. She was sitting on the dirt floor, hands and feet bound, a dirty gag in her mouth. She had long hair, the color of honey, and she had wet herself. When she saw us in the candlelight, her eyebrows raised, tears came, her nose started to run.

It was a beautiful present. I assessed the smoothness of her skin under the dirt and tears and snot. A good catch. Fizcko loaded her into the carriage and took her back to the castle. She waits in the cellar, until we decide how she may be best used.

Čachtice, March 12, 1603

My new toy arrived yesterday. She is crude, and a bit frumpy, but I welcome her. Fizcko moved her into my chambers this morning, and I will employ her tonight.

I must thank Darvulia for introducing me to this device. Of course, I had heard of iron maidens before, but I was not very interested. With all of the spikes on the inside, and the lumbering figure, like a coffin, like one of those Egyptian tombs that hide the corpse inside, what was the purpose? You could not see the punctures, the slow, bleeding death. But this one; she is not a beauty, but she will be effective. There are two trips, one behind her left ear, and one at the centre of the throat, that trigger the release of a set of large spikes. One of these spikes swings out of her back, and the other out of her chest, just below her bustline. I am told that these weapons will not cause an immediate death. Depending on where the victim stands when she trips the latch, she could suffer a fatal stab to the lungs or abdomen, or she could receive merely a flesh wound. I like this element of suspense.

She is about my height, and although she is bulky in the midsection (I suppose it is so because this is where she houses the spikes), Darvulia advised that I could tell the girls that this is my new mannequin, a new dressing model. I will tell them it is from Paris, and it is a gift from the best dressmakers. They are such stupid cows that they will be impressed by this lie.

I had Helena Jo sew some hair around her crown. She took some from one of the girls we froze in the snow last week. Now my lady wears long, straw blonde tresses that skim her cold, bulky shoulders. I believe they belonged to that skinny girl who died fast. At least we salvaged something from her feeble death.

Darvulia will be here soon, and we will go through my jewellery. I have an old silver crown, a few strings of diamonds that might be appropriate. We will lay them all out, make it truly look as if we are trying to decide on which accoutrements I will wear to the next ball in Bratislava. I can so easily trick these girls. At first, they believe the stories they have heard and fear me greatly. But once I show them the slightest kindness, make them believe they are special to me, I know they will fawn like trusting whelps. Whichever creature I pick for tonight will be enthralled that she gets to enter my chamber, or touch my jewellery.

Čachtice, March 14, 1603

It was better than I thought it could be. Helena Jo and Dorca only cleaned up my chamber late yesterday, so I have not had a chance to write about it until now. I wanted to sleep late after the previous night's treatment. I did permit them to remove the body that night, after Darvulia cut a square of its skin to add to the talisman she is creating for me. But I insisted that they leave the rest. I wanted to wake to the rust-stained floor, that acrid smell of slaughter and the darkened, dry blood caked on the mannequin's spike.

I told them to bring me that very pretty one Darvulia found for me, a girl who was beautiful enough to serve as a lady of my chamber, if I were actually to employ such ladies. I think is it kind of me, in a way, to keep up this pretence for the other girls; they still believe their fantasy that they are here to work for me, to serve me, but that it will not cost them their lives. Though it is perhaps vain of them to think they would be valuable to me for any other purpose, that the efficient manner in which they carry a tray is worth more than their blood.

When the girl entered my chamber, I wondered if she had heard the screams from the ones we killed last week in the snow. She was terrified of me, and all the more beautiful because of it. Her fear drew me like an intoxicating perfume, wafted from her fine white skin, sixteen years of uselessness. Tonight I would give her purpose. Her beauty had no titles, no muscle, no consequence, except to lure, at most, a merchant's son, or stoke my stable boys. Her hair was blonde, a false sort of gold, worthless compared to the metal that linked the diamonds on my necklace. Her grating Slovak voice was a cheap load of tin that scratched my ears when she choked out "my lady" in Hungarian, as she gave me a ragged curtsey. Helena Jo moved her out of my direct line of sight and instructed her to stand by the dressing table where I had laid out the jewellery. The mannequin was a few feet away, facing the table. The bed was close enough that I could have sat on the edge and comfortably watched the show, but I left Darvulia perched there, and I crossed over to Helena Jo and the girl.

I told Helena that I would give the orders directly. I saw that the girl trembled, so slightly, when I spoke or came near. She was dressed in a simple grey dress, and her hair waved loose around her shoulders. She kept her eyes to the ground, as she should, but I saw that she stole glimpses of me when she thought I wasn't looking. It is understandable.

"Girl," I said to her, and she jumped, looked sideways at me for a moment and then forced her eyes back to the floor. I asked her if Helena Jo had told her why she was here, that she was to dress my mannequin. I told her to start with the silver crown.

She gave another awkward curtsey and turned to the dressing table, picked up the headpiece. It was a half crown, really, heavier than a tiara, but not a full circle. It had a crude criss-cross pattern, and it bore no jewels. It was a wedding gift from Ursula, and those first few months that we lived with her, she made me wear the awful thing twice a week to dinner. But now, at least, it was going to be of use.

The girl had trouble fitting the crown on the mannequin, but she finally found a way to wedge it on, slightly askew. I let this imperfection go.

I instructed her to take the long gold chain.

She scuffled back to the dressing table, took the long, braided loop of gold and hung it around the mannequin's neck. I waited—but no click. The chain was too light to trip the latch.

I could not wait much longer. I told her to take the heavy silver and diamond choker on the table and fasten it at the nape.

She walked over to the mannequin. She stood in front of it, reached around its neck, almost as though she were giving it a hug, to fasten the clasp. At last— the click. My lady attacked.

The girl's cry thrilled me like a lover's caress as the steel spike penetrated her suckle-soft abdomen. I circled to the back of the mannequin so I could look at the girl over its shoulder. She writhed like a deliciously wounded deer. The spike must have nicked her lung, because blood bubbled out of her mouth and wet her lips. I leaned forward and collected this spill with a kiss.

. . .

My abdomen throbs where I imagine the girl was punctured by the spike. My lips tingle as I picture Báthory and the bloody kiss. The drama of the tabloid, the problems at work, even the mystery of Foster's possible accomplices, they all wither compared to Báthory's diaries.

I close the file, make more tea and check my mobile in hopes of a message from Henry. I do the dishes. I organize the pantry. The quiet evening stretches on, eleven thirty, midnight, almost one. I put on my pajamas even though I'm not sleepy. I go back to my laptop and reread the diary entry. Then I go back and reread all the others.

I want to see the rest. I want to see Maria. And the photos that prove the diaries are authentic. I reply to her email and agree to meet her on Saturday.

Chapter Twenty-One

Maria's flat is in Shakespeare Tower, part of the Barbican Centre in the City of London. Despite asking three people where the building is, I still spend forty-five minutes wandering around the Barbican before I find it. The delay makes me anxious; it pushes my desire to see her into frenetic anticipation. Only when I'm gliding upwards in the elevator to her flat do I release my tight grip on my handbag and take a few deep breaths.

"You have the perfect time," she says, as she pulls open her cream-white door and ushers me in. The opaque grey sky still streams bright light through her floor-to-ceiling windows. I blink a few times, let Maria slip off my black puffy jacket. "I just finished my phone meeting with the museum director."

"Working on a Saturday?" I say.

"Yes, it is how it must be. My term here, it is only for a little while more, so things are very tight now." She hangs my coat in a tiny closet near the door and strides back to the kitchen. "But work is over for today," she smiles. "Tea? Or—" she looks at her watch, "four is not too early for a cocktail, yes?"

I want to skip the niceties and ask her about the article. But I find myself capitulating. "Whatever you want," I say. "So, you are leaving London soon, then?"

"Not so very soon, but in the not-very-distant future." She disappears into a little pantry, and I hear her rummaging around.

"So, like, two weeks, a month?" I walk into the kitchen and lean against the counter.

She pops back out, holding a jar of olives. "It is hard to say. But do not worry. I think I will be here, at the least, for one more month. Maybe a little longer. As long as they need me. Go, sit on the sofa. I will be there in a minute."

I walk towards the sitting area, pausing by one of the windows to look at the grey patchwork of tall concrete buildings, cobblestoned streets, the dull bulk of the Barbican. Cars jerk forward, then stop suddenly for lights, the occasional pedestrian. I think of my life here without Maria. No one leaking my random comments to tabloids, dropping into my boyfriend's studio, no one trying to get me to risk my job for their whims. No one sending me a four-hundred-year-old psychopath's journals. When she leaves, it will just be me and hopefully my job, and Henry and our basement flat.

I notice several letters and printouts of emails scattered on the coffee table. I scan some of the subject lines: *Re: Báthory ms.; Working on last part; An agreement?* I hear sounds of activity from the kitchen. Has she really got a publisher for the diaries? I'm about to pick up a letter and read it through when Maria swooshes into the living room.

"Here." She puts a martini with olives in front of me and has a short crystal glass filled with transparent liquid and a lime twist for herself. She sits beside me on the sofa. "This is the girls' cocktail hour—very fun!" She raises her glass and I do the same; we clink and sip. "So, Dani. You were not upset by that silly tabloid, I hope?"

That silly tabloid. Does she have to treat it so flippantly?

"Actually, it has caused me a lot of problems at work. And it's quite upsetting to think Edward used a private conversation for personal gain."

"Edward? Oh no, Dani, you must not blame him. It was my fault entirely."

"How? And why would you talk about me like that to a tabloid? Do you know that I could get moved to another section of Stowmoor, not be allowed to work with Foster anymore?"

"You are serious? This institution, it is so difficult. Can you not explain to them it was a mix-up? Shall I call them, will that help?"

"No, no, that's not going to help." Maria on the phone with Sloane would be a disaster. "You haven't explained how this happened."

"That. Yes, I will explain. You see, it was not Edward at all." I wait for her to continue. She takes a sip of her drink.

"You've already said that. Maria, tell me how this happened."

"Dani, you sound so stressed. Yes, all right. It was after we saw you and Henry at the Tate. Edward and I, we had plans to meet at a pub with some of the people he works with. On our way over, we were talking about the day with the two of you. He mentioned your conversation. He thinks you are so brave, Dani, and so accomplished, to be at Stowmoor."

I pretend to ignore the compliment. "If it was just the two of you talking, how did it get into the *Daily Press?*"

"You see, it was accidental. We met his reporter friends at the pub. Mostly, the group, they were writers from the arts section. We had some drinks, someone called his friend, and then another friend, and soon there was a whole group of people."

"Okay, so there was a bunch of people, and . . . ?"

"We were there for some time. There were many drinks."

She shakes her head. "And one man, he was not interesting at all, I do not know why I bothered speaking to him, he was asking Edward about his reviews, about the little mention he made of the Báthory artist's opening. Edward did not so much like the show, but this man, he wanted to know all about it. He said he had heard many stories about Foster, that he was going to be paroled, that he had help from others."

"Paroled? I don't think so."

"Well, exactly, Dani. This man was so stupid. So I said, to get rid of him, 'I have a good friend, Dani, she works at Stowmoor. She says if Foster has other people, they would be very danger-ous. So I am sure if they exist, they would have done something terrible, been caught already.' You see, he was an idiot."

"Right. But then somehow this exchange morphed into a quote from me in a story?"

"Oh, Edward says that this newspaper, they will print any-thing. All their stories are 'if this, maybe that.' They twist anything, but say nothing. I am sorry I mentioned your first name. He must have looked you up, googled you and then— poof!"

"Poof?"

"Exactly. At Stowmoor, they cannot understand that?"

For the first time since Sloane and Abbas lectured me on Thursday, I smile. I imagine Maria sitting down with them, getting them to understand that—*poof!*—it was all a complete misunderstanding, and that the *Daily Press* reporter, the real villain in this story, is an idiot.

"No," I laugh, "I don't think they can."

"Ridiculous! Ah, Dani," she says, "your smile, so beautiful. It is nice to see you laugh. Henry, he told me you are on an edge lately?"

I stop laughing. "Yeah, he mentioned you came by his studio."

"Yes, I had a meeting with a client at Aquarium. It ended early, and Henry's studio, it was close by. You were at work, or we would have called you."

"And he told you he thinks I'm on edge?"

"Do not be angry with him, Dani, for telling me. I think he is worried, that is all."

After his behaviour earlier this week, I don't think *worried* is the right word. I pick one of the papers off the coffee table. "What's this all about? You have a book coming out?"

"Ah, that!" She jumps up and crosses the room to her desk. "I will show you something, it will cheer you." She comes back with a sleeve of photos and sets it on the table. "You see? The diary!"

The photos. There are three. One is of the worn cover of an old leather-bound volume; one of a tattered page with a few lines of handwriting in strong black ink. I can't decipher it, but one word looks like *Báthory*. And the third photo is of a page full of the same black-inked script. "Is this her writing? What does it say?"

"Here, I will explain. She leans close and points at the first picture. "She was, of course, nobility, so she had access to, could afford to have, a codex journal, the pages bound together. The cover, it is vellum, very delicate. And here," she points to the lines on the first page, "is her name, and here," she points to the last photo, "is the first page of the diary."

I stare at the photos. I don't know anything about rare books, but this one looks very old. And it does look like the word *Báthory* is written on the first page. Maybe this is all for real.

"As I said, I will go back, do more documentation, once I have finished the draft of the manuscript. You see," she points to the papers on the coffee table, "already, a publisher is interested." She leans back into her chair and crosses her legs.

"So, it will appear with an academic press? Small print run?"

She uncrosses her legs, sets down her drink. "Dani," she says, in a tone that is slightly admonishing, slightly amused, "you have been inside Stowmoor too long! No, no. I want a large publisher, a commercial press. Translation, distribution in multiple countries. With Foster in the news again, the time is now. People will want to, they will need to, read Báthory."

"Commercial?"

"Of course. A powerful woman, killing all those girls. For beauty. And Foster killing for her, four hundred years later. People want to know."

I put my glass, now empty, down on the table. Maria scoops it up and takes it into the kitchen. "So," she calls, "I am still looking for someone—someone who can sign their name 'doctor,' you know, the public, they like that—someone to write an afterword on Foster, on the resonation of Báthory's appeal in contemporary time." In a minute she comes back with fresh drinks. "I was going to ask if perhaps you could recommend one of your colleagues to me, but after this little silliness with the tabloid, they sound maybe too rigid."

"No, I don't have any colleagues to recommend." She'll ask me. She won't leave me out of this. "They wouldn't be interested in writing for anything that is not an academic publication. Really, they're much too stuffy."

"Well, I am not looking for stuffy."

"No. And it might be complicated, legally, to talk about a case, even speculatively, that they're currently working on."

"But surely there is someone who does not care only about academia and clinical practice and their stodgy reputation? Someone a little tired of all the dry little rules? Someone who is excited by the diaries?"

She turns her glass in her hands while she talks. The lime rind floats among the ice cubes. I wait for her to say more. The cubes clink against the glass.

"Maria," I say, "I could possibly consider . . . maybe there is a way I could be involved."

She sets her drink on the side table, puts her hands on the arms of her plush white chair and leans back. "Dani, really?" She smiles. "It could work. And this tabloid business, perhaps it is a silver lining? Now you are connected in the media to Foster. We can present you to the public as an expert."

"Wait," I say. "I'm already in enough trouble about being quoted as an 'expert' in regard to Foster. And I don't see how being quoted in a tabloid helps to make me an expert. We'd have to be very careful . . . I couldn't talk about anything conclusively."

"The general public," she makes a sweeping motion, "does not care about *conclusively*. They want professional speculation, some sort of explanation, a legitimization of Báthory's state. That she was at the extreme edge, insane. They do not need the technical terms, the *conclusively*. An educated discussion of the diaries, of obsession, of the cultural meanings around Foster's crime, that is what this project needs."

"You think this book will be a success?"

"Of course. Notorious women are always popular. And everything I do is a success." She stands up. "Dani, if you want to achieve anything, you must learn to make your own successes. This work at Stowmoor, you do not shine when you speak of it. These people you work with, they sound terrible, controlling, drab people. Leave them, make your own name."

"It's not that easy, Maria. I don't have the hours to become certified yet. If I quit at Stowmoor, I'll—"

"Dani, listen to yourself!" She sits close beside me on the

sofa. "This institution, this certification, all these rules that other people created, you let them run your life. You are better than these rules."

I think of giving up my fellowship, leaving the clinical interviews, the endless reports, the academic articles, walking out of the aging hulk of the Victorian asylum, walking past the weathered angel out front and not looking back. I feel Maria's breath on my cheek. She's the angel, blue eyes bright against pale skin, more luminous than Stowmoor's guardian statue ever was.

"Now, I shall give you all the information, so you can consider things properly." She tears a strip of paper off a notebook, grabs a pen and writes something down. She slides the paper across the table, in front of me. "It is so gauche to speak of money with friends, but for business . . . this is, approximately, what I would pay for your fee."

I pick up the paper. "Are you serious?"

"Completely. And do not forget, there are things to be gained, greater than money. There will be the promotions, the media. The right media," she says. "You will make contacts. This is an opportunity, you can make of it what you want. A new career? To be a public figure? This is a door."

This is a door.

"It would be complicated, to leave Stowmoor. I would need some time, but maybe . . ."

"There is no maybe. This is your chance. You are in a position now, one that you could never be in again. I have found the diaries. We are in the same city, have found each other again. You know Foster, and he is in the papers, many stories about him, this possible cabal or whatever they called it . . . people will be interested in what you have to say. Do you not want the spotlight?"

"Maria. I just need some time to—"

The phone rings. She jumps up, looks at the number on the display. "Dani, so sorry, I must take this." She answers and speaks quickly in Hungarian. Then she sets the receiver down beside the phone.

"This call, it will take me a while." I'm about to tell her I don't mind, that I'll wait, when she reaches into the hall closet and hands me my jacket. "Danica. We can work together, accomplish much together." She opens the door. "I will call you soon."

Chapter Twenty-Two

She hung up her coat, kicked off her white and silver python-skin boots and set them next to the small table by the door. Then her daily ritual: she stood in her bedroom before the Countess's portrait and curtsied. It still leaned against the wall beside her closet, near the bed. It would be in her flat only a few more days; she would miss coming home to it, miss the Countess's face staring at her while she slept.

She put the boutique bag on her bed and pulled out the heavy box. Dark chocolate ribbon taut against glossy cream cardboard. The box gleamed against the flower print of the cotton duvet, lilacs and roses sun-faded into a worn, muted haze. Beside the bed, on her vanity, a wave of zirconium jewellery spilled from an antique box, the faux gems iridescent under the pink-shaded lamplight. A tennis bracelet coiled at the foot of a perfume bottle. La Douleur Exquise. Her hatbox sat at the edge, purple velvet with a spun-gold tassel, lush against the light pink wall.

In her closet were the dozens of past presents, outfits hung on thin wire hangers. Red taffeta cocktail dress, a slinky black strapless, slit to the upper thigh. Electric blue tunic, calf-length gold coat. Pairs of shoes stacked neatly on a three-tier rack. Two years of gifts, two years in this place. They had taken care of everything.

Now she looked at the portrait and unzipped her dress, let it fall to the floor and stepped out of the pool of material. She gripped the gold tassel of the hatbox, lifted the lid. Inside, a stack of DVDs, a couple of books. She flipped through the discs, settled on one, loaded it into the player. Hammer's Countess Dracula *started on the flat screen mounted on the wall across from the foot of the bed. The sepia footage showed a man riding a horse near the foot of a mountain, a castle turret looming at the top. She pointed the remote at the player, fast-forwarded to the part where a girl draws the Countess a bath. There was a fight, a slap; accidentally the first girl was cut. Her blood transformed the skin of the Countess. Movie music, 1970s horror-organ crescendos.*

She turned back to the cream-coloured box on the bed. Slowly, she pulled the end of the ribbon. One loop of the bow became smaller, smaller, until it closed tight around nothing. She felt the release of the knot, unravelled the ribbon from the box and dropped it on the floor, a pile of silky chocolate snakes. She gripped the sides of the creamy box and lifted, a slick swish as the top slid off. She riffled through a flurry of baby blue tissue paper, found a small box, velvety, hinged at the back. She popped it open. A necklace, a collar of heavy dull-silver rods hooked onto a thick serpentine chain.

On the screen, the girl was dead; the Countess daubed herself with an oversized, blood-soaked sea sponge. Fast-forward to the next girl, a gypsy who snuck into the Countess's chamber and laid out tarot cards that prophesized a new love for the Countess. The Countess fetched a heavy jewelled necklace, moved behind the fortune teller to dress her with this reward.

In the bedroom, she mimicked the screen and put on the necklace, the chain snagging the fine hairs at the nape of her neck. She breathed deeply, felt the chain tight against her throat, the semicircle of heavy metal splayed over her collarbones, the unfinished edges raking her décolleté.

She dug deeper in the blue tissue. There was a dress, steel grey, beaded around the neckline and shoulder straps, rows of heavy crystal fringe dripping down the garment. She unfurled it from the box, pressed it against herself, the crystals cold on her skin.

She lay on the bed, relished the weight of the dress draped over her body. Looked at the portrait and saw the Countess gazing upon her. Then she arched her neck to watch the screen and the chain caught more of her silky hairs. The film's Báthory grabbed the ice pick she had hidden in her masses of hair. The fortune teller looked down, stroked her new jewels. The Countess sank the pick into the girl's neck.

As she watched the screen, she embraced the sting of pulled hairs, the hard crystals against her skin. Imagined that the beads were tiny knives, her body punctured, bleeding, wetting the steel grey with warm red.

She thought the girl screamed unconvincingly. She was not impressed. If she had played the role, there would be no eyes scrunched unattractively tight, no blind flailing. She would have looked at the Countess, watched her jewelled wrists, the ringed hands that held the pick. She would have kept her eyes on the lady. Would have felt her breath, smelled her skin as the Countess leaned in. She would have known what she was screaming for, would have done it beautifully as her blood slipped from her and coated the blue-white skin of the Countess.

The screen faded to black. The next scene was filled with sunshine, the now-young Countess riding to meet her lover.

She sat up. The dress fell from her torso, settled heavily in her lap. She looked in the box again, fished out a deep red card with black cursive writing: Your work lately has been impeccable. We look forward to seeing you in this soon.

Chapter Twenty-Three

I'm staring at my computer screen, trying to focus on the new batch of paperwork I'm now responsible for. But I keep thinking about Maria, about her invitation to write an afterword for the diaries. And about leaving Stowmoor, creating my own success.

I'm tempted by her offer. I would be able to think, to write about Báthory and Foster for a wide audience. I could hypothesize any way I wanted to, without worrying about following academic form. And I would be working with, be partners with, Maria. My stomach flutters with excitement and worry at this prospect.

Besides the moral and possible legal problems of what Maria's proposing, I'm not sure what I would write about Foster. Is he fabricating his accomplices—this cult, as he calls it—just to promote his fame, create speculation, manipulate public interest? To gain a legal advantage? Or is he actually hiding his involvement in something larger? Either way, with things as they are at work right now, I don't know how I'll get much opportunity to find out.

I ordered a few books online after my last conversation with Foster. I pull them out of my bag. *Bad Men Do What Good Men*

Dream. Deadly Cults: The Crimes of True Believers. Masochism and the Self. I shove the paperwork aside and start researching.

Blood cult, cabal, network, whatever you want to call it, there isn't an official clinical term. But Foster fits the profile. He's young-ish, has some university education, had a decent job at a soft-ware company before his arrest. Had a flat, lived independently. He could almost be considered conventionally good-looking, if it weren't for his unfashionable "ginger" complexion. Cults and cabals primarily recruit from a demographic sometimes referred to as "sophisticates." Relatively educated, idealistic, under thirty-five. People who are a bit lost, maybe confused about life, unsat-isfied with themselves, searching for a universal truth, a way to connect their lives to a great purpose, an extreme action, an elite understanding that eludes the masses.

According to these criteria, Foster would have been a strong candidate to be recruited into a cult. On the other hand, this description sounds like a lot of the people I knew in graduate school. And just because someone has qualities, tendencies, it doesn't mean they'll act on them.

But the violence. The meticulous planning that went into his attack. Completely possible he did it all himself. But also possible he was coached, his tendencies encouraged, the details of the killing suggested by others.

There's not enough information to know for sure. I know Maria wants me to forget about the absolutes. She wants me to indulge in the "could haves" and construct intrigue and ambiguity around Foster. To take this opportunity to create success for the book, for ourselves. But if I do that, I will not only glamorize his crime, I will benefit from it. I will benefit from the murder of that fifteen-year-old girl.

I hear my email tinkle. It's from Abbas. *Subject: Assignment of New Duties.*

I've been expecting this for days. After careful consideration of the incident, which has called into question my adherence to Stowmoor confidentiality codes, it has been determined that it would be best for me and Stowmoor patients if I were removed from working with DSPD populations. This removal may or may not last the duration of my fellowship. Starting tomorrow, I will no longer conduct assessments of or have regular contact with patients housed in the Paddock.

I close the message. I look at the covers of my books. Regardless of whether I work with Maria, whether I write about Foster in her book or in a scholarly article or never again, I want to know. I want to know if, behind all Foster's innuendo, his attempts to unsettle me, there's anything more.

I finish writing the summary for the file I'm working on. I email it to Kelly and print out a copy to file here. Technically, a copy needs to go to the nurses' station in the Paddock, too. Kelly usually drops it off. But I print out a second copy, sling my soon-to-be-void ID around my neck and walk it over myself.

I make small talk at the Paddock nurses' station. They tolerate my chit-chat while they stock the meds cart, speed in and out. No one says anything about Foster. I leave the copy at the desk and walk down the hall. Make it look like I'm on my way somewhere, passing through to deliver more important documents, attend a scheduled appointment.

I turn down Foster's hallway. Logically, I know I probably won't learn anything of value through another encounter with him. I don't even want to think about the risk I'm taking, not only for my own emotional health, but for my professional life as well. But I keep walking. I feel like I'm walking towards some space in myself, no longer an itch somewhere deep inside, but a crusted, infected wound I can't leave alone to heal.

His sideroom is the fourth one on the left. He's probably not there, likely not back from lunch yet. I walk slowly, my steps as hushed as I can make them in this dim, grey concrete corridor. Brighter light glows from the small windows in the sideroom doors; fluorescent rectangles beam into the cold hallway.

I'm at his door. I stand on my tiptoes, peep in quickly. A flash of his empty bunk, a stack of magazines. I look down the hall, right, left. No one, nothing except the red dots of light on the cameras that hang from the ceiling at either end of the hall.

I rest my hand on the cardlock beside the door handle. I touch my ID on its string around my neck. One swipe and I could be in. Five minutes in his room, with his things. I could find something. If I open the door it will show at the security station: *Sideroom 4 Open*. But what if I'm quick? It might not be noticed at all.

I stand on my tiptoes again, peer through the window at his few possessions: bed, magazines, an extra pair of socks on the floor. A stack of books, some pages of loose-leaf crammed into them. I trace my finger around my ID card. Every rule, every protocol, forbids unauthorized entry into a patient's room. But I keep staring at his things. A swipe, a turn of the handle and I could have them. I fantasize about impressing Maria with the story of me examining Foster's belongings.

There are voices down the hall. I jump back from the door and drop my folder. The voices and footsteps get louder; Foster and an orderly round the corner and start walking down the hallway.

I bend down to pick up the folder. Pretend you're on an errand, I tell myself. I stand up, straighten my jacket and start walking briskly down the hall towards them.

Foster smiles. "Dr. Winston! Lovely to see you."

I nod and don't break my pace.

He stops in the middle of the hallway. "Were you coming to see me?"

"Just passing through."

"Pity you're in a rush," he says. The orderly prods him to keep moving. "Come back anytime!" he singsongs as I pass him.

Once I'm a few feet farther down the hall, I look back. He's standing outside his room while the orderly opens his door. He's watching me. Then he steps inside and the orderly shuts him in. The window shines with a pale light, the beam piercing Stowmoor's ubiquitous grey.

Chapter Twenty-Four

When I get back to my office, there's an email waiting from Maria.

Dani,

So glad we straightened things out on Saturday. Now we can go ahead, make our own way. Here is another section. Think of us, working on this together.

x, M.

I want to write her back at once, tell her about Foster's room, tell her that I almost broke Stowmoor's rules so I could find out Foster's secrets. I imagine her sitting in front of her computer, her blue doll eyes focused on a message from me, half jealous, half impressed at my temerity. But first I open the attachment and read what she's sent me.

Čachtice, July 15, 1608

Darvulia finished the talisman today. It is a small square, made mostly of calf hide, with special tokens sewn in. There is a patch of skin from the first girl we killed with the mannequin; there is a piece of hide from one of the

spring deer, folded over pressed poppy petals from outside the castle walls. Darvulia has marked it with special
symbols and emblems that will keep me safe from the
treachery of others. The King has returned none of my
letters, and Darvulia says she has heard he is in league
with the Palatine and the clergy against me. I cannot
believe they could stop me—what would they do, burst
into my chambers and arrest me? I am a Báthory.

Darvulia has folded the patchworked material into
a small square and then sewed it in place with golden
thread. Helena Jo has begun sewing tiny pockets in
the sleeves of my dresses and blouses so that I can keep
it on my person, discreetly, at all times. I will guard it
as if it were bejewelled with diamonds.

Čachtice, November 21, 1608
I have been too tired get up from bed for the last three
days, and the headaches have returned, despite the
elixirs Darvulia has given me to prevent them. Her
eyes are not what they used to be, and I wonder if she
is giving me the right doses. She insists she is, but my
pain grows worse.

Čachtice, April 16, 1609
The worst has passed, and I am able to sit up in bed,
take some broth and some wine. I have sent Dorca and
Helena Jo to make arrangements for a trip to Piešťany.
I would not go if Darvulia did not think it necessary. I
have heard that one reeks of rotten eggs for days after
bathing in that water. But it is a sure way for a cure,
says Darvulia, for my constitution, and perhaps even
her eyes.

Helena is to ready a group of girls for us. She has
seven of them here at the castle, and she is to make
them fast until we leave. I want them wan and well-
behaved for the journey.

Darvulia says taking the waters will restore us. But
I know that the games last night are what brought me
back to myself today. That girl was almost cherubic,
with her round, dimpled cheeks and her dark golden,
curled hair. Dorca and Helena stripped her naked and
presented her at my bedside. The girl was shivering,
from cold or shame. Darvulia handed me a candle, and
I motioned for the girl to come closer. I was inches from
her ivory-pink thighs. I nodded to Helena and Dorca,
who held the girl by the arms. She startled then and
strained against them, so she did not notice that I moved
the flame to her vulva, but she jumped and squealed as I
seared her pubic hair. My women held her firmly, and I
applied the candle again, until I had burned away all the
hair, and I could see her raw labia. The pretty thing had
not yet cried, which was refreshing. Instead, she made a
repeated, high-pitched squeal, thrashed her lovely curls
and tried to kick away. It is nice to have a fighter every
now and then instead of these small, delicate girls.

Darvulia walked behind the girl and clubbed her a
few times. She was more sedate after that, so I asked
Dorca to lean the lovely thing closer to me. Now the
girl was crying, with tears running all over her face,
dripping onto her shoulders. Her skin was the colour
of sunset on the first mountainside snow. I leaned into
the round apple of her shoulder and bit. Harmlessly
at first, soft bites as if she were angel cake, or a fresh
strawberry. She shook and cried and I bit harder—wal-

nut, turnip, mutton. I felt my molars grind together, and my mouth full of blood and muscle. I spat out the first piece and went back again, near the clavicle, and again, on the top curve of a breast. She bled freely now, and I lay back, my face covered with her blood.

Darvulia and the others finished the girl with a beating. I drifted off, and woke up feeling much restored.

Čachtice, April 20, 1609

Darvulia told me she lived with a noblewoman in the east who coveted her stepdaughter's smooth, fair skin. The woman became obsessive, raved about the beauty of the girl's skin, and stared in the mirror at her own wrinkled face for hours at a time. Finally, she accepted Darvulia's counsel. She arranged for a hunter to kill the girl in the woods, then bring back her heart and liver. Darvulia boiled the organs into a stew, and served them to the woman. She said the woman's complexion brightened considerably.

The recipe to retain one's looks is simple. Destroy and consume. I have been doing this in part, with the blood treatments. But Darvulia says we must increase the momentum, the energy behind these acts. I look forward to it.

Čachtice, April 25, 1609

That stupid Helena. We drove the carriage all the way up to the castle, only to find that she has starved most of the girls almost to death. Only one could even walk. We took that one with us. We had no choice but to leave the others—they were scrawny and looked like they would die within hours.

The journey to Piešťany took an entire day and most of the night. It took me two days to recover, and the smell here is revolting, but I do feel stronger. And I saw something I would like. She's blonde and pale. Tall, with blue eyes. She is a baron's daughter, from Braşov. Darvulia says we cannot take her, that the risk is too great. But I do not think there is a real danger. Girls die from the flu, a pox, all the time. I have invited her to come back with us next week. She accepted, of course. Who would not want the honour of living in my court?

Flesh as strawberries, blood kisses. The image of Báthory biting into a girl like she's mutton plays over and over in my head like a scene from a horror movie. Báthory's is the ultimate story of extremity, obscenity. Of the violence one can inflict if obsession and action go unfettered. She is rare, a weapon and a jewel.

I think of Maria transcribing then translating these words. The diaries are the antithesis of the sanitized, measured way I've been trained to understand disorders and offenders. I'm curious what sort of freedom I might experience if I surrender to their pull.

Chapter Twenty-Five

The next day at work, Kelly knocks on my door and hands me a thick envelope. "Just came by courier. I signed for it."

I look at the return address—it's from Maria. As soon as Kelly has gone, I rip it open. Inside is a four-page contract. Maria has left a sticky note on the front page:

> *Dani,*
>
> *Just some business. Sign on pg. 4. Then we will be partners! Call me if you have any questions. See you at the ball!*
>
> *x, M.*

Despite wanting to escape the constraints of Stowmoor, I'm unsure what to do. I don't really care about becoming certified, don't want to keep working in my field indefinitely. And as Maria says, when will I get another chance like this? If I'm being honest with myself, I've been hoping for something that would force me off this path I've been on. But what she's proposing, it's so uncertain.

I look over the contract. It has nothing to do with a publisher; rather, it's some sort of working agreement between the two of us. It mentions primary author assignation (her, of course, complete with solo dust-jacket photo), that she will receive complete and sole credit for the discovery of the diaries, that she will have final say regarding all parts of the manuscript. So much for breaking free of restrictive rules, I think. I've never worked on a publication like this before, though, so maybe this isn't so unusual.

My computer tings. I have a new email, another message from Foster's lawyer, marked urgent. I didn't reply to his last one. I'd hoped that whatever he wanted—whether it was to sue me for defamation of his client or to encourage me to speak about him more—he had just forgotten about it.

Turns out, he hasn't. He still wants to meet. This time, he writes, *I am interested in discussing the possibility of hiring you as a consultant on Mr. Foster's case.* Consultant? But I couldn't do paid work for Lewison, a defence lawyer, if I'm employed at Stowmoor; it would be a conflict of interest. I hear Maria's lecture from the weekend: *You make your own success.*

I leave the email unanswered and call Maria. I have questions about this document, but I also want to see what she thinks about the lawyer's email. She answers on the second ring.

"Dani! Did you receive the package?"

"Yes. There seem to be a lot of stipulations."

"This is how I work, Dani. I had an experience once, years ago, things went very sour with a collaborator. I find it is best to lay things out, very clearly, at the start."

"It looks like you have pretty much complete control of the project."

"Dani, it is only on paper, in case of the worst. With us, it will be more like we are partners."

"Right."

"Do not worry. I will take care of us. Did you get the tickets?"

"The tickets?"

"In the envelope. Look."

There's a small envelope at the bottom of the package, with *Danica and Henry* written on the front in Maria's elegant cursive. I shake out the contents onto my desk. Two gold-embossed rectangles of heavy ivory-coloured card stock fall on top of the contract. I pick one up. *Art and Design Institute Ball,* it reads, in what looks like hand-drawn calligraphy, *Grosvenor Hotel, June 21st, cocktails 8 p.m., drinks and dancing 9 p.m. onwards.* I know that tickets to the Art Institute Ball are highly coveted. I've heard Wilson gossip about it—*Oh, the year Tracey Emin did such-and-such the night of the Art Institute Ball*—it sounded like something whimsical, magical, that I would never have the chance to attend.

"These aren't real?" I say.

"They are very real," laughs Maria.

"Where did you get them? Why do I have them?"

"I told you, I will take care of us. I thought, maybe, a perk would be good for you."

I look around my very small, bare, grey office. At the three filing cabinets I shuffle papers among. At my view onto the bland, fluorescent-lit hallway. It feels like I'm underwater here, at the bottom of a cold, rocky lake, holed in my little cave to avoid lampreys like Sloane latching onto me. I imagine leaving this place to put on a long, slinky gown, pulling up to the Grosvenor Hotel in a limo. Walking into the white light of a sparkling ballroom.

"Seriously?" I ask Maria. "Don't important or famous people go to this sort of thing?"

"Danica, soon you will be one of those people. Now, there is just one thing we must discuss—"

There is a beeping on the line, and I see a light flashing on my phone. A call from reception. Dr. Sloane walks by my hallway window and glances in. I feel like she can tell I'm on a personal call.

"I will have to get back to you on that matter," I say, straightening up and grabbing a pen off my desk, trying to look very businesslike. Dr. Sloane keeps walking. "I have a call on the other line."

"Ah yes, you are calling from work. It is best that we leave things off here. I will be in touch. We will need to go shopping for a dress."

The line clicks and she is gone.

Henry's actually home when I turn the latch. "Hey," he shouts from the loveseat. He's slouched into one corner of it, staring at the TV, and he doesn't look at me as I hang up my coat and take off my shoes. I'm excited to show him the tickets in my purse. But first, I step into the bathroom to touch up my makeup and take out my ponytail. I make sure to clear any stray hairs from the sink and counter. "I have some news," I say, as I dab a bit of gloss on my lips.

"Yeah?" he calls out, not moving his gaze from the screen.

I pull the tickets out of my purse and sit beside him. "Look!" I say, holding up the tickets.

"Hmm?" He's still riveted to the quiz show.

"Seriously," I kiss his cheek, "look!" I thrust the tickets in front of his eyes. He's momentarily annoyed, but as he reads the gold calligraphy, his mouth drops open.

"Are these legit? Are they for us? Where did you get them?" The quiz show is forgotten.

I assure him they are genuine, and for us, and that we are really going to go. "They're from Maria," I say.

"Really? Wow! Why did she give them to you?"

"It's, well, it's kind of a business perk, I guess." I say it hoping we can gloss over the specifics of "business."

"What kind of business do you have with Maria?"

"We're working on a project together. A book."

"A book?" He raises his eyebrows. "What sort of book? Why did she ask you to work on it?" He sounds defensive, almost jealous.

"It's just an afterword," I say. "To some historical documents. About Báthory." He frowns. "It's just a little project. I'm writing a small section, you know, psychologist's take, that's all."

"Oh." He flips the tickets over in his hand. "Well, that sounds like a nice little project, sweet pea. As long as you think you can juggle that and your job. We gotta cover rent."

I pretend to look for something in the fridge. This afterword is the most exciting thing I've been asked to do for a while, and he thinks it's just a little thing, less important than the rent. I think about telling him that it's not a little thing, that I'm even getting paid for it, that I'm tired of Stowmoor. That Maria is showing more interest in me than he's been lately.

"Hey, you want to go out for supper tonight? Celebrate these tickets?" He leans against the counter. "Really, that's so nice of Maria to give them to us."

"Sure." I shut the fridge door. It's been a couple of weeks since we've been out somewhere, just the two of us. I feel guilty suddenly for assuming he cares more about the rent than my happiness. I haven't exactly been forthcoming about this project with Maria. Henry and I just need to talk. It's been too busy lately.

"Cool. I'll jump in the shower and then we can head out."

I hear the shower turn on. I put the tickets back in my purse and pull out Maria's contract from my bag. *It's a door.*

Some voice keeps repeating that, Maria's, or some part of my own brain maybe. I envision my life in ten years if I don't go through this door, if I don't do the book, don't take the chance to consult for Lewison. I'll probably still be uncertified, working assistant-level jobs in places older and drearier than Stowmoor, or I'll have to go through a demoralizing job search back in Canada, and in the meantime try to study for my licence exams, which could take years. Or working with some counselling firm, talking office workers through depression and anxiety problems, eight hours a day.

My phone chirps. A text from Maria: *D, shopping for the ball this Saturday? And coffee? There are details we must discuss.*

Chapter Twenty-Six

The last time I saw Maria before she turned up in London was over a year ago. Carl had taken me to Prague, and I came down to Budapest, as Maria suggested. We began our search for the diaries the afternoon I arrived, but our lack of progress at the archives was discouraging. Frustratingly, I realized I knew very little about how to do historical research. I felt useless, and worried that Maria might think me useless too.

"Dani, but that is ridiculous," she said when I told her my concerns. "It has been long days for you, at the conference, the train ride." We were at her flat; she had wheeled my suitcase into a tiny spare room. There was a twin bed covered with a white cotton quilt. "You must have a night of rest."

The next morning, bright summer light shone through the small bedroom window. Maria, dressed in a violet peignoir, came into the room carrying a vase of lilies. She set the flowers on the nightstand. "You are awake?"

"Barely."

"The morning light, it is nice in your hair." She lay down on the bed, her head inches from mine on the pillow. "You are feeling better than yesterday?"

"Yes, much." I propped myself up on my elbow.

"Dani, to find the diaries, it would be wonderful. But your visit, it is also wonderful. And in Budapest, there are many things I can show you." She smiled.

I was relieved she was still enthusiastic about my visit. My hair shone alongside hers in the sunlight, my golden red and her deep ruby.

Maria sat up and pulled a lily out of the vase. "These are from the Great Market hall." She reached towards me and ran the soft petals down my arm. "We can visit it later." Then she stood, put the lily back in the vase, and started to walk out of the room. "This morning, I must do some errands." She paused by the door. "But you have a map of the city? Meet me outside the Gellert spa at two. "

I waited for Maria outside of the Gellert. It was a searing mid-July day. The air was humid and touched with smog; the spires of the parliament buildings on the far side of the river were softened through the haze. I could hear voices and the sound of splashing water coming from the open-air part of the spa, fenced off from public view. It was ten past two.

"So sorry, Dani," Maria was saying, another ten minutes later, as she rushed up the steps to meet me. "You know it is difficult to be on time in this heat." Her hair was slicked into a coiled braid at the nape of her neck. She took off her big sunglasses and tucked them away in a pocket of her gold shoulder bag. "Here," she said, taking my hand and leading me inside the double doors, "we must join the queue."

We stepped through the double doors, walked down a short hallway and entered another set of doors. Inside was a grand hall, the floor checked with black and white tiles, each one about a foot square. The ceiling was high, cathedral-like.

Maria got us tickets and led me towards the change area.

"I told her we need only one change room," said Maria. She put her hand on the small of my back and gave me a gentle push forward.

The cubicle was large enough for both of us. I put my bag in the corner and changed quickly, facing the wall. Maria laughed.

My bathing suit, a navy tankini, safely on, I turned around. Maria was standing with her hands on her hips, in white bikini bottoms, topless.

"Ready?" she asked.

"They allow topless bathing here?"

"Ah, you are so silly. Of course, in the women's section. We must do the hot and cold pools first, before we go outside."

She opened the door, picked up her tote and called the attendant to put our bags in a locker. Maria took the wristband with the metal disc that indicated the locker number; she slipped it over her right hand, the silver a few shades paler than her skin. I followed her down the corridor between the rows of change rooms. She had no tan lines, but I noticed a smattering of freckles across her shoulder blades.

"The hot one first." Maria took my hand and led me into the first pool on the right. I walked down marble steps into warm, clear water. Maria reached the bottom step before me, released my hand, pushed off and glided across the small pool. The water was chest-level, and I kept taking heavy, water-slowed steps in Maria's direction. She was resting, her back against the wall, the tops of her breasts breaking the surface of the water with each small wave I pushed towards her.

"Come, look at the ceiling." She motioned me over. "You are such a slowpoke."

"Now look." She pointed out the small Roman-style pillars,

the domed opaque skylight that let in muted sunshine. There was a second pool, about the same size as the one we were in, a few feet away. The wide strip of tile between the two pools led into a darker room. Young women in string bikinis walked by and into the dark room; so did large older women, some wearing nothing but a small cream bib, wet and translucent, with light cotton underwear. My tankini suddenly felt like a turtleneck.

"The cold pool, it is busy," said Maria. "We can wait here for a while—you do not mind?" She ran her hand lightly down my upper arm. "You are disappointed still, about the archives?"

"I thought things would be more straightforward," I dipped my shoulders under the warm water. "What now? Is there anyplace else to search?"

"I will look in the boxes, when they come. It is possible something is there. We must be patient." She paused and scooped water into her hands, gently splashed her face.

"But what do you think our chances are? Can you imagine if we did find them? Her words! A record of a perfect psychopath."

"Dani, you and your perfect monsters. I wonder what you would do if you ever met one, outside of your little clinics, your institutions."

She stood up, splashed me again and started to swim to the steps. "I am warm enough," she said over her shoulder. "Are you coming?"

I followed her across the pool, up the steps. Turned to follow that lightly freckled back into the dark room.

We passed through the tiled arch. On the other side, the ceiling was low and beige. Narrow metal pipes wound around the room like skinny snakes. The cold pool was to the right.

It was smaller than the others, oval and deep. There were a couple of lights under the water, halfway to the bottom. The pool glowed, pond green. A rickety metal ladder hung over the side; its small silver steps looked distorted below the surface, smudged grey planks descending into the green.

"It's good for the skin, Dani," said Maria. "Tightens the pores." She turned around to descend the ladder and took a quick breath after her first step. "And good to get the blood going," she said, looking up at me as she sank into the emerald pool. "You must come in." She slowly walked backwards towards the far wall, away from the ladder. The water was up to her chin.

"I'll try," I said. I put one foot under the water; my flesh screamed, then went numb. Another foot. Then legs, thighs. I let myself fall off the ladder and plunge in. My skin prickled, almost burned, and then nothing. The cold anesthetized me. I watched my hands moving, paddling my body over to Maria, but I couldn't feel anything. "How long do we stay in here?"

"What, too much already?" Maria laughed. "Just a few minutes, Dani. It will be good for you, you will see."

"I can't feel my skin."

"That means it's working. Here, I'll keep you distracted." She swam around to face me. "I have made plans for us, for tonight."

I forgot about the cold for half a second. "What kind of plans?"

"We will go out. First, we will meet with my friends for some drinks. But later, there is an event, a tableau vivant. It is designed by a Dutch artist who loves Báthory—you have heard of her?"

"The one who legally changed her name to Báthory? Are you serious—she's in Budapest tonight?"

"It is serendipity. We must dress up," she said as she moved closer to me.

"What painting are they presenting?" I asked.

"So many questions. You should wear something white." She leaned her head close to my ear. "It will be so striking against your hair."

I nodded. Even through the chlorine of the water, she smelled like flowers. She pulled away and moved towards the ladder.

"Enough of the cold now." She looked back over her shoulder. I paddled over and climbed up the metal rungs after her.

Maria lived on the Pest side of the river, near the Erszébet Hid (or Elizabeth Bridge, but not *our* Elizabeth, she told me). The evening was warm, and I felt happily disoriented as I looked at the curling eddies of the river during the walk from Maria's flat across the long bridge towards Buda. Zöld Pardon, where we were meeting Maria's friends before the party, was just a couple of blocks beyond the bridge.

Maria led me up the dozen or so concrete steps to Zöld's front gates. A bald bouncer with large biceps stood in front of the entrance; Maria said something briefly in Hungarian and he stepped aside, sweeping his arm towards the open gate with a flourish. Maria dropped my hand, and I followed her through.

Zöld Pardon was largely what the name described: a green, open, outdoor space. There were three different dance areas, and each featured a different style of music. Tall scaffolds held up pink and blue spotlights that speckled the dancers below. In the middle of the field was a shallow wading pool and a bar in a wooden cabana. Wooden boardwalks ran from each of the dance floors to the bar.

From our spot just inside the entrance, Zöld looked enormous. The sounds from the dance areas mashed into a frenetic beat, and I stood still for a moment, trying to sort out a melody in my head, surveying tanned women walking the boardwalks in heels, young men with shirts unbuttoned to the navel hovering nearby in case the ladies needed assistance. Maria kept walking, merged with the crowd, her magenta-red hair blending into and out of the dark, spotlit night.

I weaved through the crowd to catch her, but was swept along in a crush of drunk young dancers making their way to the pop music floor. Someone grabbed my hand and I moved with them to the edge of the grassy space. I found myself standing among a group of strangers who were motioning me to dance with them. I smiled, laughed and shook my head at their entreaties, which I couldn't understand, and they left me near the cabana bar. I looked towards the floodlit structure and saw Maria, laughing with a bartender, picking up two bottles. I headed towards her.

"Dani, but you almost lost me! Here, for you." She handed me one of the cold green bottles, the glass sweating beads of condensation. She clinked her bottle against mine. "*Egészségedre*," she said, looking me in the eye.

I laughed. "Yes, Eggy-shaggy-rats," I said and drank the cold beer.

"Ah, there are my friends, Sándor and Tünde." She pointed to a tall man in a black dress shirt and a petite woman with long, dark blonde hair. We shall go with them to dance, yes?"

We danced for about an hour, but I wasn't disappointed when it started to rain and we left for the performance. Maria started walking away from the front gates of Zöld.

"Maria, I think you're going towards the back."

"It is shorter. This is the way."

Sándor flipped open his mobile, said a few words in
Hungarian, flipped it shut again. "You see," said Maria,
"Sándor will have a car waiting."

We picked our way through groups of partiers dancing in
the rain and made it to the back fence. Sándor and Tünde led
us to a corner gate guarded by another bouncer; Sándor said
a few words and slipped the man a couple thousand forints.
The bouncer opened the gate, and there was a driver waiting
for us in a silver car. Sándor got in the front, and the three of
us crawled in the back. I was in the middle, wedged between
Maria and Tünde.

"Now, to the show," said Maria. "Your first tableau vivant.
It will be exciting for you. It is really how the French called it,
a living painting."

Tünde grabbed my hand. "I have a part, you will see." She
grinned, her professionally whitened teeth gleaming in the
dark.

"Yes, we must get these two," Maria motioned to Tünde
and Sándor, "to the location on time. They are both performers tonight." Maria draped one arm behind me along the back
of the seat. "You and I," she said, looking at me, "we will first
go to the reception, for the spectators."

I followed Maria up the steps of a grey four-storey building.
We went through the double door, and a young woman greeted
us with "Jó estét" and handed Maria a handbill. She made a
gesture towards the twisting staircase behind her. Maria was
going to pull me past the girl, but I stopped and attempted a
"Jó estét" of my own. She smiled, lips cotton candy pink, and
handed me a pamphlet as well.

"Very good, Dani," said Maria as we climbed the stairs.

I looked at my handbill. It was in Hungarian; I could make out some names on what looked like a list of performers. At the top, in larger type, was a name that seemed familiar: István Csók.

The stairs led to a large, open room with hardwood floors and a rectangular burgundy rug in the middle. A crystal chandelier hung above, and the only other illumination in the room came from groups of taper candles arranged on the window ledges. There were several vases of pale pink roses, and the air was saturated with their sweet scent. Waiters circulated with trays of glasses filled with an amber liquid. My heels sank into the deep plush of the rug. A tray drifted near to us; Maria took two glasses and handed one to me. "It is Tokaji," she said. "Only from Hungary. The wine of kings and the king of wines. You will like it."

I stayed close to Maria all night. She seemed to know most of the fifty or so people there, and most of their conversations were in Hungarian. I attempted to introduce myself in Hungarian, stumbling through "*Dani, vagyok. Ès te?*" but then I'd fall silent and watch Maria as she talked. She laughed loudly, stroked people's forearms, looked seductively at the more handsome men. A few times we drifted off by ourselves, sipped our Tokaji by one of the candlelit windowsills.

After about an hour, a man stepped into the centre of the room. The crowd hushed and he spoke three or four sentences. Then everyone started moving towards the back corner of the room, where there was another staircase.

Maria leaned close and whispered. "It is time for the show, Dani." She stepped ahead of me and I followed. We funnelled into the line of people and headed up the stairs. To the side of each stair, a tealight burned. The tiny flames were the only source of light. I kept hold of Maria's hand.

The crowd filed around two sides of a rectangular space lit

by floodlights and filled with shaved ice. Four naked women were sprawled on the ice; two were completely supine, while the others were posed with arms outstretched in a way that suggested they were trying to crawl away. Three people dressed in black robes with hoods were holding a fifth naked woman. They were trying to drag her forward, and she was hunched over in resistance. On the far side of the ice pit, a number of men in dark fur coats and hats regarded the scene. An old woman, with a full peasant skirt and a kerchief, lunged towards the naked women and held a bucket of icy water that threatened to spill onto them. Her face was contorted into a joyful sneer.

A long, red, embroidered carpet unfurled from the head of the ice pit and led beyond the glow of the floodlights into darkness. On the carpet, a few feet from the edge of the pit, a woman sat in a throne. She was dressed in a long white dress and a purple velvet, fur-lined cape jacket. White gossamer sleeves emerged from the coat and were gathered at the wrist by ruby-studded cuffs. A square, lace-trimmed collar topped her dress and overlapped the collar of her jacket. She wore a headdress of garnets and pearls that held in place a tall, stiff-looking cap. Her posture was relaxed, her head tilted back and her arm draped over the side of the throne.

"You remember Csók's painting from Čachtice?" Maria had manoeuvred us into a spot right at the front of the crowd, parallel with the supine naked woman nearest the throne.

"Yes." I wasn't sure what else to say. The women lying on the ice stayed completely still. I was surprised at the realism of the recreation. "Do you know all of the performers?"

Maria put her arm around my bare shoulders. I held my breath for an instant, wondered if she would keep it there.

"Always a question. For now, watch. Later, we can talk."

Then I heard a deep, nasal hum, like a low note on a bassoon. The sound grew louder, and more notes layered on top of it. Soon, the low tones merged with other pitches, higher-toned instruments, and a slow, sombre music began. A loop of synthesized bass notes kicked in, along with a slow drumbeat. The figures in front of us began, very slowly, to move.

The women lying on the ice began to writhe; their motions were fluid, yet they performed at one-tenth the pace of regular movement. Then the women became still, and the black-robed men on the side of the ice began to mime clapping and laughter. Only one or two figures or groups moved at a time, so I could take in every movement of each of the figures in the scene. The three men holding the naked woman started to push against her stance of resistance. Her bare feet dug into the crushed ice, and her calves and thighs tensed against the men's pressure to drag her forward. All the figures were silent, and the music continued to play, getting faster and louder.

After a minute or two of this, I asked Maria, "How long does this last?"

"It depends on how they have designed the performance."

"So what does that mean?"

"Traditional tableau vivant, the actors do not move. But this is not strictly traditional."

"Does anything else happen? Or do they just do these little motions for the whole time?" Now the Báthory figure had begun to raise her arm from the side of the throne. Her mouth pulled back slowly into a wide grin.

"Danica." Maria dropped her arm from around me and looked annoyed. "Just watch." She turned away from me and focused her attention on the scene. Suddenly, I might as well have been a lump of rock next to her. I looked at the rest of the crowd. They were all transfixed by the performance.

The old woman with the bucket started to move. She rocked back and forth, swinging her bucket to and fro painfully slowly. It was difficult to mime the inertia of swinging a washbucket full of water; on her creeping upswing, I saw her upper arms wobble under the weight. She made one more sweep back, then made a rapid upswing. Water flew from the wooden bucket and doused the women lying on the ice. The old woman became still, and the women again began to writhe. The ice they rested in had begun to melt in the warm summer night, but still their skin, illuminated by the floodlights, was bright pink gooseflesh.

The women ceased to move and the group of men who held the lone standing woman inched her closer to the edge of the pit. Her feet scraped and slipped in the icy slush as they dragged her towards the throne. The Báthory figure began to lower her hand back over the armrest, but her face stayed frozen in a wide, smug grin. One man broke from the group, grabbed the woman's hair with one hand, pushed at the small of her back with the other and caused her to fall forward, still slowly, onto the slush. His hood fell back, and I could see it was Sándor, from Zöld. The woman arched her head back from the cold surface, and her hair fell away from her face and settled over her back. It was Tünde.

A moment later, the floodlights went dark and the music stopped. The crowd was silent for a couple of seconds, then someone to my right started clapping and the rest of the people joined in. The applause was thunderous, and as my eyes readjusted to the darkness, I saw some audience members clapping with a serious, pensive look on their faces, as if they had been greatly moved by what they had viewed. Others were smiling, one or two were pumping their fists in the air, and still others were making yelling, whooping noises. I could make out the figures moving away from the scene, disappearing into the corners of the set.

"There, Dani," said Maria. Her long crystal earrings glimmered. "Your questions are now answered?"

"How often do these things happen?" We had begun to drift with the crowd towards the door to the staircase.

"You must learn to *absorb* these events," she said. She walked ahead of me slightly. "The effect will be ruined if all you think of are questions."

"But I can't absorb anything if I don't know what I'm seeing." She sighed. "Did you like it?"

"They did a good job of creating, you know, an atmosphere." I tried to think of an insightful comment. "The audience was really into it." Maria ignored me. We jostled down the stairs with the crowd. The thick scent of the roses hit us as we re-entered the main room.

Now Maria turned to me. "That is all you have to say?"

Her annoyance was palpable. "It was . . ." I stammered. "What did you think?"

"They should have staged it in the winter. The girls' flesh barely turned red. It was not very impressive. The weather, it needs to be freezing, there should be real snow, the water should turn to ice on them."

Maria continued on for a few steps, then turned around.

"Dani, do not pretend that I shock you."

"Maria, that would be cruel."

"Cruel? Why did you come here and help search for the diaries? You are not as dedicated to these things as I am?"

"That's completely different."

"I have, I think, misjudged you." She walked towards me.

"You want a story. You want to watch, but you want, at the end, things to be pretend. You fear risk. And that, what is the point? That is useless."

"Useless? What are you talking about?"

She stood inches away from my face. "I do not know if you really understand." Her blue eyes, rimmed with black liner, scrutinized my face. "If, really, you are what I look for."

I was silent. She put one hand on my waist, the other on my cheek. My heart felt like I'd taken a shot of epinephrine. Her eyes hardly blinked.

"What?" She leaned close to my ear. "Still, you have nothing to say?" Her nails dug through my dress, into my waist. She gripped my chin with her other hand, then roughly pushed me away. "You don't know how lucky you were. What I could have shown you. Pathetic!" She started to walk away.

"Where are you going?" I ran after her.

"I am leaving. I am going with my friends." She walked out of the room. I kept following her.

"Maria! You're leaving me here? I don't even know where we are. How do I call for a taxi?"

"I cannot have your ridiculous things, your pathetic self, near me any longer. I will call my doorman. He will put your suitcase downstairs," she called over her shoulder. She caught up with a group of people filing out of the building, and started laughing and talking with them, piled into one of their cars and drove away.

Chapter Twenty-Seven

On Saturday, I meet Maria for shopping. "You will love this place, Dani." The storefront's two large display windows are filled with mannequins dressed in short, sparkly, black cocktail dresses, thick, metallic-gold, patent-leather belts and magenta bobbed wigs. There is a large security man dressed in black, arms folded, standing at the door. He nods at us as we walk in. The walls of the boutique are covered in black, silver and gold sequin-like discs, the lights are dimmed, and heavy electronica broadcasts from speakers suspended from the ceiling. It's like I've stepped into a club, except that instead of cocktail bars, racks of clothing line the perimeter of the irregularly shaped space. Maria heads for an alcove on the right of the store, and I follow.

She flicks through the clothes with precision; in ten minutes, she's got a fitting room started and three outfits to try on. I'm still trying to figure out whether the garment I'm holding, which has one fringed shoulder, is a dress or a shirt. I finally just hand it to one of the impeccably coiffed salesgirls and head into the fitting room, where the light is dimmer still.

As I change, I catch the looped fringe of the dress/shirt on one of the shiny discs that line the cubicle wall.

"Dani, your outfit, do you have it on?" I hear Maria call from outside my curtain.

"Uh, yeah, I'm almost ready," I reply, trying to unhook the loop from the disc. The back of my left shoulder is caught on the wall, and it's difficult to reach my right hand around to free it.

"You all right in there?" the salesgirl asks.

"Oh, yeah, fine, thanks." I wait until I hear her walk away. "Uh, Maria?"

"I am ready for my next one, and you have not seen the first," she answers.

"Yeah, I know. Can you come here?"

"What is it?" She's standing right outside my curtain. I pull the material aside a bit and try to step away from the wall. The fringe holds me back, and I clatter into the discs.

"What are you doing?" laughs Maria.

"I need some help," I say, motioning her into the cubicle. "I'm stuck."

"Yes, I see that you are. There," she says, as she leans in and unhooks me. "Much better. Now, come out—tell me what you think of this," she says, as she walks out of the dressing room, twirling a little. She's wearing a zebra-print spaghetti-strap cocktail dress, with a wide silver belt held together by three tightly fastened straps. The belt cinches her waist tight; she is a tiny hourglass.

"Too much?" she asks, piling her hair on top of her head and twisting to look at herself in the mirror over her shoulder. She lets her platinum waves fall and turns to face front, hands on hips.

I'm momentarily mute. It's not that she looks stunning. She does, but it's not only her physicality that impresses me. It's an indefinable element, the sum of her thoughts and her movements, the way she sweeps around me, the jingle of the silver hoop bracelets she's worn today. I'm tethered to her.

"Yes," she says, answering her own question before I recover from my reverie. "But only a little. I will try the next one." She takes a look at me in the fringed monstrosity. "I do not think that suits you, Dani," she says, before she disappears behind the curtain.

I look in the mirror. The "dress" I have on barely comes below my bum, and the material is so sheer across my tummy that you can plainly see my belly button. A tight, wide band runs around the bottom, and the material balloons from there, taut and translucent from front to back and very roomy from side to side. When I hold my arms out straight, it looks like I have bat wings. With fringe hanging down one side. I take it off and pull on my jeans and sweater.

"Now this, this is good," I hear Maria say. "It is not right for the ball, but perhaps I will buy it anyway?" I collect my jacket and purse and pop out. She's kept the silver belt, but put it over a tight, strapless black dress that hits just above the knee. It's an outfit you'd notice come into a room, I tell her.

"It is not always the outfit, Dani, it is whether the woman wears it properly. And this," she says, turning her shoulder to the mirror, tossing her hair, "I can."

"Is it for anything special?" I ask, once she's back in the change room.

"Oh, there is always someplace, something, and you will need a new outfit."

"Or do you mean someone?" I say teasingly. "Edward, perhaps?"

Maria sweeps aside the curtain and steps out with the outfit draped over her arm. A salesgirl hurries over, confirms with Maria that she should take it to the cash. "Dani, you do not choose your fashion for a man." She looks at me seriously, puts a hand on my shoulder. "You are not a doll. If you do, you will likely be both ill-dressed and pathetic."

"Yes, of course," I say, unsure exactly what has triggered this lecture. "I was just trying to be funny. You know. It's just that you and Edward are usually together, so I assumed you'd wear the outfit around him."

"Usually together? That is not so."

"Oh, I guess it just seems like it. And at the Tate, he mentioned to me that you two were getting serious."

"Oh, Dani," she sighs, "so adorable. But this is really what you think? I believe it is true, yes, that you know me better than that? I have other interests." She walks me out of the change area to the cashier. There is no cash register on the large, smooth desk where the girl is folding the dress and belt into a little parcel. Maria slides her credit card across the shiny surface.

"Yes, I know, your work and everything."

"See, it is as I said."

"But he seems very nice. And he's completely in love with you."

She signs the bill, collects the red-ribboned black bag and heads towards the door. "They always are, to begin." The security guard nods at us as we step out to the street. "But it changes, yes? If they think you love them back." She links her arm through mine and picks up our pace.

"Well, that's not true. You're too cynical," I say.

"Am I?" She pulls her arm back and begins to walk faster.

"I'm sorry. I didn't mean to offend—"

"What you say, I do not take offence. I think only you are wrong. Listen," she turns towards me, "you start to try to please, to need them to be pleased. Soon, you are won, and the game is over."

"What about being in love? You said you were married when

you were younger, right? So you must have been in love then, to go through with it." I know I'm pushing her.

She prickles. "To you, marriage equals love? You are more naïve than I thought," she says, sighing loudly. I'm taken aback by the dramatics, but now I feel bad that I've said something to make her react so strongly. I start to apologize again, but she beats me to it.

"Forgive me, Dani. It is nice, in a way, that you are still able to believe things like that. Perhaps I am only jealous of it."

I want to say something kind, to make up for upsetting her. "But Maria, maybe Edward doesn't think of you as a thing to be won."

"Yes, now he may not know he thinks like that. But if you are wealthy or powerful or very smart or very beautiful—especially if you are all of these things—you always are something someone will desire to possess. To win."

I am not sure what to say. Her comment about my naïveté aside, for the first time ever I feel I want to comfort Maria. Maybe she's more vulnerable than I think.

"But let us talk of something else," she says. "Maybe you are right, I am only too cynical. Your Henry, things are good there?"

"Sure. Henry is doing very well in his residency. He's always at his studio, and his work is going well." This, at least, is true.

"Yes, he has a very nice studio—you have been?"

"Yeah. It's a great space for him. And great for him to have Andreas close by, too—they seem to get on well." I'm babbling a bit now, and don't factor in the tension that seemed to erupt between Henry and Andreas after the review business. But it feels good to talk about something positive that's come out of our move here.

"Andreas? That man that had the show on the same night as Henry?" says Maria. "But he has moved—Henry has not told

you? When I went by a couple of weeks ago, a girl, I think her
name was Nicola, she had moved her things there."

Nicola. "Ah, no, he hadn't mentioned it."

"Yes, it was something to do with Andreas's next project,
he needed a bigger space or some such thing. But the switch
agrees with Henry. Nicola seemed very friendly."

"That's great," I say, looking down at the pavement.

An hour later, I'm standing in front of a well-lit three-sided
mirror, in a meadow green strapless party dress. Sweetheart
neckline, tight waist. The skirt is made of layers of tulle, falls
just above the knee and is covered with tiny pink satin roses.
The dress swishes and flutters when I do a twirl.

"Here, with the shoes." Maria motions to the saleslady, who
sets a pair of shiny lilac pumps in front of me. I slip them on.
"Perfect," says Maria. She moves behind me and scoops up
my hair in one hand. "Hair up, definitely. Then you will see
the back," she says, tracing the edge of the bodice against my
shoulder blades. "Look," she says, gesturing with her head. I
turn and see the reflection in the mirror and nod, as much as
her grip on my hair will allow.

"This colour, it is perfect for you. The green, with your
hair. You glow, a wood nymph."

"It suits your skin tone," says the saleslady.

"Very elegant," says Maria, letting my hair fall. "Yet still
youthful. Yes."

The dress is about the same price as my share of the rent,
but I'm swayed. I let the saleslady box it up and hand her my
credit card before I think too hard about it.

"You wear it very well," says Maria, as we exit the store. "I
cannot wait to see you at the ball."

"Me, too," I say, swinging the carrier bag as we walk down the street. I feel like skipping. I can't wait to put it on. And for Henry to see me in it.

"Now that is taken care of, I have some business we need to discuss," says Maria. "Shall we have a coffee?"

Ten minutes later we're ensconced in a booth at the back of a café. Maria hands me a large envelope. "This is the last entry now." She sips at a tiny cup of espresso, then sets it down.

"Thank you. Maria, I haven't decided about this project." I expect her to give me another lecture. I want her to convince me completely.

Instead, she says simply, "But you will. There is no question."

"There's something that's come up. Foster's lawyer, he's offered to hire me to consult on the case."

"Danica, you see? You are meant to work with him! Think of everything you will learn, everything you can put into the book. You can tell everyone his story. You, not those silly tabloids, will know about him, if he is part of a cult, how he became obsessed with Báthory." She doesn't seem surprised or excited by this news; she talks about it like it was inevitable.

"I suppose."

"You will see. There is something else, Danica, I must tell you. I have delayed speaking with you about this matter for some time."

Oh god. Something about Henry. Or another tabloid episode about me and Foster.

"It is necessary to tell you now—because we are to be partners, when you return the contract—and so that I will not surprise you."

"Surprise me?" I close my eyes, wait with dread.

"Yes, at work." She handles the little cup delicately, spins it around in her brick red fingernails. "I have done my best to involve you in this matter as little as possible. Not that it matters much, because you will not be there much longer. But I wanted to share this news with you."

"Okay," I say, "just tell me what's going on."

"This book, Dani, it is my vision, you know, to include material on Foster. The project will not have as much currency if it does not."

"Yes, or gain as much publicity," I say, leaning back from the table. "That's why I'm writing my section."

"Exactly. But you must understand, the diaries are my discovery." I feel a slight prick of jealousy. She continues, "I must be informed about all aspects of this book."

"Yes. I'll inform you."

"That is nice. But it is not what I meant, exactly. You are starting to see?"

"Not really. Explain it for me."

"I understand that you were not able to help me gain visitation to Foster, especially after you had the troubles with the tabloid."

The troubles she was mainly responsible for, I think, but I stay quiet.

"I have undertaken that task myself," she says. "I have an appointment to see him in two weeks."

"You're *seeing* him? How?" My throat feels dry.

"You are surprised that I am so resourceful?"

"How are you doing this? How did you get approved?" No doubt she's gone about this in a less than ethical manner, but immediately I'm resentful that she's been able to arrange it without my help, or even my knowledge. And now I'll almost certainly have to quit Stowmoor, very soon. If Sloane and Abbas hear about my association with Maria, with the book, that will be it. It will look like Maria and I have been working together, that I've been speaking to her about Foster from the start.

"Well, I knew a person, who introduced me to somebody; we had some common interests. His lawyer, he is a very reasonable man. He understands the value of Foster's fame. I am going to meet with Foster as a specialist in media privacy."

"First, how did you meet his lawyer? And Maria, you are not a specialist in media privacy." What *is* media privacy anyway? It doesn't sound like it would fit the agenda of Foster's lawyer. He seems like he'd bring in the whole reporting staff of the *Daily Press* to visit Foster if he could.

"Dani, I have many skills. You do not know everything about me." She hooks the polished nail of her index finger through her cup's tiny handle. "I only tell you now so you would not be confused if you saw my name on the visitors' roster."

She's serious. Perhaps I've overlooked the benefits of spending the next thirty-odd years in a routine clinical job. Better than being convicted of fraud. "Maria," I sputter, trying to find enough words, the right ones. All I manage is, "You are not a 'media privacy' specialist, if such a thing even exists. That's completely fraudulent. Totally illegal."

"Laws should be taken with a grain of salt. Mr. Lewison, he knows laws must be interpreted creatively."

"You're insane."

"Now, Dani, that is a rather politically incorrect thing to say to me, especially given your profession." She leans back, half-smiles, arches a finely plucked eyebrow. I catch myself almost weakening at her teasing.

"Well, then, why would you even tell me, if you have it all set up? Have you thought about how this could affect me?"

"How exactly? You are going to resign."

"I'm not sure about that, and I definitely wasn't going to resign before next week."

"You will resign. You were always going to resign. Next week, the week after, it does not matter. You will do it."

Her certainty annoys me. "Why do you need to see him, anyway? I'm handling his part of the book. Why can't you trust me with that?"

She looks exasperated. I feel it's a small victory.

"I had thought you might be excited," she says. "If I speak to him as well, we can compare notes, discuss things."

As if he would confide in her. She thinks speaking to him will be easy, that anyone will talk to her, that she's entitled to anything she wants.

"Maria, have you disclosed to Foster your reasons for seeing him? If not, you're asking me to be complicit in allowing you to deceive and manipulate a patient. That's against several institutional rules, not to mention the moral issues of—"

"I did not know you liked rules so much," says Maria. "You must know, I always find ways around such things."

"What could you get out of talking to him, anyway? You're not trained to interview forensic patients."

"I do not need to be trained. I am after what is genuine. After beauty."

"You're delusional." I say it out of frustration, and it's probably true. But somehow I'm still unwilling to believe it completely.

"Excuse me, are you finished with that?" A thirty-something guy points at the newspaper crumpled up on the far side of our table. Maria hands it to him. "Always lovely to have a paper when you're sitting on your own, having a nice cup of coffee."

He addresses this comment solely to Maria, and gestures in the direction of his table. She smiles, and he stands there, looking at her, until she says, "Yes, enjoy your afternoon." He looks back at her twice as he returns to his chair.

"What were you saying, Dani?"

"But you haven't considered at all how this will affect me. You don't think about ethics, you think you can get around laws if you don't like them."

"But, Dani, I do think about you. Maybe you should think, too. The rules tell you, do not pursue your intuition. You cannot tell me you do not want to know more about Foster's story, if there is a cult. Can you imagine if it were true? Sublime."

I pause for a moment. She is right, I do want to know. It is horrible, but I want to know everything there is to know about Foster, about his crime, his fixation with Báthory. And if a cult did exist . . . it would make the story deliciously bigger, perfect. It would be, as Maria said, sublime.

I'm silent. I wish I knew how to flout the rules. To know what it feels like to do exactly what you please. How can she be so absolute in her confidence, her entitlement?

As if she were reading my mind, she says, "Dani, all of the world works on connections. And I have them."

I want to give in to her. I want to let go of the edge and dive into her world view, where laws are mere suggestions and delusions of grandeur constitute a healthy self-confidence. She believes herself to be invincible, entirely in control. I recognize that these are extremely maladaptive, even dangerous, traits, but still I'm tempted. I wonder what it would be like to move through the world with that feeling, delusional or not, of power and beauty.

"Trust me, Dani. We can be great. You can be great."

I've been trained well. I can't completely ignore all the

warning signs, all the coincidences. Even though I want to believe in her, I can't discount that things aren't right. I leave her there, walk through the café door onto the street, my coat unbuttoned and billowing.

The flat is dark. I turn on the kitchen light, then throw the carrier bag onto the bed. I hurl a pillow at the bag, then a shoe, and another, then my old copy of the DSM that I keep on a shelf by the sofa. Maria has never really cared about me, has only been interested in me for whatever self-aggrandizing agenda she wants to push. Right now, this realization is as much as I can manage. I know there's more, that it goes deeper, but I don't want to look. I'm afraid of the magnitude of dis-illusionment that awaits me.

The glossy bag is now creased and dull, weighed down by a pile of my dreary belongings. I imagine the dress inside: a pile of soft green leaves, now crushed. I stop myself from hurling a cheap glass vase at the end table, and instead flop down on the bed and crumple into a heap on top of the bag. I don't cry, and I try not to think. I lie motionless and concentrate on the sensation of the corner of the DSM jabbing into my forearm, a heel grazing my tummy, the crumpled green meadow I'm resting upon.

The phone rings. I don't move, let it ring and ring, the sound bouncing off the walls of the small room. The caller leaves a message on the machine, her voice soaking into me: "Henry, it's Nicola. Thought I'd catch you at home before tonight. I'll be a half-hour later than I said. See you soon."

It's like someone scooped out my stomach with a melon baller. I crumple a little more, get a little smaller. Twenty min-utes later, I hear Henry turn his key in the latch. I pick myself up, tread into the bathroom and close the door.

Chapter Twenty-Eight

Later that night, I'm alone in the flat. Henry said the message was about a "program thing" that he had to go to this evening. I flip through terrible shows, watch California girls who go to beach parties, cry about boys, have standing invitations to VIP sections in Las Vegas bars. They all have varying shades of blonde hair. On weekdays, they go to fashion design class, meet with each other in perfect sidewalk cafés, fight over who started which rumour about whom.

I remember the envelope that Maria gave me. I hold it in my lap. I want to rip open the seal, lose myself in Báthory's tortures.

Maybe Maria's plan to see Foster isn't any worse than my badgering him in the library, spying on him in his room. I almost bribed him with the diaries. I tried to manipulate him, repeatedly acted in my own interests instead of considering his. It's not just that I don't have a calling as a clinician, it's that I've been abusing my position. And I'm supposed to be on his side, to help him, provide him with resources for his rehabilitation. Is Maria's plan any worse? Is his lawyer any worse? I tell myself I'm not in a position to judge.

The envelope burns my palms. I pop the flap.

For you, something you want to see. The conclusion. Your
afterword will be brilliant. Yours, x, M.

Čachtice, January 17, 1611
It has been too much. Too much to think of writing until
now.

Darvulia is dead. They arrested her in the raid and
put her in a cell with the rest of my servants. They
let them starve, and it was too much for her old body.
Most of them, they tell me nothing, but there is one
guard who will talk. He says they will force Dorca and
Fizcko to testify at a trial. Then Helena is to be next.
And then they will kill them all.

I know it is because of the money they owe me,
and because the Palatine actually listens to the clergy,
thinks anything they say is as important as Scripture.
They are all corrupt. They could not have cared about
that girl; her father was only a noble of the counties.
What would she have amounted to in life?

I am shut up here, in my tower, but the guards peep
in when they think I am sleeping. I am still the most
beautiful woman in Europe. And I will have that last
beautiful memory to keep with me here, until I am
released.

We shackled her in the cellar, arms above her head,
her feet cuffed and chained to a spike in the ground.
Darvulia had told Dorca to use the new knife she had
brought to cut off the girl's nipples. That pale, tall
torso was streaked with blood, and she was crying for
us to stop. Then I took the knife.

She passed out when I approached her. I understand; it must be overwhelming to be at once so afraid
of someone yet so in awe. Helena heated a poker and
jabbed her thighs to rouse her.

I was inches away from her face when she came to
her senses. Her soft hair was matted with blood, and
her pale, pale skin stained with splatter. Her blue eyes
opened wide and shone through the mess of her. If
only they could be made into jewels, if only they kept
their colour after the heart stopped beating. But they
would never be more beautiful than at that moment.
And I decided no one should see them again. I plunged
the knife first into her stomach, then into her neck,
where Darvulia showed me I could hit that great vein.
The warm salt-iron leapt up at me and coated my face.
I waited until the eyes shifted, when that slight dull
cloud claimed them—I cannot tire of that, the moment
when their tiny life expires.

I never heard the pounding at the door. When I
turned around, they already had Fizcko and Dorca.
They clamoured around the girl, undid her bonds, but
it was far too late. She was one of mine.

I collect the paper into a neat pile and put it back in the envelope. I drop the envelope in my bag and pace around the small
room. I know I should not reread them. I know I should think
more critically about Maria, her motives, the circumstances I
presently find myself in.

On my third lap across the flat I stop. I grab my laptop, take
the envelope from my bag and pore through the diaries again.

Chapter Twenty-Nine

"The taxi said he'd be here in ten," says Henry over his shoulder. He's lounging on the couch, arm over the upholstered back, left ankle resting on right knee, bottle of Old Hooky in his hand.

It's seven fifteen. The ball starts at eight. And no one arrives at a party right at the start. I don't even have my false lashes glued on yet. "Why did you call one already? There's still lots of time. Can you call them back and see if they can come a bit later?" I don't want to get this evening off to a bad start, but he didn't even check to see if I was close to ready.

"It's Saturday night, Dani. It's better to go early before they're swamped. If we'd gotten a ride with Wilson and Nicola," he says, getting up from the sofa, "we wouldn't even have to take a cab."

Wilson and Nicola. Henry told me yesterday that the two of them were also going. Wilson got tickets from some gallery owner who came down with the flu, and he was taking Nicola with him as "an educational field trip." I tried not to be annoyed that, rather than make this a more romantic outing, Henry wanted us to pile into the microscopic back seat of Wilson's car in our fancy clothes. But I was not going to scramble out of the back seat of a hatchback and flash my underwear to passersby

in front of the Grosvenor Hotel, in the most expensive and beautiful dress I'd ever worn in my life, on the way to my first black-
tie ball. So I'd insisted on the cab.

"Fine, I'll be ready," I say, smiling into the mirror to make
my voice sound cheery.

"Looks like you're almost finished anyway," he says, leaning against the open bathroom door.

"Hey!" I put down the sparkly hairpin in my hand and
push him out the door. "No peeking until I'm done." I wanted
to emerge, even if it had to be from the bathroom, beautiful
and polished, maybe see that *you're gorgeous* look from him
that I'd missed for a while.

"All right, Cinderella, just don't make us late for the ball."
I hear his bottle of ale, empty, clunk down on the kitchen
counter.

A few minutes later, I have lashes on, earrings in, sparkly
barrettes fastened in hair. I needed this ritual of getting ready,
this distraction. I've been treading water at work. I've ignored
three more of Foster's lawyer's calls. I haven't spoken to Maria
since she told me about her plan to see Foster. I even thought
about taking back the dress, the shoes, and not going to the
party, but Henry couldn't be talked out of it. And when I
opened the dress box and saw the beautiful green bodice of
the dress, the tiny rosebuds on the skirt, I wanted so badly to
wear it to the ball, despite the misgivings I had about how I
got the tickets. So I went through the week like an automaton
at work, ignoring everything but the photocopying and filing
my daily routine has been largely reduced to. While I filed, I
thought of the green tulle and of fluttery false eyelashes and of
dancing with Henry in a ballroom.

"I think the taxi's here. I'll go up and hold it—hurry!" says
Henry. I hear the door shut.

I put on my blue and gold brocade trench coat. It has princess sleeves and a rectangle of rhinestones for a belt buckle. I found it in a vintage store years ago, but it's too fancy for everyday. I slide into it, happy as the brocade falls over my skirt, as I cinch the rhinestone belt around my waist.

Even though the taxi's waiting, I pause to take one last look in the mirror. I've swept my eyelids with light gold and peacock shadow. Heavy doe-lashes. I imagine getting out of the cab at the hotel, Henry helping me slip off my coat when we enter the ballroom, tracing his fingers across the back of my soft green bodice. Chandeliers of azure crystal. He leads me slowly, deliberately, to the dance floor, my lilac heels clicking on marble, the band in white tuxedos playing ballads.

We walk through the tall iron gates of the Grosvenor. In the courtyard to the right there's a line of sports cars and bright film lights hoisted overhead. Photographers snap, flashy-heeled women and dark-suited men mill about, stride through the front doors of the building. I look up at the tall stone facade, see illuminated windows dressed with gossamer curtains dotting the building in an erratic constellation. I wonder who's inside, why they're staying here, what they're doing in London. The rooms that are dark, I wonder if they're occupied, where the guests are for the evening.

We're in the cloakroom and Henry's just handed the attendant his jacket. "Hey, Wilson," he shouts, waving his hand high above his head. He rushes into the ballroom.

"Here, miss, let me take that," the attendant says, as I unbelt my brocade trench. "Lovely dress." I thank him, then walk into the ballroom after Henry. I tell myself he's probably just excited to be here, to get into the room.

The ballroom is more opulent than I'd imagined. High ceilings, ornate mouldings curl around the walls. A massive chandelier commands the centre of the room, suspended above the hardwood floor. It's a tightly coiled spiral of crystal curtains illuminated in the centre by a soft, dusky light. Waiters circulate with impossibly ornate hors d'oeuvres on silver trays. The crowd is still thin, but the stream of arrivals steadily picks up and the atmosphere is growing more boisterous.

I catch up to Henry and Wilson. "Hey," I say, linking my arm around Henry's, "it's all just stunning, isn't it?"

"Ah, first time in a ballroom like this, is it?" says Wilson. "Well, you look gorgeous tonight—like this sort of thing is old hat to you."

"Thanks," I say, and glance at Henry. He's scanning the room and suddenly smiles. I look in the direction of his gaze. A young woman is walking towards us. She's tall, even minus the silver stiletto heels she's wearing. Her dress is steel-coloured and covered with layers of tiny, swinging crystals. It's sleeveless, with a plunging V-neck. The skirt is straight, with a broad U-shaped cutout in the front that rises to her toned upper thighs, inches below her crotch. Her legs are long, her hair below her shoulders and very dark, almost black.

"Nicola," says Wilson. "Found the ladies' room all right, then?"

"Yes," she says, drawing a long nail down his shoulder. "Henry, hello, darling." She leans forward and kisses him on both cheeks.

"Very good to see you," he says softly. "So, would you like a drink?"

"Wonderful," says Nicola. "Champagne would be brilliant."

"Right on it," says Wilson. "Dani, I'll grab you one too,

love." He and Henry head off to the bar. I'm left, unintro-
duced, with Nicola.

"Um, hi," I say. "I'm Danica. Henry's girlfriend."

"Oh, right," she says, sounding a little bored. She doesn't
extend her hand, so I keep mine at my side, but I attempt to
make some conversation.

"So, you're in the residency with Henry?"

"That's right."

"You have studios nearby each other, I think?"

"Yes, we do."

I wait a few beats and hope that she elaborates. Nothing.

"So, what sort of art do you do?" Henry's told me that he
always hates it when someone asks him this, but I'm desperate.

"Photographs, mostly."

"What's your main subject?"

"Whatever interests me. Currently, I'm interested in the
male form. I like to experiment with applying different sub-
stances to the body, then photographing in varying light."

I decide to be encouraged that she's spoken more than
three words in a row to me, so I follow up. "What sort of sub-
stances? Different kinds of materials or outfits or something
like that?"

"No outfits. Things like oil, or milk, or even things like
canned tuna or dog shit, right onto the nude male."

"Does the tuna even stay on the skin?" I ask.

"It doesn't matter if it stays *on*," she says, sounding exasperated, "it's about the *method,* the theoretical understanding
of committing and documenting a certain event."

"Right, I didn't mean to suggest . . ."

A waiter comes by. "Ladies?" He holds out his tray of
salmon canapés. I take one; Nicola waves the waiter away.

"Darling, you are here!" At the sound of Maria's voice I

turn around. She's wearing a Grecian-style gown, with Edward trailing behind her. "Wonderful!" She kisses me on the cheek. "Hello," she says to Nicola. "We met at Henry's studio."

Nicola nods at her and continues to look uninterested.

"Dani, you have been here long?" I haven't spoken to her since the day we went shopping.

"Not too long," I say. I'm grateful that she's joined Nicola and me. "Wilson and Henry are here too, at the bar."

"If you excuse me, I'm going to see how they're doing with that champagne," says Nicola. She turns and stalks across the floor. The back of her dress is also cut low, to the top of her hips. She's not wearing a bra.

"Pretty girl," says Maria. She takes a tiny sip of her drink. "That dress—it looks like Swarovski crystal."

"Yes, it's interesting," I say. I look down at my outfit, which seemed so chic before. Now the tulle and roses all seem child-like.

"Dani, you look sad, almost," says Maria. "What, you do not like your dress now?"

"No, no, it's fine. Anyway, you look great. Beautiful gown."

"Yes, it is. On loan, only." She twirls, strikes a pose that showcases a thigh-high slit. "But Dani, you are silly to worry about your dress. You are beautiful tonight. As always, but you shine especially tonight."

I smile and I feel like hugging her despite our disagreements. I try to forget about the crotch-cutout no-bra outfit on Nicola, and instead remember my manners and say hello to Edward.

"Good to see you again," he says, smile perfect and white against his lightly tanned face.

Another waiter comes by with flutes filled with champagne. Edward holds one out to me.

"Oh, I think Henry's actually getting me one," I say.

"Then he's too slow," he says with a grin and puts it in my hand.

"Come with me," says Maria to me, "there are some people we should meet."

For the next hour and a half, Maria and I whisk around the ballroom. We meet the latest Turner Prize winner, a food writer for the *Guardian* and the host of *The X Factor.* The actress who plays Baby in *Dirty Dancing* compliments me on my dress. Maria tells everyone we're collaborating on a book. Waiters buzz by with prosciutto-wrapped melon balls, brie and cranberry tartlets, and trays and trays of champagne and wine. By the end of my third glass, a Pinot Grigio Edward insisted I try, I am awash in all the warmth and glamour that I'd expected from this night. Except I haven't seen Henry since he went to get me a drink almost two hours ago. I look around the room and spot him over by the illuminated multicoloured bar, talking to Nicola. I excuse myself from my current conversation partners—Maria, a novelist named Tessa whom I've heard of but whose books I've never read, and a rich museum patron—to go and see if he might dance.

"Of course, darling," says Maria, walking with me a few steps out of the group. "But you are enjoying yourself, yes?"

"It's perfect, Maria. Thank you for the tickets."

She smiles and puts her hand on my arm. "You are most welcome. See, Dani, you shine tonight. We are a good pair."

It might be the wine or the light or how beautiful and earnest Maria looks, but I think she could be right. She's pinned a spray of tiny white flowers behind her ear; the petals twine with her shiny curls. Her diamond pendant glitters. She leans towards me, eyes wide and waiting for a reply.

"Yes," I finally say, "we are."

"I will catch up with you later," she says, her voice light and happy. "Go and dance with your Henry."

He doesn't notice me walking up, so I tap him on the arm to get his attention. "Oh, hi," he says, looking uncomfortable.

"Coming in! Here's fresh drinks," says Wilson, approaching with a cocktail in either hand. He gives a pink one to Nicola, who hasn't looked at me. "Oh, Dani," he says, "I would have got you one too—didn't know you were here."

"It's all right, I just came over. To see if I could finally steal Henry away for a dance?" I circle my arm around his and tilt my head to the dance floor.

"Uh, well, maybe later, Dani. Nicola and I were discussing . . . business."

"Business?" I can't keep the sharpness out of my voice.

Wilson hands the other glass he's holding to Henry and puts his hand on the small of my back. "I'd be happy to take a spin," he says, and leads me away from the two of them. "No need to get upset, Dani." He manoeuvres me to the middle of the ballroom and into a tight hold.

"Right, right."

"It's not like you guys are married or anything."

"What does that mean?" I lean away from him.

"It's just that monogamy isn't a priority for you guys at this time in your lives," he says, moving his hand back around my waist and pulling me in. "You're still young. There's so many choices out there."

"Choices?" My eyes sting.

"Exactly. I mean, you can't blame Henry, really. He's just doing what he needs to, personally, creatively. You've gotta relax, Dani," he says, twirling me around quickly and laughing.

"*Just doing what he needs to?*" I say, trying not to scream out the words. But the bowling-ball feeling I've had in the pit of my stomach tells me that I have a very good idea what he means. Wilson's words finally make it real, make it something I can't continue to ignore.

"Come, now, you have to know. Nicola is beautiful and well-connected. And Henry's clearly attracted to her, not that that's a news flash." Over his shoulder, I catch the light bouncing off Nicola's crystal dress, see her leaning close to whisper something to Henry. He's smiling, looking downwards, close to her chest.

"Don't worry, Dani," continues Wilson. "You'll figure out if you and Henry will keep up an open arrangement, or if you'll just finish with each other. Or whatever. Don't worry so much about defining things. You have lots of options." He slides his right hand below my waist and rests it low on my hip, and strokes my neck, lightly, with his left. "You look smashing tonight, Dani. So fresh, cute." He pushes his pelvis against mine and keeps his hand on my bare neck, pulling me towards him. I smell his Hugo Boss cologne, and my field of vision fills with his frosted-tipped hair and a gold hoop earring. I feel a little like I might vomit.

"Wilson—" I push away from him and leave the dance floor. I force myself not to run, instead manage to keep it at a brisk walk until I find the ladies'. Then I dash into a stall, lock the door and sit down on the closed lid. I gather my skirt between my legs and bend over my knees so that my tears drop straight down on the pretty mauve-tiled floor and don't run down my face and ruin my makeup.

The bathroom door swings open and two women click-clack in. I try to stop sniffling and remain as quiet as possible. The stall, or little room rather, that I'm in is fully enclosed, with a proper door, so hopefully they won't take notice of me crying. I hear the snap and pop of compacts and lipsticks being opened.

"Did you see that woman wearing that hideous rust-coloured dress? The one that looked like a hoop skirt?" says one.

"I tried not to. I can't believe anyone would go out in public like that."

"I know," says woman number one. I hear fabric rustling, imagine she's adjusting her acceptably stylish dress. "But," she continues, "looks like you've been pretty occupied all night."

"Perhaps," the other woman says coyly.

"I would have thought you'd be farther along with things by now. Are you dragging things out on purpose?"

"No," says the second woman, sounding exasperated. "It's only that Henry has some little girlfriend trailing around after him."

I stop breathing.

"What, is she here? I didn't notice her."

"You wouldn't. She's plain as. Wearing some goody-goody fifties green thing. With a sweetheart neckline."

"Ugh."

"And she's a ginger. Awful hairdo. She's been schlepping around the place all night."

I want to scream, to burst out of the stall and take her down. She's pretty skinny; I bet she's not that strong. But she's mean. She'd probably be a hair-puller. I close my eyes and will myself to keep very still.

"Doesn't sound like much of a problem, then," says Nicola's friend.

Nicola laughs. "No, not really. Now, if you'll excuse me, I don't want to keep the poor man waiting too long." They both giggle and swish out the door.

I stay frozen in my position, head between knees, staring down at the little puddle of tears on the tile. My mind is numb; it feels like I've had an injection of novocaine between the eyes. I can't move until I figure out what I'm going to do once I leave this bathroom stall. What I'm going to say to Henry when I go back out there.

The door swings open again, and I hear a group of women, laughing and talking loudly, pile into the room. One of them rattles my stall door, trying to open it. "Oh, sorry," she says, after a second try to push in the door, "someone in there?"

"Out in a minute," I manage to say, my voice strained and croaky.

I walk out of the bathroom in a daze and head down the hallway towards the ballroom, still not sure who I'm going to talk to, what I'm going to say. I pass by the cloakroom and pause. I consider getting my coat and leaving. Then I hear a woman giggle, and Henry's voice telling someone how beautiful she is. I open the door a crack.

Henry's kissing Nicola; he's pressed her up against the wall, and one of her legs is wrapped around his waist. He's pushing her dress up. I slam the door open. He turns and sees me.

"Where, why—you're not supposed to be here."

Not even an apology. Not even like he's doing anything wrong groping another woman in the cloakroom. Instead, it's my fault, because I'm not supposed to be here. Just like every time I was overreacting or in a bad mood. I take two steps forward.

"Fuck you," I say. "You wouldn't even be here at this ball if it weren't for me!" I grab a handful of coat hangers and wing them at him. I keep walking forward. "What the hell do you think you're doing? You fucking asshole." I throw some more hangers, then shove them both back against a rack of coats. I get my fingernails into Nicola's shoulder, scrape them down her arm. Henry steps in front of her and takes hold of both my wrists. Nicola touches her upper arm for a second. She looks straight at me, smirks and readjusts her underwear.

"Don't touch her." Henry shakes me. "You're being hysterical."

"I'm not even close to hysterical." I twist my wrists free and shove his shoulders again. I want to grab his thin hair and hit his head into the wall. He grabs me by the forearm and pushes me into the middle of the room.

"Calm down. You're making a scene."

There are a few people peeping through the open door of the cloakroom.

"This has been a long time coming," he says. "You can't say you're really surprised."

"A long time coming? We've been living together for what, three months? We haven't *had* a long time. I moved here—we were starting a life here together."

"That was your idea, Dani."

I am acutely aware of how ridiculous I must seem. A joke. Even Nicola's looking at me with an expression close to pity, or disdain. I start to back away from Henry.

"There you are, Dani!" Maria sweeps in, puts her arm around me. "I have been looking everywhere for you." She looks around the room and knows intuitively what's going on. Someone like Maria always knows what's going on, while someone like me bumbles along, believing that she and her boyfriend are going through a rough patch, when actually she's been a blind idiot.

"Come with me," she says, pulling me closer to her. She

keeps her arm around my waist, says good night to the spectators who have gathered and walks me out the door. We head
towards the ballroom.

"Maria, I can't go out there. I'm a mess."

"No, no, there is a spot, a little alcove, hardly anyone sits
there. We will talk."

I'm sitting on a plush, gold-trimmed chaise longue in an alcove
with a huge bay window. I hear the din of people talking and
having fun on the dance floor. This should have been a perfect
night. Instead, I've shoved and slapped two people in public
and now I'm hiding in an alcove, crying, mascara dripping.
In a designer dress. At the Art Institute Ball at the Grosvenor
Hotel in London.

"Dani, this is all beneath you," says Maria. She's perched
on the window seat. "That Henry, he was never good enough
for you."

"But I thought you liked him. You always went to his studio, Edward liked his work."

Maria hops off the window seat and sits beside me. "I was
only friendly to him because he was your boyfriend. I wanted
to get to know him so I could know more about your life. Be
in your life. It has always been about you." She wipes the last
undried trail of mascara off my face. "There, beautiful as ever."

"But that girl said—"

"That girl is of no importance."

"But you said she was nice, pretty. She's more than pretty.
And her dress was—"

"Too obvious. She is a pretty mannequin. That is all."

"What I am going to do?" I've driven my life into a brick
wall. I moved across the ocean to make risky career choices

and to be with my boyfriend, who has now dumped me in the most humiliating fashion possible at a posh ball. I am so stupid. So stupid. "I've ruined everything."

"Dani. But you are being ridiculous. Stop. Henry, he did you a favour. You could never be happy with him. Better now than another year from now. You do not have to waste any more time. This is an opportunity."

"For what?"

"For whatever you want to happen. Quit Stowmoor, do the afterword, the consulting. Go where you please. Now," she says, standing up and taking my hand, "you will not go back home to deal with that man tonight. Come to my place, text Henry to move his things out tomorrow. Tell him I will send Edward to move them out if he will not. You sign my contract, and resign from Stowmoor. Then you will be free."

The diamonds sparkle at her throat. Maybe she's right.

Chapter Thirty

A ray of early afternoon light jabs the room. I hear a rattle, a clunk. A curtain sweeps back; the room floods with brightness.

"Come, now," says Maria, walking towards me with a tray. Her footsteps are punctuated with a *clink-clink* of teapot against china plate. "A little food, yes?"

She sets the tray on the nightstand beside the bed. I peep out of the covers, eyes not yet adjusted to the afternoon sun. I see the tag of a tea bag, a bunch of purple grapes, a stack of arrowroot biscuits. I don't move; instead, I answer her with an unintelligible moan, a half growl, half whine. My head still pounds from last night's champagne and crying.

Maria pulls back the feather duvet. I blink, try to bury my head into the pillow. Tea pours from pot to cup.

"Drink," says Maria, holding the steaming tea in one hand, drawing me into a sitting position with the other. My body follows her lead; I sit up, take the cup. She hands me an arrowroot. I gnaw the edges between sips of tea.

"I checked your phone. Henry agreed, he is moving his things today." Maria sets the mobile on the tray. I nod absently, too numb to be annoyed at this invasion of privacy. "It will soon be done, Dani. You will see." She tries to finger-comb my hair, which is tangled, half matted from sleeping on my updo. I nod again and she hugs me.

A few hours later, I've managed to get dressed, in an old cotton jersey empire-waist sundress of Maria's. I'm sitting on her beige sofa with a vodka martini, extra olives. I haven't showered, but I've pulled the bobby pins out of my hair and piled them like a ceremonial heap of bones on the end table. A movie about a teenage American girl who has eight months to live flickers on Sky TV. She meets a boy, they fall in love and she still dies, but it's okay because his love was her miracle. My martini glass is dry. I go to the kitchen to see if Maria will make me another.

"No, not yet." She's deep in the pantry, whispering on the phone. "It is under control. No, all is fine. For her, this heartbreak is delicate." Pause. "She will. It will. Trust me. Let me talk to Sándor." Maria starts speaking at full volume, in Hungarian. I jump, and the martini glass clatters against the granite countertop.

Maria stops speaking. Instinctively, I fumble in a drawer, pretend I'm looking for something. She strides out of the pantry, hand cupped over the receiver.

"You are all right?" Her voice is tense, an elastic ready to snap.

"Yes, yes." The drawer is full of take-away pamphlets, a couple of cookbooks. "I'm looking for a shot glass. I need another." I shake the martini glass from side to side. "Something stronger." I play it half sad, half tipsy.

She smiles, reaches out and strokes my cheek. "I will help you. Only a moment." She speaks a few short, clipped syllables into the receiver, then snaps the mobile shut. "Let me," she says, unscrewing the cap of the bottle.

Twenty minutes later I'm sitting at the table, halfway through a large glass of vodka. Maria sits beside me, arm around my shoulders. The contract is on the table. She smiles at me, serenely.

"Let us finish with this business. Officially, let us become partners."

She hands me a pen. I take it, click the ballpoint in, out. I'm swaying from the drinks and Henry's betrayal; the scene last night makes me feel like my heart's been wolf-mauled, left for carrion. Somehow, this rip, the pain, gives me a clarity; there is no more balancing act, nothing to keep from falling apart. It has all already fallen.

I look at Maria. Her light hair pulled back, grey cashmere sweater, diamonds still sparkling in that divot between her collarbones. She is luminous. But for the first time, she can't court me. For the first time, I can acknowledge what I kept pressed down for so long, what I didn't want to believe. She loves only herself. She wants me for something.

"I can't sign it." I take another slurp of vodka, slam the tumbler down. I stand, take a step away from the table. Maria's face twitches out of her smile for a moment, twitches back in. She takes a few steps towards me, caresses my cheek.

"Dani, darling. You are upset. But this, we discussed. It is for you, for the best."

"No." I don't move, just stare at her.

"Dani, darling." She moves closer, faint smell of gardenias. She presses her silky cheek to mine, circles out, kisses me on the bridge of my nose. "You are so beautiful," she whispers into my ear. "Come." She takes my hand, tries to lead me back to the chair. "Trust me."

I shake her hand free of mine.

Her phone rings. She answers, her voice elastic-band tight again, speaks in clipped monosyllables: *yes, no, I will soon, I will look.* She checks her email while still barking into the phone. A minute later, she comes back to me.

"Dani, you must not be feeling well."

"Actually, I feel fine."

"That was Edward. I must go out. See yourself to bed. You will sign this later, when you've slept. And, you do have work tomorrow."

Tomorrow. Her visit with Foster.

"Later. Of course, Maria." I sit down.

Ten seconds after the door clicks shut, I'm searching. First I go through the reams of paper she's left on the table. Nothing but the contract and the diaries she's already shown me. I move to her desk, rifle through the side drawer. Blank letterhead from the Museum of London. A stack of her business cards, heavy stock, cream-coloured: *Maria János, Archivist,* her email, her mobile. I move to the centre drawer: bills, electric, phone. I sit down on the iron lattice-back chair, straighten the papers into a neat pile.

Then it drops from the sheaf of white bills. A deep red business card. In black, cursive font, it reads *The Beauty of Báthory.* The next line, a website: *bathorybeauty.net.* I flip the card over. Handwritten in black ink, an address on Old Street. And a word, looks Hungarian: *gyilkosság.*

It has to be a research group, I think. Please let it be a research group, a study group. I move over to the keyboard, type in the website.

A dark red screen appears, with the word *Beauty* in black

gothic font. I click on the word. A login window pops up. ID and password.

I rifle through Maria's papers again. It could be anything. I run through the obvious: *Báthory, Elizabeth, Hungary, Countess. Maria.* What for a password: *blood, beauty?* The word on the card?

I try a trick I learned when I first started at Stowmoor and couldn't keep straight all the IDs and passwords I needed. I switch on the autofill option on the computer. Then open up browser history. Go back to the last time Maria logged in, which looks like this afternoon. Then I try the ID box again.

I go through about thirty words, from *Budapest* to variations on Maria's name. Foster's comments about "the network" keep wiggling their way into my mind. I don't want to think this is connected. But if it is, if it is. I mustn't panic. I am a trained psychologist, I tell myself, so think. What would Maria pick? She wouldn't use something directly about herself. But she'd keep everything related.

I type in *t-h-r* . . . and the autofill punches out the rest: *throne1.*

The curser blinks, black, black, black. I type *s-t-o-w* . . .

The word *stowmoor* appears in the password box.

The login page dissolves and for a moment the screen is black. A picture of Báthory materializes in the middle and floats to the top right-hand corner. Then a graphic of the letter *B* surrounded with vines appears and floats to the top left-hand corner. A menu bar slides down. In red, cursive font, it lists only four options: *events, news, classifieds, links.* Then a white box pops up in the centre. A window to a chat room.

The window is blank, and I stay away from it. I turn to the menu, click on Events. A calendar for this week opens up. Sunday, a cryptic listing: *A, LDN, 9 p.m.*

A. What place in London begins with *A*?

I scan the table, try to think of any word, any place Maria ever mentioned that started with *A*. I pick up the red business card, anxiously tap it against the edge of the keyboard, think, think. The address. I flip the card over, type the Old Street address into Google.

Aquarium. The place she'd mentioned, where she met a client before having drinks with Henry. I look at my watch. It's five to nine.

There is a *ting*. Some text has appeared in the window, from username csok23: *M, you almost here? Hope this is you on your blackberry, not from home.*

I grab the mouse, search for a logout button, find one under the Báthory picture. The website clicks, goes black, then returns to the home page. I go back into the browser history and clear everything.

I gulp back the rest of my drink, go into the kitchen and put my hand on the blue cap of the vodka bottle, think of pouring another. Everything swims. Budapest, the tableau vivant. Dogs barking, a ruined castle strewn with poppies. Maria, plucking me out of receptions. Foster. Maria with her blonde-blonde hair on Henry's throne.

I take the red card and walk out the door.

I come out the wrong exit of the Old Street tube station and have to cross the street above ground, damp asphalt and air thick with exhaust. A hundred yards ahead, I see a massive brick building painted aqua. It's half a block long. I stop at the first entrance, a silver garage door, pulled closed and locked. A piece of paper, framed in glass, hangs on the turquoise brick. It's a list of days of the week and Aquarium's opening hours.

*Sunday: 10 p.m.–4 a.m. Music prescription: Dirty, minimal elec-
tronica.* My watch reads nine twenty-five.

I continue down the length of the building. It runs until the
end of the block, three more silver garage doors bolted shut.
Finally, some windows, with *Aquarium Pub* stencilled across
the top in white, frosted letters. I lean into the window, cup
my hands around my eyes to block out the glare of the street
lights. Black, nothing. Charcoal soundproofing foam and the
backs of speakers line the windows. I put an ear to the glass;
no sound, no rattle of booming bass.

I must have misunderstood the message or got the place
wrong. The yellow-orange street lamps shed enough light for
me to see my reflection in the dead-end windows. I'd tossed on
my coat and shoes from the night before and hadn't washed my
face or touched a comb or a toothbrush the whole day. My hair
is a hairspray-tangled mess of frizzed-out curls. The hem of my
blue and gold brocade coat doesn't match up in the front; I've
fastened the buttons wrong. Immediately, I undo the belt at my
waist and rebutton.

Again, I step closer to the glass. My face looks sallow, sagged
out. I wonder if the reflection is accurate, or if it's distorted by
the poor light. I notice a clump of black makeup under my right
eye. I scrape it off with my fingernail; it's flakey and sticky, a
remnant of my false eyelash glue. The skin under my eyes looks
shadowy and crinkled. When I took off from Maria's, I grabbed
my green rhinestone purse from last night. I dig around inside
and find a compact and some concealer. I just finish covering up
the bags under my eyes and have started to put on a bit of pink
lip gloss when I see a flash of black reflected in the compact.
Footsteps clicking down the footpath. A man's face in the mirror. Just a quick smear as he turns down the side street behind
me, but I feel a jolt of recognition. I'm sure I know him.

I shove gloss and compact into my purse and clip-clop to the edge of the Aquarium building, trying to be light on the pavement in my lavender heels. I watch as the man knocks on another garage-style door, around the side. The door rolls up. A muscled arm attached to a large sculpted shoulder leans on the door's interior handle, ushers the man inside.

I run towards the entrance. The silver door is rolling down, is halfway to the ground. I bang on the metal.

"Excuse me," I say. "Wait a minute." The door starts to slide up. My heart flutters like a hummingbird and I have no idea what I'm going to say to whoever is on the other side. Excuse me, I'm looking for a beautiful blonde woman, probably insane, who is obsessed with a Hungarian countess and ritual killings? Happen to know if she's meeting with some friends here tonight?

The door rises to reveal the man I saw in the street, tall, a gloved hand holding the bottom edge of the door. He stares at me.

"Milo?" I say, half to myself.

For a moment he looks confused. Looks at my shoes, my hair. Stares at my face a few seconds. Then his brows relax. "Oh, yes. You are Danica, right? Maria introduced us, in Toronto."

"Right." I say this in an *of course* tone, pray he believes I should be here.

"I didn't know you had officially joined us." He leans towards me, a kiss on each cheek.

I hope the peppermint scent of my lip gloss masks the smell of my unbrushed teeth. Even with the concealer and gloss, I must still look a wreck. "Oh, yes. Just running a bit late. Had to stop off for some cough drops. Fighting a cold, you know." I smile, look him straight in the eyes.

"Well, it's worth coming out for. A big night. My work is

on display." He stands squarely in the door, doesn't make a motion to invite me in.

"So Maria has been promising me. I wouldn't miss it for anything." I tuck a frizzy tendril behind my ears, put the other hand on my hip. My heart thrums. I shift my weight to my heels, try to stop my calves from shaking. Keep my eyes on his. Maintain eye contact with the subject. Smile, but not too much.

Milo steps to the side, puts his hand on the small of my back. "Well, we're late. Better get in there."

I step inside. A large, muscled man in a black T-shirt, the owner of the arm I saw earlier, sits on a stool by the door. He's wearing earbuds and is flipping through an iPod, but he stands up when he sees me. Milo gives him a nod and he sits back down.

We walk down a dark, narrow hallway. I smell chlorine. My heels click loudly on the concrete floor as I try to keep up with Milo. The hallway turns left, right, has only the occasional light to keep me from veering into the wall.

The hallway brings us to a large room. Silver stools line a deep red bar with a backlit array of liquor bottles: blues, reds, greens. Down a few steps, in the middle of the room, white chaise longues are clustered around a deep blue rectangular pool. Lights shine from the bottom of the pool; the pearly chaises are dappled with a sapphire glow that emanates from the water. I slow down, look for Maria. The place is empty except for a waiter wiping the long red bar.

"Pretty room, but we're down this way." Milo puts his arm around my shoulder and turns me towards a door to our left. "Wait a sec, Dani." He stops me, looks at my face. Reaches out and cups my chin.

"You've got a bit of . . ." He wipes his thumb across the edge of my lip, pulls his hand away.

Gloss, smeared outside my lip line. His thumb is shiny pink. I'm waiting for him to realize I'm a mess, I'm a fake. He just smiles.

"You girls have a lot to keep straight," he says, putting his arm around my shoulders and leading me through the next door. I follow him down another narrow, concrete-floored hallway. There's a second bouncer guarding a heavy metal door.

"Good evening," he says, getting up from a little stool and standing directly in front of the door. He's about six foot four.

"Evening," says Milo. Then a little more formally, "We're here for Báthory."

"Password?"

Milo looks at me, gives me a half smile and a nod. "Go on, first time."

My heart no longer thrums, it thuds, a racehorse pounding down a short-haul track. "Oh," I say, "I'm probably pronouncing this wrong, but . . ." I claw through my mind for every Hungarian pronunciation rule I learned back in Budapest, hope that indeed, the word is Hungarian. Or the password at all. "*Gyilkosság?*"

The tall man smiles and cracks open the door.

There are candles everywhere. Soft light on thick moss carpet. My heel catches on a loop as I walk into the room. I grab Milo's arm to keep from falling. A crowd is gathered, hushed, their backs to us. Everyone is staring at a large projector screen at the far end of the room.

A naked white thigh, two sets of bite marks. A piece of skin ripped out, blood streaked down the calf. The screen flips to another image: an asphalt path, yellow dividing line interrupted by a pool of dark liquid. Next photo: a girl, crumpled and supine on a tiled floor, bloody leg poking out of a navy school uniform skirt. Dark, matted hair covers her face. Her shirt collar is stained red, her head and shoulders cushioned in a puddle of blood. Her palms are branded with the letter *B*. The crowd murmurs approvingly.

I'm still hanging on to Milo's arm. He breathes in deeply, slides his arm around my waist, puts his hand on my hip. "This was just before my time, too, but it's legendary. Beautiful, don't you think?"

My skin crawls. I try not to shake. I'm sure he can feel the gooseflesh through my dress. It takes all my focus not to flinch away from him. How did they get photos of Foster's victim? Are these his admirers, the fans he talks about?

A voice broadcasts from a microphone at the front of the room. "This is, of course, very good work." Maria. "He is extremely dedicated."

The screen goes dark for a moment. Then, a triptych of photos on the screen. Three girls, each around fourteen. One carrying a hockey bag, walking out of a rink. Another busing dishes in a diner. The last in a library, reading a book.

"Our finalists," says Maria. "Photos courtesy of our dear Milo. Please cast your vote with our new solicitor by the end of the evening."

Vote. They are sending Foster the photos, suggesting another victim. I check my purse. No phone; Maria took it out, put it on the bedside table. No camera. I need evidence.

Milo leans toward me. I stiffen when I feel his breath on my ear. "Tough call. Took me three months to get those photos. I still haven't made up my mind."

I step away, pretend I'm trying to see the screen better. I grab my stomach, will myself to breathe.

I stand on my tiptoes, strain to see Maria. The crowd is clustered tight. Then her small white hand pops above the throng. She waves towards someone.

"A toast. To welcome our new friend. Come, you must come up here!" she says.

In front of me, to my right, someone begins to move towards the front. The crowd flutters, parts, weaves together again. But for a second, I see him. Heavy black glasses, a severe expression. I've seen him before, somewhere.

"Now," Maria continues, *"egészségedre!"* She raises her hand again, slim ringed fingers holding a champagne flute. The crowd echoes her, then applauds. The crowd shifts and I see him again. Bryan Lewison. Foster's lawyer.

"Would you like a drink, Dani?" Milo asks.

I'm straining to get another look at the man at the front. Maybe I'm wrong. I want to be wrong.

"Dani," Milo says again, his hand on my shoulder. "A drink?" He points to the side of the room. There's a full bar, granite top, stocked with a host of coloured bottles. On the wall, in the middle of the bottles, a picture of Báthory. Like the one at Čachtice.

"Champagne, wine?"

I'm still staring at the picture. Velvet bodice, turquoise cuffs at the wrists. "Is that the one?" I ask.

I hear him laugh. "You find it that mesmerizing? Some do, I guess."

"It's the original?"

"Smuggled out of the Čachtice museum in the nineties." He moves between me and the picture, puts a hand on my forearm. "Even with a cold, you're still very pretty," he says. "Champagne, then?" He heads to the bar.

The crowd starts to break up. I turn around, survey the people. I don't know what I expected to see: ragged clothing, knives, people stumbling around glassy-eyed, mumbling about blood, shouting insensibly about girls shackled, tortured, covered in ice? Everyone is dressed in heels, suits, sports coats. Drinks in hand, talking. Well-coiffed guests at a regular cocktail party.

I hear Maria's laugh. She's sitting on a cream divan across the room. Beside Nicola. The two are sipping on their flutes, laughing like old girlfriends. Part of me wants to confront them, smash their glasses, see Maria's shock that I've found my way into her secret, sick world. But the pictures of the girls still loom on the screen: I'm in a room full of Foster's accomplices.

Milo's still waiting at the bar. I have to find a way out, before he comes back, before Maria looks over. I start to make my way to the door.

"Dani?" Maria calls out, her voice a dart gun. My heart races and I keep moving.

"Dani!" She rushes beside me and grabs my elbow. "Let's step over here."

I wrench my arm free, almost elbow her in the gut. But then I notice that people are starting to stare. I let her lead me to the edge of the room. "What is this, Maria," I lean in close. "You're best friends with Nicola? And that's Foster's lawyer?"

She tightens her grip. "How did you get here?"

"You have Foster's lawyer. What are you doing with him?"

"Dani. How did you get in here?" Her nails dig into my arm. She's wearing a silver cuff studded with unpolished turquoise. The stones scrape my skin.

"You thought I wouldn't figure things out?" I dig in my purse with my free hand, pull out the red card. "Thought I wouldn't even think to search your place? Maybe you should have hidden this a bit better."

She eyes the card, takes a deep breath. "Well, what, exactly, do you think you have discovered?"

I squeeze the card tight and put it back in my purse. "He did have help. You're the cult. Foster's network."

"Dani, this is important. I was going to tell you everything, bring you into everything, when you were ready. When you understood."

"I understand. You told him to hurt that girl. You're going to get him to do it again, aren't you? If he gets out. When Lewison gets him out."

"Dani, these things you say. Unfounded accusations. We are an interest group."

"Where did you get those pictures? They're of Foster's crime scene, aren't they? What sort of *support* do you give?"

"Danica, as I said, I was going to tell you everything, when it was the time." She relaxes her shoulders, reaches out a hand and cradles my hip. Over her shoulder, I see Nicola still sitting there, watching us, long legs crossed, swinging her foot to and fro.

"And what's with Nicola? And Henry, is he here too?"

"Henry? No, no. Danica, you do not understand. You know, I have told you, I only look out for you. I did you a favour. Nicola, she works for me. For us. Henry, he was not for you. He strayed, so easy. I showed you, helped you."

"You asked her to be with him?" Of course she did. How could I be so stupid? She blinks, dark lashes framing her blue Siamese cat eyes. I used to think of her eyes as cornflowers, or pieces of summer sky. Now they look like cheap plastic marbles.

"There you are," Milo's voice calls out. He walks towards us, a champagne flute and a highball in hand. "So," he hands me the bubbly, "our newest member?" He raises an eyebrow towards Maria.

"Yes, yes. Actually, we have business to discuss." She takes my hand again, starts to curl her fingers into my hair. "Excuse us."

She pulls me away from Milo, away from the crowd and into a far corner of the room. "You should not be here, Dani. Not yet."

"Let go of me."

"Listen. Now you are here, we will work together. We must. Otherwise, it could be dangerous for you. You do not know—"

"I know enough. Let go."

She unwraps her fingers, moves her hand up to caress my hair again. I flinch.

"You must let me explain. Our philosophies. How we see beauty. You, too, you are fascinated with Báthory. You will understand."

"I'm fascinated in a different way. In an intellectual way. You're not well. You are—"

"I am what? We do what we believe in, we do not sit only, read in books. You sit, you watch, you think you know about the people in your little asylum. Play everything safe. Have you ever seen a murder? Do you know what it is, really, that you are so fascinated with?"

"I'm leaving."

"Danica, do you not see me? See who I am? Now you are here, you must stay. There is no leaving." She steps closer to me.

I put both of my hands on her shoulders and push. She grabs my hand, clenches it, pulls me towards her again. *Do you not see me.* I push again, harder, slip out of her hold and run to the door.

The bouncer is still on the other side. "Leaving already?" he asks, and stands in front of me.

"Ah, you caught her." Maria's followed me. "Very good. She was about to slip away and yet I have important things to discuss." She smiles at the bouncer, pushes a stray tendril behind her ear. "We will just step outside for a moment, yes? We need some privacy."

She pushes the small of my back, guides me out the door. We walk down the hallway and I think of running. But I don't know where; not back into the party, and the first bouncer is probably still at the front door. I need her to let me out, let me go.

We emerge from the hallway into the main section of the club. We walk past the silver stools, the red bar, descend the few steps to the poolside. No one is around; the bar is unattended.

"You must listen, Dani. You do not understand what I offer you."

"What? You're a murderer. You're trying to get Foster out. I want nothing from you."

"Dani. I will explain. Sit, please." She sits on one of the chaise longues, the sapphire light from the pool dancing over her. "I ask only for five minutes of your time."

I sit beside her. I realize every patient I've met in Stowmoor, even Foster, has been nothing compared to her. I know I shouldn't, but I want to hear what she has to tell me.

"Yes, there is a project to recover Foster. Normally, we wouldn't spend the time and resources for such a recovery. But for years, we had problems when it came time for the murders. No one did it properly, some failed completely, no one who was caught was worth saving."

I nod for her to go on. I try to pretend I'm speaking to just another patient. But this interview is anything but sanitized or controlled.

"With Foster, he is the perfect tool. He loves his fame, he is devoted to us. And what he wants is to serve us. Serve me. Báthory, she had her servants, Dorca, Fizcko. They never failed her, brought her girls, helped to kill. Foster is my servant. He is loyal, and we are loyal in return. Here," she raises her chin slightly towards the secret back room, "we research and curate the attack; he executes it. It is a beautiful system. We build on Báthory's work. I improve it."

"You improve it?" I try to understand the enormity of this statement. She thinks she's more capable, more powerful, than Báthory. "How are you going to get him out? It will take years to parole him."

"Dani, I do not wait. I will get him out. All these rules, these laws, these people who you run after at your little job, they are nothing. I told you, I always succeed. And look what I have done for you."

"What you've done for me?"

"For you, I have set everything up. The newspaper article, the consulting. I have freed you from the everyday world, from that unoriginal drone Henry."

She slides her hand up my thigh and kisses my neck. "After Budapest, I thought we were done. But when you came here, for Foster, I knew you were not pathetic. You would understand, like Darvulia understood Báthory. Now we can work together." She puts her lips close to my ear and whispers. "You can shine."

Maria is the extreme experience I thought I wanted, the event after which you're never the same. Part of me wants to melt into her touch, her desire. To ignore conscience, to reject rules, to move through the world, through people, as effortlessly and violently as Maria. With Maria.

My body vibrates. I grab her wrist and push her away from me.

The club's sound system revs up and loud electronica blares over the speakers. A disco ball by the bar starts to turn. A door slams and the bartender emerges, walks to his post.

"Ah, the main club, it is opening." Maria stands up, offers me her hand.

My entire body shakes. I take her hand. I have to ask one more question. "Maria, the diaries . . . are they real?"

She lunges, leans a leg between my thighs. "Danica. They are as real as I am."

Another staff person walks by and starts to set tealights on nearby tables. Maria steps back. "Now," she says, "I must return, the meeting will be ending. Are you coming?"

I drop her hand, steady myself on the back of a chaise. I shake my head.

"That is fine. You will change your mind." She leans close again and whispers, "But you should hope, Danica, by the time you realize what you want, that I still want you."

I feel a breeze as she strides past me. I close my eyes, keep my grasp tight on the back of the chaise until I'm certain she has gone.

I walk halfway home, then finally duck into the underground and take the tube the rest of the way to Shepherd's Bush. I dig for my keys, turn the latch, like an automaton. The place looks bigger, Henry's pile of stray art supplies gone from the corner, his shoes, jackets, no longer strewn everywhere. I sit on the couch for almost an hour, trying to think logically, trying to process every piece of the weekend. Trying to decide what to do now. I hear Sloane's reprimands in my head. Carl's lectures. What could I tell them? Come to that, what could I tell the police? I crashed a cocktail party, they were showing disturbing photos, and I saw Foster's lawyer there? That I suspect the people throwing the party were not very nice and one of them slept with my boyfriend? That they are a historical-interest group fascinated with a long-dead serial killer, or maybe they're really a support group for mentally ill convicts and I've been fraternizing extensively with their leader? The painting—that might be evidence of theft. And Maria, if she comes for her scheduled meeting with Foster tomorrow, that would be reasonable cause for concern.

I pull the red card out of my purse, type *gyilkosság* into an online Hungarian–English dictionary.

Gyilkosság is murder.

Chapter Thirty-One

I don't remember falling asleep, but I wake to find myself half-slumped on the couch. According to the clock it's seven a.m. I glance in the mirror. Dark circles, hair worse than yesterday. I've slept in Maria's sundress, but I don't waste time changing, just throw on flats and a cardigan over the dress. I phone Abbas and get his voicemail. Same with Sloane. I call again, leave what I hope is a non-hysterical-sounding message: "Dr. Abbas, this is Danica Winston. It is imperative we cancel Martin Foster's meeting with Maria János this morning. I will explain. Please cancel." I leave a similar message with Sloane, then call Kelly at reception. No answer. I run out the door to catch the tube.

I get in at quarter to nine. Kelly is at the desk.

"We need to cancel Martin Foster's appointment with his new consultant."

She looks at me like I'm a puppy with an injured paw. "There are some messages here for you," she says in a slow, soft voice. "From Henry. Something about forgetting a set of brushes at his old place? And there was another call from a friend of yours? You left your mobile at her flat. And she wanted to speak to you, see how you were holding up after the breakup."

"She wanted what?"

"She was very concerned," says Kelly. She leans towards me, says in a hushed tone, "Sounds like it was very messy. Terrible. In public, no less. Do you need to take a personal day?" She reaches over the reception desk and pats my hand. "You look a bit out of sorts."

"No, you don't understand. I need to talk to Abbas or Sloane. We need to cancel the visit today with Martin Foster." I'm speaking fast, my palms spread out on the desk.

"Danica, it must be terrible. Your friend told me all about it. I was a wreck when my boyfriend and I split last year, and he wasn't cheating on me in public with a supermodel. I can't imagine. I mentioned the whole situation already to Dr. Abbas, when he came in this morning. I am sure he'll understand if you need to take a day to yourself. Get some sleep," she says, gesturing towards my face. "Have a shower. You know, clean yourself up a bit."

I catch my reflection in the mirror behind Kelly's desk. I haven't combed my hair since Saturday. And since last night, I've gone from possibly passing as messy-chic to looking unhygienic. There are deep purple bags under my eyes. The cardigan I've pulled on is brown with pink-and-blue racing stripes across the shoulders. It clashes horribly with the cotton dress, which, since I slept in it, is even more bagged out than yesterday. I fidget in my white ballet flats.

"Look, I'm really all right," I say. "I'll take it easy today, though." I smile at her. More flies with honey. "Thanks so much for being so kind to me. You're right. I'm going to head back and speak with Dr. Abbas."

"Oh, I think that's a good idea," she says. "You don't want to push yourself, after such a terrible weekend." She pulls out a cherry-smelling gloss and smears some on her lips. "If you

ever want to talk, I can commiserate. When my boyfriend and
I split last year—"

"You know, that is so kind of you. I will definitely let you
know if I need to talk. I wonder," I continue, "if, for now, you
can cancel János's appointment?"

Her smile collapses. She snaps a drawer open, tosses the
gloss inside, slams it shut with a sigh. "You know I can't cancel
anything unless Abbas and Sloane say so. Besides, I thought
you weren't working with that patient anymore." She looks
at the computer, "Anyway, she's probably here already. The
appointment's at nine fifteen. Probably parking her vehicle in
the Paddock lot. What's the big deal, anyway?"

I knock on Abbas's door. "Yes?" he says, not looking up from
his desk.

"Dr. Abbas. Did you get my voicemail?"

"Danica. Yes. It was rather odd. What's this about Ms.
János?"

"We need to cancel the appointment." I'm standing in the
doorway, interns and nurses rushing in the hallway behind
me. "Can I come in?"

He finally looks up, motions for me to come in. I close the door
behind me, sit down before he invites me. I feel lightheaded and
nauseated. I blurt it all out. "She's a fake. Foster did have help. I
can almost prove it. She's part of the network Foster mentioned
in the police report. I know I'm not supposed to worry about
that, it's the police's job, but still, I know she is. So is his new
lawyer, Lewison. There is a whole network of people, it's like a
cult, a cabal, they have secret meetings. They must have coached
him on the crime. They want him to do it again."

"Danica." Abbas takes off his reading glasses. "First, you

have been taken off Mr. Foster's assessment team. He is no longer your patient. Also, these are some strong allegations—and,
in Lewison's case, against a member of the legal profession.
This sounds like something from the tabloids, and you know
first-hand how they distort things. Really, Lewison is well
within protocol. This woman is a sort of consultant he wants
on the case. Of course they are going to try to get him paroled.
It is their job."

"But I saw it. This woman, my friend—well, I thought she
was my friend . . ." If I could just get the appointment can-
celled, maybe I could fix everything. "Anyway, she knows
these people, she's involved. They're dangerous."

Dr. Abbas folds his hands together, places them on his desk
and leans towards me. "Kelly said you had a very bad weekend. That you and your partner have had a falling out. She
intimated it was quite an acrimonious split? A public row,
and you engaged in some violence towards him and another
woman?"

"I'm doing fine. I'm still a professional. We need to cancel
the appointment."

"Danica, I appreciate your concern for our patients. As I
said, these are serious allegations you are making. They must
be taken up with the police. And you know I can't cancel an
appointment based on some hearsay. It would be unprofessional."

I start to wonder if he's connected to the cult, too. "Well,
then I'll speak to the authorities."

"I think you should. If this information you have turns out
to be valid, they must know. You are obligated to tell them. I'll
have Kelly set up an appointment for a detective to come interview you this afternoon."

"But this is urgent."

"Which is why we will have you speak to someone today. We must go through the proper channels, Danica."

"Of course." My eyes well up.

"Take it easy today. Why don't you stay in your office and catch up on some filing until the detective comes this afternoon?"

I find a white lab coat in my office, put it over my mismatched outfit. There's a memo from Kelly stuck to my desk: *A police detective will see you in your office at 2 p.m.* The clock above my desk says ten past nine. I grab a stack of papers and head to the lobby.

"Just doing some photocopying, Kelly," I call out to her as I pass by the desk. "Taking it easy. Just catching up on some filing." I carry the paper high, tight to my chest.

"You can use the one back here."

"I need the one down a floor. It has some special features on the collation thingy." I keep walking, get around the corner and slip out into the stairwell. I gallop downstairs and out the back doors. Race across the lawn to the Paddock.

I pray Kelly hasn't already managed to spread the gossip of my public meltdown as far as the Paddock. I pass through the doors as one of the orderlies walks out. I smile, motion to my ID. I know he won't stop to check it; I don't ask to check his. I say a polite hi to the nurses on duty. They give me a quick hello back as they're loading up the meds cart for rounds. I wave to two special-help aides passing behind the station on their way to the patients' shower rooms. Like I'm supposed to be here, just passing through.

Twenty feet past the station, just around a bend in the hall-way, are the elevator doors. If she's parking in the lot below, Maria has to come up here.

A minute later, the elevator pings and the doors slide open. It's Maria, escorted by an orderly. She's wearing tailored black dress pants, a baby blue bell-sleeved jacket.

"I'm Dr. Winston," I tell the orderly. "I'm supposed to escort Ms. János as well."

"Oh. I'm Nick. I thought I was to bring 'er up to Bill."

"Yes, I know," I say, straightening the staff badge around my neck. "It's just that some new information, things Mr. Foster's solicitor should know about, came through today. I'll debrief Ms. János before she meets with her client."

Maria looks half annoyed, half amused. "Nick, it is fine," she says. She smiles and tilts her head. "We are almost there, yes?"

"Yep," Nick says, "Bill's just on the other side of that door there." He points. The door's about fifteen feet away from us.

"Oh, it is so close. Then I will go with the doctor, here. Thank you so much for escorting me this far."

"My pleasure, Ms. János," Nick gives her a smile and a little salute before he walks away.

"The orderlies, they are so handsome here, Dani. You did not mention it." Maria begins walking towards the door.

I block her path. "Leave. If you leave now, I won't give your name to the police."

She laughs. "Danica. You will not talk to the police. Take me to Foster and everything will be fine."

"No, Maria. I'm speaking to the police this afternoon. Leave now. Don't make it worse."

"Dani," she reaches a black-gloved hand into her large leather portfolio. "I care for you. I wanted what was best for

you. You were good enough, I did think, to be a part of us."
She walks towards me, pulls her hand out of the bag. "I did
not want to hurt you. I always wanted you." Her arm is under
my lab coat; I feel something sharp press against my abdomen.
"That feeling," murmurs Maria, "it is a blade against you. One
push, I stab you. I know where to cut a girl so that she bleeds."

I'm silent. My stomach churns like a cauldron. It's probably
not a knife. Probably not.

"You got a knife through security? Through the metal
detector?"

"Ah, security." She raises her eyebrows high, opens her
bright blue eyes wide. "Yes, it has been such a strong point
over the years here, yes?" She smiles and pushes the object
against me, harder. It feels strong, sharp.

"Zirconium oxide blade," says Maria. "The metal detector,
not a problem. Walk."

Maria knocks on the door and Bill lets us in. "This must be
the visitor for Martin Foster," he says, all polite formalities.
"You escorting her in, Dr. Winston? Thought an orderly was
bringing her up. Didn't think you were seeing this patient any
more."

I nod. "The orderly did escort Ms. János here, but Dr.
Sloane and Dr. Abbas decided they wanted an observer from
Stowmoor staff. Everyone was busy on short notice except
me."

"Oh?" says Bill.

I feel pressure against my lower back. "Some new information has come up. I'm to debrief her." I smile, look him in the
eye.

"Hmm. Okay." He pauses, about to say something, then
closes his mouth. "If those are the orders . . ." He leads us
down the hallway to the interview room.

Maria walks slightly behind me, still holding the blade to my abdomen and pushing me ahead of her. She's hiding the knife from Bill in her bell sleeve. I imagine the blade biting through the fibres of my sweater and dress, finding my skin.

"Just a moment, ma'am," Bill says to Maria as we arrive at the door. "I'm sure they told you downstairs, but I'm going to have to keep your briefcase outside here while you consult with Mr. Foster. Just take in your notebook, pens, what have you."

"Are you quite sure?" Maria doesn't look at him.

"I will have to insist." Bill sounds annoyed, maybe even suspicious.

I look at him again, try to mouth "weapon" behind Maria's back.

She hands him the case with her free hand. He takes it, but sees her arm around me.

"Ma'am," he begins to drop the case and pull out his night-stick. "Could you step away from—"

She's fast. A blur, I don't even see her arm move. But the pressure of the blade against my torso lifts and the knife is in his neck, to the hilt. She rips it sideways, then pulls it out. Blood runs out from Bill's neck like a tipped glass of water. He tries to speak, to scream, but he can't get his breath, can't push out a sound. A froth of saliva and blood seeps over his lips. He falls.

Do something, I think. Now is the time to do something. But I stand there, staring at Bill. I've never seen a stabbing before. There's movies, of course, TV. I watch the news, see footage of bodies on gurneys. In anatomy class, there were cadavers, washed, preserved, splayed on stainless steel. But when I see Bill fall down, blood spilling out, litres of it—one moment he's talking, breathing, the next his neck ripped open—I know until now I've seen nothing.

In a few seconds, first aid training kicks in. I take off my coat, ball it up and try to press it against Bill's neck. Maria's arm slides around my neck. She presses the blade, warm and wet, against my neck.

"There's nothing you can do. Take the keys. Get up." She increases the pressure against my skin. "Quiet. Be quiet."

The lab coat is scarlet. I'm breathing hard, I'm crying.

"Now, Danica."

I unhook the keys from Bill's belt and open the door. At the end of the hallway, I see a surveillance camera. Is anyone watching?

Foster jumps up from the table. "You came. Are we leaving?"

"Darling, of course. We're going now."

"What's happening with her?" He points to me. "I always enjoyed your visits, Dr. Winston. You're very pretty."

I start to bargain. "You don't need to kill me. Just walk out. Walk out. You don't need to hurt anyone else."

"We haven't decided yet, darling," Maria says to Foster.

Foster walks over to me. He looks at the knife Maria has to my neck, wipes his index finger along the blade. He pulls it away, red with Bill's blood.

"Whose is this?"

"Darling, I had to remove the guard out there. We must hurry."

"Just an old man's blood. No good." He steps close to my face. Drags his bloody finger along my cheek.

Maria pushes me down the few feet of hallway to the elevator. "Not a sound, Danica." How long since she stabbed Bill? Almost a minute? The cameras must have picked up something.

I glance back, think of Bill slumped there. Maybe he's still alive, maybe the lab coat has stopped the bleeding. The nurses' station is just down the hall, just around the corner. Maria's moved the blade down, holds it against my abdomen again. I look in the direction of the station. No one comes around the corner. The line of blood Foster smeared on my cheek has dried and begins to itch. The elevator pings, doors open. Foster steps through first.

"In, Danica." I take a quick step forward, move sideways, try to move back from the blade. I scream.

I've let out maybe half a second of sound when Maria shoves me from behind into the metal wall of the elevator, hard. She's small, but holds me easily against the brushed steel, grabs my hair and bangs my head against the wall. The doors close behind us and the car moves down.

"That was not a good thing to do, Dr. Winston," says Foster. "Should we kill her now?" he asks Maria.

"Danica, why do you make things difficult for me? Always, my only wish is to help you. For us to work together. " Her lips graze my earlobe.

I hear the doors open. Musty, exhaust-tinged air. Maria twists my hand behind my back, returns the blade to my neck. She turns me around. "Out." Then to Foster, "To the right. Twenty feet, the garage door. Go."

He runs out of the elevator. Maria tells me to follow him. I count seconds in my head, calculate. If the nurses heard me, how long until they make it down the hall, until they find Bill? I walk, slowly.

"Faster, Danica."

"You'll never make it out." I tell her. A siren starts to ring through the car park. The alarm. Someone pulled the alarm. "Hear that? They're coming."

"Who is coming? Is this not the alarm they test every Monday?"

We're steps away from the garage door. It's closed, Foster waits beside it.

"They'll figure it out," I say. "The cameras." The alarm half-drowns out my words. We're at the door. It starts to roll up, stops halfway. I see car tires outside.

"Go," says Maria. "Outside."

Foster ducks down, bounds out. Maria kicks the backs of my knees and I fall on the concrete. She presses the knife against my shoulder, hard, a hot saw digging through the acrylic knit of the cardigan. The alarm must be real. Security, the police, someone must be coming. It can't just be the test.

I crawl under the door. I run into a pair of legs, a man's black shoes. I look up. A handgun, pointed at me. "I've got her, Maria," says a polite English voice.

Edward.

Foster is standing next to the door of a white van, the type they use for laundry. Its engine is idling. "You're really here," he keeps saying. "I'm really getting out." Maria scoots under the garage door, stands beside Edward.

"What do you want to do with her?" says Edward. "We've got to leave, fast."

"Just a moment." She strokes Edward's arm, the one that's pointing the gun towards me.

He lowers the gun. "Only a second, Maria. I'll get Foster in the van." He walks over to Foster, puts his arm around his shoulders. "They treat you all right in there?" Foster smiles.

"It wasn't too bad. But I'm very ready to get back to the world." He laughs.

"Then let's go." Edward opens the back seat door and Foster

gets in. He watches me through a small window at the back of the van.

"Danica." Maria kneels down to me. "This is our last chance. Will you come with me?"

"Come with you? Maria, you just killed a man. You're breaking out a patient. You were probably there when Foster killed that girl."

"Danica, you know that together we can do good work." She has her hands in my hair, pulling my face close to hers. She kisses me on the cheek, her lips warm.

Her gardenia perfume is cloying. "Good work? Like murder? You're insane."

"You still do not understand? You read the diaries. It is not about murder. Murder is an incidental."

"An incidental?"

"Yes. It serves something bigger. Our ideas, our aesthetics. You say you love Báthory and still you understand nothing?" She stands up. For the first time, I see her emotional, upset. She looks like she might cry. Then, in an instant, she becomes calm, stony-faced. "You do not see."

See?

"Maria, in the van, now. Is she coming?" Edward waves the gun at me.

She really believes she is indestructible.

"Edward, she is not. She is nothing."

"I'll take care of it." He kisses her on the forehead. "Get in with Martin." She walks away, gets in the front seat.

"I'm quite sorry you had to be wrapped up in all of this, Dani," says Edward. "I always told her I didn't think you had it in you."

Foster opens a side window and sticks his head out. "Ooh, a show."

Edward raises the gun. I close my eyes, hear Foster giggling. I'm crying, almost hyperventilating.

A bang. I wait for pain, for a feeling of my blood spilling. I just feel my lungs rasping hard, in, out. I open my eyes.

Edward is on the ground. Foster sees his crumpled body, jumps out of the van. He gets down and embraces him, his arms, his head nestled near Edward's wound. Another shot. Foster screams in anger. He's got Maria's knife in his hand.

More shots from somewhere. Maria hits the gas. Stray bullets ricochet off the bumper, but the van doesn't stop. Foster starts to scream. "Don't leave!" Then, to me, "You ruined everything." He picks up the knife and lunges.

I try to get up, to run backwards. I am trying. I see a blood-splattered fist raised above me, a thickly freckled arm. I hear the *clonk* of my head hitting concrete. The alarm is still ringing; what if this is a test, this is only a test. I feel something rip down my arm.

Epilogue

I was in the hospital for ten days. Edward was dead. So was Bill. Foster was back in custody.

Maria was gone.

I saw the headlines on Sky News. Watched the small, bolted-to-the-wall TV in my hospital room. "More on the story unfolding from Stowmoor," said the news anchor. "The security guard critically injured in an escape attempt yesterday morning from the renowned psychiatric hospital has succumbed to his injuries." The newswoman pressed her lips together, looked grave for a moment. "It is believed that members of an alleged cult organized the attempted escape of Martin Foster, who was convicted last year of the brutal slaying of fifteen-year-old Moira Price. Stowmoor security fatally shot one member of the group. A source has told Sky News that a second member remains at large."

"You've got that thing on all the time! You've watched enough now," said Julie, the nurse who worked nights. She eased the remote out of my hand and shut off the TV. Every report mentioned the "alleged cult" or "the alleged suspect." Alleged allowed for a better story. I wondered how Sloane and Abbas were handling Foster's assessment now.

The police interviewed me repeatedly.

"You say this woman's name is Maria, and she was working on contract at the Museum of London?" The detective flipped his notepad open. "According to our investigation, the Museum of London did not have any such person working for them, either on contract or as full- or part-time staff. Are you sure?"

"Yes, I heard her on the phone with them once. In her flat, beside the Barbican."

"Yes, that. We checked it out. Owners were subletting the place, but to someone named Pieter. Arranged over Craigslist while they were away, so they didn't meet their tenant in person. We couldn't find anything that indicated the name of the occupant, no mail, no computer."

"No computer?"

"Is there anything else you can tell us? Did you see any of her credentials, any sort of alias she might have used?"

They found partial trails of her, different names, no full record. Not here, not in Budapest.

"Are you quite sure you are remembering the facts correctly?" asked the detective. "Did you ever see any identification, did you visit her at a workplace?"

I was in her flat. I visited her in Hungary. But the texts, the calls, the meetings. The more I thought about it, the more I realized that everything she told me was a lie. I'd never seen her at work, she didn't present a paper at the conference. All the jobs, the contracts, they didn't exist. The Museum of London letterhead, probably stolen or photoshopped. All the people I met, cabal members backing up each other's stories. The conferences, every time I had a chance meeting with her at a reception, the timetables were online. She'd said she tracked me down in London through Carl, but Carl said he'd never been contacted by her. All the information she had she got from my staff webpage, the phone directory, Google or good guesswork. And I didn't see it. She'd fabricated it all and I'd believed her.

After a few days, Henry came to the hospital and dropped off some of my things. "They say you'll be out soon," he said. "I'm staying in Wilson's spare room for now." He looked down at the scruffy floor tiles.

"What," I said, unable to keep an edge out of my voice, "Nicola wouldn't put you up?" At least, I thought, Henry was taken in too.

He shifted in his chair, kicked at the floor with his thick, rubber-soled boots. "She and I, well. You know. We're moving into a bigger place, the two of us, the beginning of next month."

"You're serious?" I almost yelled. "When you know she's hooked up with Maria? After all she did?" The cereal I had for breakfast an hour before threatens to come up.

"Maria," he said. "Maria, or whoever she really is, is genius."

"What? She's a killer. She's the reason I'm in here."

"You've been through a lot. But I'm sure she didn't intend for things to get this out of hand." He leaned forward, lowered his head. "And I mean, the news is making everything sound so sensational. We don't really know the whole story."

I used to think Henry was beautiful. Now, I saw his thinning hair, his shiny, oily forehead. His eyes, which I used to tell myself were intense, I now recognized as small, too close-set. Feral. The colour of shit. I used to tell myself that his art was brilliant. Now I saw it for what it was. That throne, over-grown dollhouse furniture. All of it, the work of a child playing with Plasticine and crayons. A weak puppet.

"And it probably wouldn't be a bad idea, you know," he said, "to be a bit more discreet with the police."

I sat up, the stitches in my arm puckering as I moved. "Have you heard from her?"

He stood, dropped a folded piece of paper on my lap and left the room.

Danica,

I have, often, a talent for picking girls. You were there, in Vienna, tucked away in that corner with your titian hair and clear eyes and skin without any freckles. But you did not appreciate what I did for you. Without me, you were a pretty little girl, but you had no muscle. Without me, you were ordinary, your beauty a false promise of something rare. I thought you were something stronger, but you broke like all the others. You never saw who I am.

You know now how powerful I am. And that I no longer want you. If you try to follow me, persist to speak about me, you will understand how much my previous affection was worth in terms of your physical safety.

I felt like a gardenia plucked and crushed under a pestle, oil for her perfume. I crumpled the paper, shoved it under my pillow. I rolled over, pressed the button to release more pain-killers into my IV and waited for sleep.

When I got out, the authorities told me I had to stay in the country indefinitely. Reporters were waiting for me outside the hospital. Press followed me everywhere for over two weeks, to the pharmacy, to the grocery. TV crews, cameras.

I did not enjoy the spotlight.

The police looked at my emails with Maria, trying to find clues, to decide if I was her accomplice or if she had tricked me, used me. Dr. Abbas supported me, told them that I did report my suspicions to him. Said he believed I had good intentions. Was under a lot of stress. New job, new country, relationship troubles. Even Dr. Sloane spoke on my behalf, said I never properly adjusted to the stress of my position at Stowmoor. I am not sure whether they or the police believed what they were saying. Six months went by and they had no leads on her whereabouts.

I didn't have a work permit, refused to take a loan from my family. I lived in a tiny bedsit in Hackney and helped one of my neighbours staff her stall at Petticoat Lane market on Sundays for a bit of money under the table. I cut my hair short, wore a lot of scarves, baggy tops, trainers. Tried to look as plain, as inconspicuous, as possible. I stayed home as much as I could. The few times I did go out, I kept an eye on store windows, on mirrors and glass doors, for a flash of blonde. Finally, they told me I could go home.

It's been over a year. For a while, Carl called, tried to convince me I could go back to work someplace. Finally I emailed him, told him I'd moved cities, was going to enroll in a fashion design course at community college. He doesn't call anymore.

Maria. I still fantasize about her. Mashing her blonde head against pavement, her perfect waves matted and rusty.

Chasing her through a field of snow. I cut her leg, hit an artery, she's hemorrhaging through her white silk slip, deep red sinking into icy ground. Her bare feet, her arms, are raw from the cold. I crouch, press a glass shard against her smooth neck.

She's bruised, tangled in thick vines, a laceration on her temple. A trail of blood runs down her pale cheek, drips onto her breasts. The thorns of the vines prick her each time she writhes to get free. A lion, leashed, circles her. He hasn't eaten for a day, swipes the vines with his claws, strains to lunge at her. I hold his chain.

I know I'm on a threshold between what you might call normalcy and disorder. Since her, something's closing inside me, some room in my mind that housed possibility, that let me love the sparkle of icicles in the sun, the delicate fur of a newborn kitten. Now a new room is opening, a place that sees the power in that ice shard, the weakness of a baby animal. A place that wouldn't stop you from killing something weaker, more beautiful, than you.

I'm fighting to stay out of this room. Most days, I can get through half a cup of coffee, draw a serrated knife through the rind of a grapefruit before I remember that I'm tainted, her bruises under my skin. I'm searching for a host of leeches, a bloodletting, to draw her stain away.

Acknowledgements

I extend heartfelt gratitude to my agent, Samantha Haywood. A deep and sincere thank you to insightful editors Jennifer Lambert and Alex Schultz, and to everyone at HarperCollins Canada. Thanks also to Claiborne Hancock and Jessica Case at Pegasus Books, U.S.

Many people lent their energy and support to this novel; my gratitude to everyone who contributed to its development. In particular, thank you to Robert Kroetsch, Jeanette Lynes, Alice Kuipers, David Carpenter, Leona Theis, Jennifer Still, Katia Grubisic, Mari-Lou Rowley, Noelle Gallagher, Mark Anthony Jarman, Ross Leckie, Steven Galloway. Thank you to psychologists Dr. Don Sharpe and Dr. Andrew Lubusko for sharing their expertise and patiently answering my many questions. To the many helpful people I met during my time in London and Eastern Europe. Also, Tony Thorne's and Raymond T. McNally's research on Báthory was extremely helpful. For financial support, thank you to the Saskatchewan Arts Board. Also to the Sage Hill Writing Experience, the Emma Lake writers and artists retreat, the Burney Centre, the Banff Centre and my fellow writers and colleagues at each of these places/programs.

Love and appreciation to my amazing, supportive friends and family.